THE PORT OF MISSING MEN

THE PORT
OF MISSING MEN

By

MEREDITH NICHOLSON

Author of

The House of a Thousand Candles
The Main Chance
Zelda Dameron
etc.

With Illustrations by

CLARENCE F. UNDERWOOD

> Then Sir Pellinore put off his armour;
> then a little afore midnight they heard
> the trotting of an horse. Be ye still, said
> King Pellinore, for we shall hear of some
> adventure.—*Malory.*

INDIANAPOLIS
THE BOBBS-MERRILL COMPANY
PUBLISHERS

Shirley Claiborne

To the Memory of

Herman Kountze

THE SHINING ROAD

*Come, sweetheart, let us ride away beyond the city's
    bound,*
*And seek what pleasant lands across the distant hills
    are found.*
*There is a golden light that shines beyond the verge of
    dawn,*
*And there are happy highways leading on and al-
    ways on;*
*So, sweetheart, let us mount and ride, with never a back-
    ward glance,*
To find the pleasant shelter of the Valley of Romance.

*Before us, down the golden road, floats dust from charg-
    ing steeds,*
*Where two adventurous companies clash loud in mighty
    deeds;*
*And from the tower that stands alert like some tall,
    beckoning pine,*
*E'en now, my heart, I see afar the lights of welcome
    shine!*
*So loose the rein and cheer the steed and let us race
    away*
To seek the lands that lie beyond the Borders of To-day.

Draw rein and rest a moment here in this cool vale of
  peace;
The race half-run, the goal half-won, half won the sure
  release!
To right and left are flowery fields, and brooks go sing-
  ing down
To mock the sober folk who still are prisoned in the
  town.
Now to the trail again, dear heart; my arm and blade
  are true,
And on some plain ere night descend I'll break a lance
  for you!

O sweetheart, it is good to find the pathway shining
  clear!
The road is broad, the hope is sure, and you are near
  and dear!
So loose the rein and cheer the steed and let us race
  away
To seek the lands that lie beyond the borders of To-day.
Oh, we shall hear at last, my heart, a cheering welcome
  cried
As o'er a clattering drawbridge through the Gate of
  Dreams we ride!

CONTENTS

THE PORT OF MISSING MEN

THE PORT OF MISSING MEN

CHAPTER I

"EVENTS, EVENTS"

Time hath, my lord, a wallet at his back
Wherein he puts alms for oblivion.
                    —*Troilus and Cressida.*

"The knowledge that you're alive gives me no pleasure," growled the grim old Austrian premier.

"Thank you!" laughed John Armitage, to whom he had spoken. "You have lost none of your old amiability; but for a renowned diplomat, you are remarkably frank. When I called on you in Paris, a year ago, I was able to render you—I believe you admitted it—a slight service."

1

Count Ferdinand von Stroebel bowed slightly, but did not take his eyes from the young man who sat opposite him in his rooms at the Hotel Monte Rosa in Geneva. On the table between them stood an open despatch box, and about it lay a number of packets of papers which the old gentleman, with characteristic caution, had removed to his own side of the table before admitting his caller. He was a burly old man, with massive shoulders and a great head thickly covered with iron-gray hair.

He trusted no one, and this accounted for his presence in Geneva in March, of the year 1903, whither he had gone to receive the report of the secret agents whom he had lately despatched to Paris on an errand of peculiar delicacy. The agents had failed in their mission, and Von Stroebel was not tolerant of failure. Perhaps if he had known that within a week the tapers would burn about his bier in Saint Stephen's Cathedral, at Vienna, while his life and public services would be estimated in varying degrees of admiration or execration by the newspapers of Europe, he might not have dealt so harshly with his hard-worked spies.

It was not often that the light in the old man's eyes was as gentle as now. He had sent his secret agents away and was to return to Vienna on the following day. The young man whom he now entertained in his apartments received his whole attention. He picked up the card which lay on the table and scrutinized it critically, while his eyes lighted with sudden humor.

The card was a gentleman's *carte de visite,* and bore the name John Armitage.

"I believe this is the same alias you were using when I saw you in Paris. Where did you get it?" demanded the minister.

"I rather liked the sound of it, so I had the cards made," replied the young man. "Besides, it's English, and I pass readily for an Englishman. I have quite got used to it."

"Which is not particularly creditable; but it's probably just as well so."

He drew closer to the table, and his keen old eyes snapped with the intentness of his thought. The hands he clasped on the table were those of age, and it was pathetically evident that he folded them to hide their slight palsy.

"I hope you are quite well," said Armitage kindly.

"I am not. I am anything but well. I am an old man, and I have had no rest for twenty years."

"It is the penalty of greatness. It is Austria's good

fortune that you have devoted yourself to the affairs of government. I have read—only to-day, in the *Contemporary Review*—an admirable tribute to your sagacity in handling the Servian affair. Your work was masterly. I followed it from the beginning with deepest interest."

The old gentleman bowed half-unconsciously, for his thoughts were far away, as the vague stare in his small, shrewd eyes indicated.

"But you are here for rest—one comes to Geneva at this season for nothing else."

"What brings you here?" asked the old man with sudden energy. "If the papers you gave me in Paris are forgeries and you are waiting—"

"Yes; assuming that, what should I be waiting for?"

"If you are waiting for events—for events! If you expect something to happen!"

Armitage laughed at the old gentleman's earnest manner, asked if he might smoke, and lighted a cigarette.

"Waiting doesn't suit me. I thought you understood that. I was not born for the waiting list. You see, I have strong hands—and my wits are—let us say—average!"

Von Stroebel clasped his own hands together more firmly and bent toward Armitage searchingly.

"Is it true"—he turned again and glanced about—"is it positively true that the Archduke Karl is dead?"

"Yes; quite true. There is absolutely no doubt of it," said Armitage, meeting the old man's eyes steadily.

"The report that he is still living somewhere in North America is persistent. We hear it frequently in Vienna; I have heard it since you told me that story and gave me those papers in Paris last year."

"I am aware of that," replied John Armitage; "but I told you the truth. He died in a Canadian lumber camp. We were in the north hunting—you may recall that he was fond of that sort of thing."

"Yes, I remember; there was nothing else he did so well," growled Von Stroebel.

"And the packet I gave you—"

The old man nodded.

"—that packet contained the Archduke Karl's sworn arraignment of his wife. It is of great importance, indeed, to Francis, his worthless son, or supposed son, who may present himself for coronation one of these days!"

"Not with Karl appearing in all parts of the world, never quite dead, never quite alive—and his son Frederick Augustus lurking with him in the shadows. Who knows whether they are dead?"

"I am the only person on earth in a position to make that clear," said John Armitage.

"Then you should give me the documents."

"No; I prefer to keep them. I assure you that I have sworn proof of the death of the Archduke Karl, and of his son Frederick Augustus. Those papers are in a box in the Bronx Loan and Trust Company, in New York City."

"I should have them; I *must* have them!" thundered the old man.

"In due season; but not just now. In fact, I have regretted parting with that document I gave you in Paris. It is safer in America than in Vienna. If you please, I should like to have it again, sir."

The palsy in the old man's hands had increased, and he strove to control his agitation; but fear had never been reckoned among his weaknesses, and he turned stormily upon Armitage.

"That packet is lost, I tell you!" he blurted, as though it were something that he had frequently explained before. "It was stolen from under my very nose only a month ago! That's what I'm here for—my agents are after the thief, and I came to Geneva to meet them, to find out why they have not caught him. Do you imagine that I travel for pleasure at my age, Mr. John Armitage?"

Count von Stroebel's bluster was merely a cloak to hide his confusion—a cloak, it may be said, to which he did not often resort; but in this case he watched Armitage warily. He clearly expected some outburst of indignation from the young man, and he was unfeignedly relieved when Armitage, after opening and closing his eyes quickly, reached for a fresh cigarette and lighted it with the deft ease of habit.

"The packet has been stolen," he observed calmly; "whom do you suspect of taking it?"

The old man leaned upon the table heavily.

"That amiable Francis—"

"The suggestion is not dismaying. Francis would not know an opportunity if it offered."

"But his mother—she is the devil!" blurted the old man.

"Pray drop that," said Armitage in a tone that caused the old man to look at him with a new scrutiny. "I want the paper back for the very reason that it contains that awful indictment of her. I have been uncomfortable ever since I gave it to you; and I came to ask you for it that I might keep it safe in my own hands. But

the document is lost,—am I to understand that Francis
has it?"

"Not yet! But Rambaud has it, and Rambaud and
Francis are as thick as thieves."

"I don't know Rambaud. The name is unfamiliar."

"He has a dozen names—one for every capital. He
even operates in Washington, I have heard. He's a
blackmailer, who aims high—a broker in secrets, a scan-
dal-peddler. He's a bad lot, I tell you. I've had my best
men after him, and they've just been here to report another failure. If you have nothing better to do—" began the old man.

"Yes; that packet must be recovered," answered Armitage. "If your agents have failed at the job it may be
worth my while to look for it."

His quiet acceptance of the situation irritated the
minister.

"You entertain me, John Armitage! You speak of
that packet as though it were a pound of tea. Francis
and his friends, Winkelried and Rambaud, are not chas-
ers of fireflies, I would have you know. If the Archduke
and his son are dead, then a few more deaths and Francis would rule the Empire."

John Armitage and Count von Stroebel stared at each
other in silence.

"Events! Events!" muttered the old man presently, and he rested one of his hands upon the despatch box, as though it were a symbol of authority and power.

"Events!" the young man murmured.

"Events!" repeated Count von Stroebel without humor. "A couple of deaths and there you see him, on the ground and quite ready. Karl was a genius, therefore he could not be king. He threw away about five hundred years of work that had been done for him by other people—and he cajoled you into sharing his exile. You threw away your life for him! Bah! But you seem sane enough!"

The prime minister concluded with his rough burr; and Armitage laughed outright.

"Why the devil don't you go to Vienna and set yourself up like a gentleman?" demanded the premier.

"Like a gentleman?" repeated Armitage. "It is too late. I should die in Vienna in a week. Moreover, I *am* dead, and it is well, when one has attained that beatific advantage, to stay dead."

"Francis is a troublesome blackguard," declared the old man. "I wish to God *he* would form the dying habit, so that I might have a few years in peace; but he is forever turning up in some mischief. And what can you do about it? Can we kick him out of the army without a scandal? Don't you suppose he could go to Budapest to-morrow and make things interesting for us if he pleased? He's as full of treason as he can stick, I tell you."

Armitage nodded and smiled.

"I dare say," he said in English; and when the old statesman glared at him he said in German: "No doubt you are speaking the truth."

"Of course I speak the truth; but this is a matter for action, and not for discussion. That packet was stolen by intention, and not by chance, John Armitage!"

There was a slight immaterial sound in the hall, and the old prime minister slipped from German to French without changing countenance as he continued:

"We have enough troubles in Austria without encouraging treason. If Rambaud and his chief, Winkelried, could make a king of Francis, the brokerage—the commission—would be something handsome; and Winkelried and Rambaud are clever men."

"I know of Winkelried. The continental press has given much space to him of late; but Rambaud is a new name."

"He is a skilled hand. He is the most daring scoundrel in Europe."

Count von Stroebel poured a glass of brandy from a silver flask and sipped it slowly.

"I will show you the gentleman's pleasant countenance," said the minister, and he threw open a leather portfolio and drew from it a small photograph which he extended to Armitage, who glanced at it carelessly and then with sudden interest.

"Rambaud!" he exclaimed.

"That's his name in Vienna. In Paris he is something else. I will furnish you a list of his *noms de guerre.*"

"Thank you. I should like all the information you care to give me; but it may amuse you to know that I have seen the gentleman before."

"That is possible," remarked the old man, who never evinced surprise in any circumstances.

"I expect to see him here within a few days."

Count von Stroebel held up his empty glass and studied it attentively, while he waited for Armitage to explain why he expected to see Rambaud in Geneva.

"He is interested in a certain young woman. She reached here yesterday; and Rambaud, alias Chauvenet, is quite likely to arrive within a day or so."

"Jules Chauvenet is the correct name. I must inform my men," said the minister.

"You wish to arrest him?"

"You ought to know me better than that, Mr. John Armitage! Of course I shall not arrest him! But I must get that packet. I can't have it peddled all over Europe, and I can't advertise my business by having him arrested here. If I could catch him once in Vienna I should know what to do with him! He and Winkelried got hold of our plans in that Bulgarian affair last year and check-mated me. He carries his wares to the best buyers—Berlin and St. Petersburg. So there's a woman, is there? I've found that there usually is!"

"There's a very charming young American girl, to be more exact."

The old man growled and eyed Armitage sharply, while Armitage studied the photograph.

"I hope you are not meditating a preposterous marriage. Go back where you belong, make a proper marriage and wait—"

"Events!" and John Armitage laughed. "I tell you, sir, that waiting is not my *forte*. That's what I like about America; they're up and at it over there; the man who waits is lost."

"They're a lot of swine!" rumbled Von Stroebel's heavy bass.

"I still owe allegiance to the Schomburg crown, so don't imagine you are hitting me. But the swine are industrious and energetic. Who knows but that John Armitage might become famous among them—in politics, in finance! But for the deplorable accident of foreign birth he might become president of the United States. As it is, there are thousands of other offices worth getting—why not?"

"I tell you not to be a fool. You are young and—fairly clever—"

Armitage laughed at the reluctance of the count's praise.

"Thank you, with all my heart!"

"Go back where you belong and you will have no regrets. Something may happen—who can tell? Events —events—if a man will watch and wait and study events—"

"Bless me! They organize clubs in every American village for the study of events," laughed Armitage; then he changed his tone. "To be sure, the Bourbons have studied events these many years—a pretty spectacle, too."

"Carrion! Carrion!" almost screamed the old man, half-rising in his seat. "Don't mention those scaven-

gers to me! Bah! The very thought of them makes me
sick. But"—he gulped down more of the brandy—
"where and how do you live?"

"Where? I own a cattle ranch in Montana and since
the Archduke's death I have lived there. He carried
about fifty thousand pounds to America with him. He
took care that I should get what was left when he died—
and, I am almost afraid to tell you that I have actually
augmented my inheritance! Just before I left I bought
a place in Virginia to be near Washington when I got
tired of the ranch."

"Washington!" snorted the count. "In due course it
will be the storm center of the world."

"You read the wrong American newspapers," laughed
Armitage.

They were silent for a moment, in which each was
busy with his own thoughts; then the count remarked, in
as amiable a tone as he ever used:

"Your French is first rate. Do you speak English as
well?"

"As readily as German, I think. You may recall that
I had an English tutor, and maybe I did not tell you in
that interview at Paris that I had spent a year at Harvard University."

"What the devil did you do that for?" growled Von Stroebel.

"From curiosity, or ambition, as you like. I was in Cambridge at the law school for a year before the Archduke died. That was three years ago. I am twenty-eight, as you may remember. I am detaining you; I have no wish to rake over the past; but I am sorry—I am very sorry we can't meet on some common ground."

"I ask you to abandon this democratic nonsense and come back and make a man of yourself. You might go far—very far; but this democracy has hold of you like a disease."

"What you ask is impossible. It is just as impossible now as it was when we discussed it in Paris last year. To sit down in Vienna and learn how to keep that leaning tower of an Empire from tumbling down like a stack of bricks—it does not appeal to me. You have spent a laborious life in defending a silly medieval tradition of government. You are using all the apparatus of the modern world to perpetuate an ideal that is as old and dead as the Rameses dynasty. Every time you use the telegraph to send orders in an emperor's name you commit an anachronism."

The count frowned and growled.

"Don't talk to me like that. It is not amusing."

"No; it is not funny. To see men like you fetching and carrying for dull kings, who would drop through the gallows or go to planting turnips without your brains—it does not appeal to my sense of humor or to my imagination."

"You put it coarsely," remarked the old man grimly. "I shall perhaps have a statue when I am gone."

"Quite likely; and mobs will rendezvous in its shadow to march upon the royal palaces. If I were coming back to Europe I should go in for something more interesting than furnishing brains for sickly kings."

"I dare say! Very likely you would persuade them to proclaim democracy and brotherhood everywhere."

"On the other hand, I should become king myself."

"Don't be a fool, Mr. John Armitage. Much as you have grieved me, I should hate to see you in a mad-house."

"My faculties, poor as they are, were never clearer. I repeat that if I were going to furnish the brains for an empire I should ride in the state carriage myself, and not be merely the driver on the box, who keeps the middle of the road and looks out for sharp corners. Here is a plan ready to my hand. Let me find that lost document, appear in Vienna and announce myself Frederick Augustus, the son of the Archduke Karl! I knew both men intimately. You may remember that Frederick and I were born in the same month. I, too, am Frederick Augustus! We passed commonly in America as brothers. Many of the personal effects of Karl and Augustus are in my keeping—by the Archduke's own wish. You have spent your life studying human nature, and you know as well as I do that half the world would believe my story if I said I was the Emperor's nephew. In the uneasy and unstable condition of your absurd empire I should be hailed as a diversion, and then—events, events!"

Count von Stroebel listened with narrowing eyes, and his lips moved in an effort to find words with which to break in upon this impious declaration. When Armitage ceased speaking the old man sank back and glared at him.

"Karl did his work well. You are quite mad. You will do well to go back to America before the police discover you."

Armitage rose and his manner changed abruptly.

"I do not mean to trouble or annoy you. Please pardon me! Let us be friends, if we can be nothing more."

"It is too late. The chasm is too deep."

The old minister sighed deeply. His fingers touched the despatch box as though by habit. It represented power, majesty and the iron game of government. The young man watched him eagerly.

The heavy, tremulous hands of Count von Stroebel passed back and forth over the box caressingly. Suddenly he bent forward and spoke with a new and gentler tone and manner.

"I have given my life, my whole life, as you have said, to one service—to uphold one idea. You have spoken of that work with contempt. History, I believe, will reckon it justly."

"Your place is secure—no one can gainsay that," broke in Armitage.

"If you would do something for me—for me—do something for Austria, do something for my country and yours! You have wits; I dare say you have courage. I don't care what that service may be; I don't care where or how you perform it. I am not so near gone as you may think. I know well enough that they are waiting for me to die; but I am in no hurry to afford my enemies that pleasure. But stop this babble of yours about democracy. *Do something for Austria*—for the Empire that I have held here under my hand these difficult years

" Do something for Austria!" *Page 18*

—then take your name again—and you will find that
kings can be as just and wise as mobs."

"For the Empire—something for the Empire?" murmured the young man, wondering.

Count Ferdinand von Stroebel rose.

"You will accept the commission—I am quite sure
you will accept. I leave on an early train, and I shall
not see you again." As he took Armitage's hand he scrutinized him once more with particular care; there was a
lingering caress in his touch as he detained the young
man for an instant; then he sighed heavily.

"Good night; good-by!" he said abruptly, and waved
his caller toward the door.

CHAPTER II

—the Englishman who is not an Englishman and therefore doubly incomprehensible.—*The Naulahka.*

The girl with the white-plumed hat started and flushed
slightly, and her brother glanced over his shoulder toward the restaurant door to see what had attracted her
attention.

" 'Tis he, the unknown, Dick."

"I must say I like his persistence!" exclaimed the
young fellow, turning again to the table. "In America I
should call him out and punch his head, but over here—"

"Over here you have better manners," replied the girl,
laughing. "But why trouble yourself? He doesn't even
look at us. We are of no importance to him whatever.
We probably speak a different language."

"But he travels by the same trains; he stops at the
same inns; he sits near us at the theater—he even af-
fects the same pictures in the same galleries! It's grow-

20

ing a trifle monotonous; it's really insufferable. I think
I shall have to try my stick on him."

"You flatter yourself, Richard," mocked the girl.
"He's fully your height and a trifle broader across the
shoulders. The lines about his mouth are almost—yes,
I should say, quite as firm as yours, though he is a
younger man. His eyes are nice blue ones, and they are
very steady. His hair is"—she paused to reflect and
tilted her head slightly, her eyes wandering for an instant to the subject of her comment—"light brown, I
should call it. And he is beardless, as all self-respecting
men should be. I'm sure that he is an exemplary person
—kind to his sisters and aunts, very willing to sacrifice
himself for others and light the candles on his nephews'
and nieces' Christmas trees."

She rested her cheek against her lightly-clasped hands
and sighed deeply to provoke a continuation of her brother's growling disdain.

The young gentleman to whom she had referred had
seated himself at a table not far distant, given an order
with some particularity, and settled himself to the reading of a newspaper which he had drawn from the pocket
of his blue serge coat. He was at once absorbed, and the
presence of the Claibornes gave him apparently not the
slightest concern.

"He has a sense of humor," the girl resumed. "I saw him yesterday—"

"You're always seeing him: you ought to be ashamed of yourself."

"Don't interrupt me, please. As I was saying, I saw him laughing over the *Fliegende Blätter*."

"But that's no sign he has a sense of humor. It rather proves that he hasn't. I'm disappointed in you, Shirley. To think that my own sister should be able to tell the color of a wandering blackguard's eyes!"

He struck a match viciously, and his sister laughed.

"I might add to his portrait. That blue and white scarf is tied beautifully; and his profile would be splendid in a medallion. I believe from his nose he may be English, after all," she added with a dreamy air assumed to add to her brother's impatience.

"Which doesn't help the matter materially, that I can see!" exclaimed the young man. "With a full beard he'd probably look like a Sicilian bandit. If I thought he was really pursuing you in this darkly mysterious way I should certainly give him a piece of my American mind. You might suppose that a girl would be safe traveling with her brother."

"It isn't your fault, Dick," laughed the girl. "You

know our parents dear were with us when we first began to notice him—that was in Rome. And now that we are alone he continues to follow our trail just the same. It's really diverting; and if you were a good brother you'd find out all about him, and we might even do stunts together—the three of us, with you as the watchful chaperon. You forget how I have worked for you, Dick. I took great chances in forcing an acquaintance with those frosty English people at Florence just because you were crazy about the scrawny blonde who wore the frightful hats. I wash my hands of you hereafter. Your taste in girls is horrible."

"Your mind has been affected by reading these fake-kingdom romances, where a ridiculous prince gives up home and mother and his country to marry the usual beautiful American girl who travels about having silly adventures. I belong to the Know-nothing Party —America for Americans and only white men on guard!"

"Yes, Richard! Your sentiments are worthy, but they'd have more weight if I hadn't seen you staring your eyes out every time we came within a mile of a penny princess. I haven't forgotten your disgraceful conduct in collecting photographs of that homely daughter of a certain English duke. We'll call the incident closed, little brother."

"Our friend Chauvenet, even," continued Captain Claiborne, "is less persistent—less gloomily present on the horizon. We haven't seen him for a week or two. But he expects to visit Washington this spring. His waistcoats are magnificent. The governor shies every time the fellow unbuttons his coat."

"Mr. Chauvenet is an accomplished man of the world," declared Shirley with an insincere sparkle in her eyes.

"He lives by his wits—and lives well."

Claiborne dismissed Chauvenet and turned again toward the strange young man, who was still deep in his newspaper.

"He's reading the *Neue Freie Presse*," remarked Dick, "by which token I argue that he's some sort of a Dutchman. He's probably a traveling agent for a Vienna glass-factory, or a drummer for a cheap wine-house, or the agent for a Munich brewery. That would account for his travels. We simply fall in with his commercial itinerary."

"You seem to imply, brother, that my charms are not in themselves sufficient. But a commercial traveler hardly commands that fine repose, that distinction—

that air of having been places and seen things and known people—"

"Tush! I have seen American book agents who had all that—even the air of having been places! Your instincts ought to serve you better, Shirley. It's well that we go on to-morrow. I shall warn mother and the governor that you need watching."

Shirley Claiborne's eyes rested again upon the calm reader of the *Neue Freie Presse*. The waiter was now placing certain dishes upon the table without, apparently, interesting the young gentleman in the least. Then the unknown dropped his newspaper, and buttered a roll reflectively. His gaze swept the room for the first time, passing over the heads of Miss Claiborne and her brother unseeingly—with, perhaps, too studied an air of indifference.

"He has known real sorrow," persisted Shirley, her elbows on the table, her fingers interlocked, her chin resting idly upon them. "He's traveling in an effort to forget a blighting grief," the girl continued with mock sympathy.

"Then let us leave him in peace! We can't decently linger in the presence of his sacred sorrow."

Captain Richard Claiborne and his sister Shirley had

stopped at Geneva to spend a week with a younger brother, who was in school there, and were to join their father and mother at Liverpool and sail for home at once. The Claibornes were permanent residents of Washington, where Hilton Claiborne, a former ambassador to two of the greatest European courts, was counsel for several of the embassies and a recognized authority in international law. He had been to Rome to report to the Italian government the result of his efforts to collect damages from the United States for the slaughter of Italian laborers in a railroad strike, and had proceeded thence to England on other professional business.

Dick Claiborne had been ill, and was abroad on leave in an effort to shake off the lingering effects of typhoid fever contracted in the Philippines. He was under orders to report for duty at Fort Myer on the first of April, and it was now late March. He and his sister had spent the morning at their brother's school and were enjoying a late *déjeûner* at the Monte Rosa. There existed between them a pleasant comradeship that was in no wise affected by divergent tastes and temperaments. Dick had just attained his captaincy, and was the youngest man of his rank in the service. He did not know an orchid from a hollyhock, but no man in the army was a better judge of a cavalry horse, and if a Wagner recital bored him to death his spirit rose, nevertheless, to the bugle, and he drilled his troop until he could play with it and snap it about him like a whip.

Shirley Claiborne had been out of college a year, and afforded a pleasant refutation of the dull theory that advanced education destroys a girl's charm, or buoyancy, or whatever it is that is so greatly admired in young womanhood. She gave forth the impression of vitality and strength. She was beautifully fair, with a high color that accentuated her youthfulness. Her brown hair, caught up from her brow in the fashion of the early years of the century, flashed gold in sunlight.

Much of Shirley's girlhood had been spent in the Virginia hills, where Judge Claiborne had long maintained a refuge from the heat of Washington. From childhood she had read the calendar of spring as it is written upon the landscape itself. Her fingers found by instinct the first arbutus; she knew where white violets shone first upon the rough breast of the hillsides; and particular patches of rhododendron had for her the intimate interest of private gardens.

Undoubtedly there are deities fully consecrated to

the important business of naming girls, so happily is that task accomplished. Gladys is a child of the spirit of mischief. Josephine wears a sweet gravity, and Mary, too, discourses of serious matters. Nora, in some incarnation, has seen fairies scampering over moor and hill and the remembrance of them teases her memory. Katherine is not so faithless as her ways might lead you to believe. Laura without dark eyes would be impossible, and her predestined Petrarch would never deliver his sonnets. Helen may be seen only against a background of Trojan wall. Gertrude must be tall and fair and ready with ballads in the winter twilight. Julia's reserve and discretion commend her to you; but she has a heart of laughter. Anne is to be found in the rose garden with clipping-shears and a basket. Hilda is a capable person; there is no ignoring her militant character; the battles of Saxon kings ring still in her blood. Marjorie has scribbled verses in secret, and Celia is the quietest auditor at the symphony. And you may have observed that there is no button on Elizabeth's foil; you do well not to clash wits with her. Do you say that these ascriptions are not square with your experience? Then verily there must have been a sad mixing of infant candidates for the font in your parish.

Shirley, in such case, will mean nothing to you. It is a waste of time to tell you that the name may become audible without being uttered; you can not be made to understand that the *r* and *l* slip into each other as ripples glide over pebbles in a brook. And from the name to the girl—may you be forever denied a glimpse of Shirley Claiborne's pretty head, her brown hair and dream-haunted eyes, if you do not first murmur the name with honest liking.

As the Claibornes lingered at their table a short stout man espied them from the door and advanced beamingly.

"Ah, my dear Shirley, and Dick! Can it be possible! I only heard by the merest chance that you were here. But Switzerland is the real meeting-place of the world."

The young Americans greeted the new-comer cordially. A waiter placed a chair for him, and took his hat. Arthur Singleton was an American, though he had lived abroad so long as to have lost his identity with any particular city or state of his native land. He had been an attaché of the American embassy at London for many years. Administrations changed and ambassadors came and went, but Singleton was never molested. It was said that he kept his position on the score of his wide acquaintance; he knew every one, and he was a great peddler of gossip, particularly about people in high station.

The children of Hilton Claiborne were not to be overlooked. He would impress himself upon them, as was his way; for he was sincerely social by instinct, and would go far to do a kindness for people he really liked.

"Ah me! You have arrived opportunely, Miss Claiborne. There's mystery in the air—the great Stroebel is here—under this very roof and in a dreadfully bad humor. He is a dangerous man—a very dangerous man, but failing fast. Poor Austria! Count Ferdinand von Stroebel can have no successor—he's only a sort of holdover from the nineteenth century, and with him and his Emperor out of the way—what? For my part I see only dark days ahead;" and he concluded with a little sigh that implied crumbling thrones and falling dynasties.

"We met him in Vienna," said Shirley Claiborne, "when father was there before the Ecuador Claims Commission. He struck me as being a delightful old grizzly bear."

"He will have his place in history; he is a statesman of the old blood and iron school; he is the peer of Bismarck, and some things he has done. He holds more secrets than any other man in Europe—and you may be quite sure that they will die with him. He will leave no memoirs to be poked over by his enemies—no post-mortem confidences from him!"

The reader of the *Neue Freie Presse,* preparing to leave his table, tore from the newspaper an article that seemed to have attracted him, placed it in his card-case, and walked toward the door. The eyes of Arthur Singleton lighted in recognition, and the attaché, muttering an apology to the Claibornes, addressed the young gentleman cordially.

"Why, Armitage, of all men!" and he rose, still facing the Claibornes, with an air of embracing the young Americans in his greetings. He never liked to lose an auditor; and he would, in no circumstances, miss a chance to display the wide circumference of his acquaintance.

"Shirley—Miss Claiborne—allow me to present Mr. Armitage." The young army officer and Armitage then shook hands, and the three men stood for a moment, detained, it seemed, by the old attaché, who had no engagement for the next hour or two and resented the idea of being left alone.

"One always meets Armitage!" declared Singleton.

"He knows our America as well as we do—and very well indeed—for an Englishman."

Armitage bowed gravely.

"You make it necessary again for me to disavow any allegiance to the powers that rule Great Britain. I'm really a fair sort of American—I have sometimes told New York people all about—Colorado—Montana—New Mexico!"

His voice and manner were those of a gentleman. His color, as Shirley Claiborne now observed, was that of an outdoors man; she was familiar with it in soldiers and sailors, and knew that it testified to a vigorous and wholesome life.

"Of course you're not English!" exclaimed Singleton, annoyed as he remembered, or thought he did, that Armitage had on some other occasion made the same protest.

"I'm really getting sensitive about it," said Armitage, more to the Claibornes than to Singleton. "But must we all be from somewhere? Is it so melancholy a plight to be a man without a country?"

The mockery in his tone was belied by the good humor in his face; his eyes caught Shirley's passingly, and she smiled at him—it seemed a natural, a perfectly inevita-

ble thing to do. She liked the kind tolerance with which
he suffered the babble of Arthur Singleton, whom some
one had called an international bore. The young man's
dignity was only an expression of self-respect; his ap-
preciation of the exact proprieties resulting from this
casual introduction to herself and her brother was
perfect. He was already withdrawing. A waiter had
followed him with his discarded newspaper—and Armitage took it and idly dropped it on a chair.

"Have you heard the news, Armitage? The Austrian
sphinx is here—in this very house!" whispered Singleton impressively.

"Yes; to be sure, Count von Stroebel is here, but he
will probably not remain long. The Alps will soon be
safe again. I am glad to have met you." He bowed to
the Claibornes inclusively, nodded in response to Singleton's promise to look him up later, and left them.

When Shirley and her brother reached their common
sitting-room Dick Claiborne laughingly held up the copy
of the *Neue Freie Presse* which Armitage had cast aside
at their table.

"Now we shall know!" he declared, unfolding the
newspaper.

"Know what, Dick?"

"At least what our friend without a country is so interested in."

He opened the paper, from which half a column had been torn, noted the date, rang the bell, and ordered a copy of the same issue. When it was brought he opened it, found the place, laughed loudly, and passed the sheet over to his sister.

"Oh, Shirley, Shirley! This is almost too much!" he cried, watching her as her eyes swept the article. She turned away to escape his noise, and after a glance threw down the paper in disgust. The article dealt in detail with Austro-Hungarian finances, and fairly bristled with figures and sage conclusions based upon them.

"Isn't that the worst!" exclaimed Shirley, smiling ruefully.

"He's certainly a romantic figure ready to your hand. Probably a bank-clerk who makes European finance his recreation."

"He isn't an Englishman, at any rate. He repudiated the idea with scorn."

"Well, your Mr. Armitage didn't seem so awfully excited at meeting Singleton; but he seemed rather satisfied with your appearance, to put it mildly. I wonder if he had arranged with Singleton to pass by in that purely incidental way, just for the privilege of making your acquaintance!"

"Don't be foolish, Dick. It's unbecoming an officer and a gentleman. But if you should see Mr. Singleton again—"

"Yes—not if I see him *first!*" ejaculated Claiborne.

"Well, you might ask him who Mr. Armitage is. It would be amusing—and satisfying—to know."

Later in the day the old attaché fell upon Claiborne in the smoking-room and stopped to discuss a report that a change was impending in the American State Department. Changes at Washington did not trouble Singleton, who was sure of his tenure. He said as much; and after some further talk, Claiborne remarked:

"Your friend Armitage seems a good sort."

"Oh, yes; a capital talker, and thoroughly well posted in affairs."

"Yes, he seemed interesting. Do you happen to know where he lives—when he's at home?"

"Lord bless you, boy, I don't know anything about Armitage!" spluttered Singleton, with the emphasis so thrown as to imply that of course in any other branch of human knowledge he would be found abundantly qualified to answer questions.

"But you introduced us to him—my sister and me. I assumed—"

"My dear Claiborne, I'm always introducing people! It's my business to introduce people. Armitage is all right. He's always around everywhere. I've dined with him in Paris, and I've rarely seen a man order a better dinner."

CHAPTER III

DARK TIDINGS

The news I bring is heavy in my tongue.—Shakespeare.

The second day thereafter Shirley Claiborne went into a jeweler's on the Grand Quai to purchase a trinket that had caught her eye, while she waited for Dick, who had gone off in their carriage to the post-office to send some telegrams. It was a small shop, and the time early afternoon, when few people were about. A man who had preceded her was looking at watches, and seemed deeply absorbed in this occupation. She heard his inquiries as to quality and price, and knew that it was Armitage's voice before she recognized his tall figure. She made her purchase quickly, and was about to leave the shop, when he turned toward her and she bowed.

"Good afternoon, Miss Claiborne. These are very tempting bazaars, aren't they? If the abominable tariff laws of America did not give us pause—"

He bent above her, hat in hand, smiling. He had con-

37

cluded the purchase of a watch, which the shopkeeper was now wrapping in a box.

"I have just purchased a little remembrance for my ranch foreman out in Montana, and before I can place it in his hands it must be examined and appraised and all the pleasure of the gift destroyed by the custom officers in New York. I hope you are a good smuggler, Miss Claiborne."

"I'd like to be. Women are supposed to have a knack at the business; but my father is so patriotic that he makes me declare everything."

"Patriotism will carry one far; but I object both to being taxed and to the alternative of corrupting the gentlemen who lie in wait at the receipt of customs."

"Of course the answer is that Americans should buy at home," replied Shirley. She received her change, and Armitage placed his small package in his pocket.

"My brother expected to meet me here; he ran off with our carriage," Shirley explained.

"These last errands are always trying—there are innumerable things one would like to come back for from mid-ocean, tariff or no tariff."

"There's the wireless," said Shirley. "In time we shall be able to commit our afterthoughts to it. But lost views can hardly be managed that way. After I get home I shall think of scores of things I should like to see again—that photographs don't give."

"Such as—?"

"Oh—the way the Pope looks when he gives his blessing at St. Peter's; and the feeling you have when you stand by Napoleon's tomb—the awfulness of what he did and was—and being here in Switzerland, where I always feel somehow the pressure of all the past of Europe about me. Now,"—and she laughed lightly,—"I have made a most serious confession."

"It is a new idea—that of surveying the ages from these mountains. They must be very wise after all these years, and they have certainly seen men and nations do many evil and wretched things. But the history of the world is all one long romance—a tremendous story."

"That is what makes me sorry to go home," said Shirley meditatively. "We are so new—still in the making, and absurdly raw. When we have a war, it is just politics, with scandals about what the soldiers have to eat, and that sort of thing; and there's a fuss about pensions, and the heroic side of it is lost."

"But it is easy to overestimate the weight of history and tradition. The glory of dead Cæsar doesn't do the

peasant any good. When you see Italian laborers at work
in America digging ditches or laying railroad ties, or
find Norwegian farmers driving their plows into the new
hard soil of the Dakotas, you don't think of their past
as much as of their future—the future of the whole human race."

Armitage had been the subject of so much jesting between Dick and herself that it seemed strange to be talking to him. His face brightened pleasantly when he
spoke; his eyes were grayer than she had mockingly described them for her brother's benefit the day before.
His manner was gravely courteous, and she did not at
all believe that he had followed her about.

Her ideals of men were colored by the American
prejudice in favor of those who aim high and venture
much. In her childhood she had read Malory and Froissart with a boy's delight. She possessed, too, that poetic
sense of the charm of "the spirit of place" that is the
natural accompaniment of the imaginative temperament.
The cry of bugles sometimes brought tears to her eyes;
her breath came quickly when she sat—as she often did
—in the Fort Myer drill hall at Washington and
watched the alert cavalrymen dashing toward the specta-
tors' gallery in the mimic charge. The work that brave

men do she admired above anything else in the world. As a child in Washington she had looked wonderingly upon the statues of heroes and the frequent military pageants of the capital; and she had wept at the solemn pomp of military funerals. Once on a battleship she had thrilled at the salutes of a mighty fleet in the Hudson below the tomb of Grant; and soon thereafter had felt awe possess her as she gazed upon the white marble effigy of Lee in the chapel at Lexington; for the contemplation of heroes was dear to her, and she was proud to believe that her father, a veteran of the Civil War, and her soldier brother were a tie between herself and the old heroic times.

Armitage was aware that a jeweler's shop was hardly the place for extended conversation with a young woman whom he scarcely knew, but he lingered in the joy of hearing this American girl's voice, and what she said interested him immensely. He had seen her first in Paris a few months before at an exhibition of battle paintings. He had come upon her standing quite alone before *High Tide at Gettysburg,* the picture of the year; and he had noted the quick mounting of color to her cheeks as the splendid movement of the painting —its ardor and fire—took hold of her. He saw her again in Florence; and it was from there that he had deliberately followed the Claibornes.

His own plans were now quite unsettled by his inter-view with Von Stroebel. He fully expected Chauvenet in Geneva; the man had apparently been on cordial terms with the Claibornes; and as he had seemed to be master of his own time, it was wholly possible that he would appear before the Claibornes left Geneva. It was now the second day after Von Stroebel's departure, and Armitage began to feel uneasy.

He stood with Shirley quite near the shop door, watching for Captain Claiborne to come back with the carriage.

"But America—isn't America the most marvelous product of romance in the world,—its discovery,—the successive conflicts that led up to the realization of de-mocracy? Consider the worthless idlers of the Middle Ages going about banging one another's armor with battle-axes. Let us have peace, said the tired warrior."

"He could afford to say it; he was the victor," said Shirley.

"Ah! there is Captain Claiborne. I am indebted to you, Miss Claiborne, for many pleasant suggestions."

The carriage was at the door, and Dick Claiborne came up to them at once and bowed to Armitage.

"There is great news: Count Ferdinand von Stroebel was murdered in his railway carriage between here and Vienna; they found him dead at Innsbruck this morning."

"Is it possible! Are you quite sure he was murdered?"

It was Armitage who asked the question. He spoke in a tone quite matter-of-fact and colorless, so that Shirley looked at him in surprise; but she saw that he was very grave; and then instantly some sudden feeling flashed in his eyes.

"There is no doubt of it. It was an atrocious crime; the count was an old man and feeble when we saw him the other day. He wasn't fair game for an assassin," said Claiborne.

"No; he deserved a better fate," remarked Armitage.

"He was a grand old man," said Shirley, as they left the shop and walked toward the carriage. "Father admired him greatly; and he was very kind to us in Vienna. It is terrible to think of his being murdered."

"Yes; he was a wise and useful man," observed Armitage, still grave. "He was one of the great men of his time."

His tone was not that of one who discusses casually

a bit of news of the hour, and Captain Claiborne paused
a moment at the carriage door, curious as to what Armitage might say further.

"And now we shall see—" began the young American.

"We shall see Johann Wilhelm die of old age within
a few years at most; and then Charles Louis, his son,
will be the Emperor-king in his place; and if he should
go hence without heirs, his cousin Francis would rule in
the house of his fathers; and Francis is corrupt and
worthless, and quite necessary to the plans of destiny
for the divine order of kings."

John Armitage stood beside the carriage quite erect,
his hat and stick and gloves in his right hand, his left
thrust lightly into the side pocket of his coat.

"A queer devil," observed Claiborne, as they drove
away. "A solemn customer, and not cheerful enough to
make a good drummer. By what singular chance did he
find you in that shop?"

"I found *him,* dearest brother, if I must make the
humiliating disclosure."

"I shouldn't have believed it! I hardly thought you
would carry it so far."

"And while he may be a salesman of imitation cut-
glass, he has expensive tastes."

"Lord help us, he hasn't been buying you a watch?"

"No; he was lavishing himself on a watch for the foreman of his ranch in Montana."

"Humph! you're chaffing."

"Not in the least. He paid—I couldn't help being a witness to the transaction—he actually paid five hundred francs for a watch to give to the foreman of his ranch—*his* ranch, mind you, in Montana, U. S. A. He spoke of it incidentally, as though he were always buying watches for cowboys. Now where does that leave us?"

"I'm afraid it rather does for my theory. I'll look him up when I get home. Montana isn't a good hiding-place any more. But it was odd the way he acted about old Stroebel's death. You don't suppose he knew him, do you?"

"It's possible. Poor Count von Stroebel! Many hearts are lighter, now that he's done for."

"Yes; and there will be something doing in Austria, now that he's out of the way."

Four days passed, in which they devoted themselves to their young brother. The papers were filled with accounts of Count von Stroebel's death and speculations as to its effect on the future of Austria and the peace of

Europe. The Claibornes saw nothing of Armitage. Dick asked for him in the hotel, and found that he had gone, but would return in a few days.

It was on the morning of the fourth day that Armitage appeared suddenly at the hotel as Dick and his sister waited for a carriage to carry them to their train. He had just returned, and they met by the narrowest margin. He walked with them to the door of the Monte Rosa.

"We are running for the *King Edward,* and hope for a day in London before we sail. Perhaps we shall see you one of these days in America," said Claiborne, with some malice, it must be confessed, for his sister's benefit.

"That is possible; I am very fond of Washington," responded Armitage carelessly.

"Of course you will look us up," persisted Dick. "I shall be at Fort Myer for a while—and it will always be a pleasure—"

Claiborne turned for a last word with the porter about their baggage, and Armitage stood talking to Shirley, who had already entered the carriage.

"Oh, is there any news of Count von Stroebel's assassin?" she asked, noting the newspaper that Armitage held in his hand.

"Nothing. It's a very mysterious and puzzling affair."

"It's horrible to think such a thing possible—he was a wonderful old man. But very likely they will find the murderer."

"Yes; undoubtedly."

Then, seeing her brother beating his hands together impatiently behind Armitage's back—a back whose ample shoulders were splendidly silhouetted in the carriage door—Shirley smiled in her joy of the situation, and would have prolonged it for her brother's benefit even to the point of missing the train, if the matter had been left wholly in her hands. It amused her to keep the conversation pitched in the most impersonal key.

"The secret police will scour Europe in pursuit of the assassin," she observed.

"Yes," replied Armitage gravely.

He thought her brown traveling gown, with hat and gloves to match, exceedingly becoming, and he liked the full, deep tones of her voice, and the changing light of her eyes; and a certain dimple in her left cheek—he had assured himself that it had no counterpart on the right—made the fate of principalities and powers seem, at the moment, an idle thing.

"The truth will be known before we sail, no doubt," said Shirley. "The assassin may be here in Geneva by this time."

"That is quite likely," said John Armitage, with unbroken gravity. "In fact, I rather expect him here, or I should be leaving to-day myself."

He bowed and made way for the vexed and chafing Claiborne, who gave his hand to Armitage hastily and jumped into the carriage.

"Your imitation cut-glass drummer has nearly caused us to miss our train. Thank the Lord, we've seen the last of that fellow."

Shirley said nothing, but gazed out of the window with a wondering look in her eyes. And on the way to Liverpool she thought often of Armitage's last words. "I rather expect him here, or I should be leaving to-day myself," he had said.

She was not sure whether, if it had not been for those words, she would have thought of him again at all. She remembered him as he stood framed in the carriage door —his gravity, his fine ease, the impression he gave of great physical strength, and of resources of character and courage.

And so Shirley Claiborne left Geneva, not knowing

the curious web that fate had woven for her, nor how those last words spoken by Armitage at the carriage door were to link her to strange adventures at the very threshold of her American home.

CHAPTER IV

JOHN ARMITAGE A PRISONER

All things are bright in the track of the sun,
  All things are fair I see;
And the light in a golden tide has run
  Down out of the sky to me.

And the world turns round and round and round,
  And my thought sinks into the sea;
The sea of peace and of joy profound
  Whose tide is mystery.
                              —*S. W. Duffield.*

The man whom John Armitage expected arrived at
the Hotel Monte Rosa a few hours after the Claibornes'
departure.

While he waited, Mr. Armitage employed his time to
advantage. He carefully scrutinized his wardrobe, and
after a process of elimination and substitution he packed
his raiment in two trunks and was ready to leave the
inn at ten minutes' notice. Between trains, when not
engaged in watching the incoming travelers, he smoked
a pipe over various packets of papers and letters, and

50

these he burned with considerable care. All the French
and German newspaper accounts of the murder of Count
von Stroebel he read carefully; and even more particularly he studied the condition of affairs in Vienna con-
sequent upon the great statesman's death. Secret
agents from Vienna and detectives from Paris had vis-
ited Geneva in their study of this astounding crime, and
had made much fuss and asked many questions; but
Mr. John Armitage paid no heed to them. He had held
the last conversation of length that any one had enjoyed with Count Ferdinand von Stroebel, but the fact
of this interview was known to no one, unless to one or
two hotel servants, and these held a very high opinion
of Mr. Armitage's character, based on his generosity in
the matter of gold coin; and there could, of course, be
no possible relationship between so shocking a tragedy
and a chance acquaintance between two travelers. Mr.
Armitage knew nothing that he cared to impart to detectives, and a great deal that he had no intention of
imparting to any one. He accumulated a remarkable
assortment of time-tables and advertisements of transatlantic sailings against sudden need, and even engaged
passage on three steamers sailing from English and
French ports within the week.

He expected that the person for whom he waited would go direct to the Hotel Monte Rosa for the reason that Shirley Claiborne had been there; and Armitage was not mistaken. When this person learned that the Claibornes had left, he would doubtless hurry after them. This is the conclusion that was reached by Mr. Armitage, who, at times, was singularly happy in his speculations as to the mental processes of other people. Sometimes, however, he made mistakes, as will appear.

The gentleman for whom John Armitage had been waiting arrived alone, and was received as a distinguished guest by the landlord.

Monsieur Chauvenet inquired for his friends the Claibornes, and was clearly annoyed to find that they had gone; and no sooner had this intelligence been conveyed to him than he, too, studied time-tables and consulted steamer advertisements. Mr. John Armitage in various discreet ways was observant of Monsieur Chauvenet's activities, and bookings at steamship offices interested him so greatly that he reserved passage on two additional steamers and ordered the straps buckled about his trunks, for it had occurred to him that he might find it necessary to leave Geneva in a hurry.

It was not likely that Monsieur Chauvenet, being now

under his eyes, would escape him ; and John Armitage, making a leisurely dinner, learned from his waiter that Monsieur Chauvenet, being worn from his travels, was dining alone in his rooms.

At about eight o'clock, as Armitage turned the pages of *Figaro* in the smoking-room, Chauvenet appeared at the door, scrutinized the group within, and passed on. Armitage had carried his coat, hat and stick into the smoking-room, to be ready for possible emergencies; and when Chauvenet stepped out into the street he followed.

It was unusually cold for the season, and a fine drizzle filled the air. Chauvenet struck off at once away from the lake, turned into the Boulevard Helvétique, thence into the Boulevard Froissart with its colony of *pensions*. He walked rapidly until he reached a house that was distinguished from its immediate neighbors only by its unlighted upper windows. He pulled the bell in the wall, and the door was at once opened and instantly closed.

Armitage, following at twenty yards on the opposite side of the street, paused abruptly at the sudden ending of his chase. It was not an hour for loitering, for the Genevan *gendarmerie* have rather good eyes, but Armitage had by no means satisfied his curiosity as to the na-

ture of Chauvenet's errand. He walked on to make sure
he was unobserved, crossed the street, and again passed
the dark, silent house which Chauvenet had entered.
He noted the place carefully; it gave no outward appearance of being occupied. He assumed, from the general
plan of the neighboring buildings, that there was a
courtyard at the rear of the darkened house, accessible
through a narrow passageway at the side. As he studied
the situation he kept moving to avoid observation, and
presently, at a moment when he was quite alone in the
street, walked rapidly to the house Chauvenet had entered.

Gentlemen in search of adventures do well to avoid
the continental wall. Mr. Armitage brushed the glass
from the top with his hat. It jingled softly within
under cover of the rain-drip. The plaster had crumbled
from the bricks in spots, giving a foot its opportunity,
and Mr. Armitage drew himself to the top and dropped
within. The front door and windows stared at him
blankly, and he committed his fortunes to the bricked
passageway. The rain was now coming down in earnest,
and at the rear of the house water had begun to drip
noisily into an iron spout. The electric lights from
neighboring streets made a kind of twilight even in the

darkened court, and Armitage threaded his way among
a network of clothes-lines to the rear wall and viewed the
premises. He knew his Geneva from many previous
visits; the quarter was undeniably respectable; and
there is, to be sure, no reason why the blinds of a house
should not be carefully drawn at nightfall at the pleasure of the occupants. The whole lower floor seemed utterly deserted; only at one point on the third floor was
there any sign of light, and this the merest hint.

The increasing fall of rain did not encourage loitering in the wet courtyard, where the downspout now
rattled dolorously, and Armitage crossed the court and
further assured himself that the lower floor was dark and
silent. Balconies were bracketed against the wall at the
second and third stories, and the slight iron ladder leading thither terminated a foot above his head. John
Armitage was fully aware that his position, if discovered, was, to say the least, untenable; but he was secure
from observation by police, and he assumed that the
occupants of the house were probably too deeply engrossed with their affairs to waste much time on what
might happen without. Armitage sprang up and caught
the lowest round of the ladder, and in a moment his tall
figure was a dark blur against the wall as he crept

warily upward. The rear rooms of the second story were as dark and quiet as those below. Armitage continued to the third story, where a door, as well as several windows, gave upon the balcony; and he found that it was from a broken corner of the door shade that a sharp blade of light cut the dark. All continued quiet below; he heard the traffic of the neighboring thoroughfares quite distinctly; and from a kitchen near by came the rough clatter of dishwashing to the accompaniment of a quarrel in German between the maids. For the moment he felt secure, and bent down close to the door and listened.

Two men were talking, and evidently the matter under discussion was of importance, for they spoke with a kind of dogged deliberation, and the long pauses in the dialogue lent color to the belief that some weighty matter was in debate. The beat of the rain on the balcony and its steady rattle in the spout intervened to dull the sound of voices, but presently one of the speakers, with an impatient exclamation, rose, opened the small glass-paned door a few inches, peered out, and returned to his seat with an exclamation of relief. Armitage had dropped down the ladder half a dozen rounds as he heard the latch snap in the door. He waited an instant to make sure he had not been seen, then crept back to the balcony and found that the slight opening in the door made it possible for him to see as well as hear.

"It's stifling in this hole," said Chauvenet, drawing deeply upon his cigarette and blowing a cloud of smoke. "If you will pardon the informality, I will lay aside my coat."

He carefully hung the garment upon the back of his chair to hold its shape, then resumed his seat. His companion watched him meanwhile with a certain intentness.

"You take excellent care of your clothes, my dear Jules. I never have been able to fold a coat without ruining it."

The rain was soaking Armitage thoroughly, but its persistent beat covered any slight noises made by his own movements, and he was now intent upon the little room and its occupants. He observed the care with which the man kept close to his coat, and he pondered the matter as he hung upon the balcony. If Chauvenet was on his way to America it was possible that he would carry with him the important paper whose loss had caused so much anxiety to the Austrian minister; if so, where was it during his stay in Geneva?

"The old man's death is only the first step. We require a succession of deaths."

"We require three, to be explicit, not more or less. We should be fortunate if the remaining two could be accomplished as easily as Stroebel's."

"He was a beast. He is well dead."

"That depends on the way you look at it. They seem really to be mourning the old beggar at Vienna. It is the way of a people. They like to be ruled by a savage hand. The people, as you have heard me say before, are fools."

The last speaker was a young man whom Armitage had never seen before; he was a decided blond, with close-trimmed straw-colored beard and slightly-curling hair. Opposite him, and facing the door, sat Chauvenet. On the table between them were decanters and liqueur glasses.

"I am going to America at once," said Chauvenet, holding his filled glass toward a brass lamp of an old type that hung from the ceiling.

"It is probably just as well," said the other. "There's work to do there. We must not forget our more legitimate business in the midst of these pleasant side issues."

"The field is easy. After our delightful continental

capitals, where, as you know, one is never quite sure of
one's self, it is pleasant to breathe the democratic airs
of Washington," remarked Chauvenet.

"Particularly so, my dear friend, when one is blessed
with your delightful social gifts. I envy you your capacity for making others happy."

There was a keen irony in the fellow's tongue and the
edge of it evidently touched Chauvenet, who scowled
and bent forward with his fingers on the table.

"Enough of that, if you please."

"As you will, *carino;* but you will pardon me for
offering my condolences on the regrettable departure of
la belle Americaine. If you had not been so intent on
matters of state you would undoubtedly have found her
here. As it is, you are now obliged to see her on her native soil. A month in Washington may do much for
you. She is beautiful and reasonably rich. Her brother,
the tall captain, is said to be the best horseman in the
American army."

"Humph! He is an ass," ejaculated Chauvenet.

A servant now appeared bearing a fresh bottle of
cordial. He was distinguished by a small head upon a
tall and powerful body, and bore little resemblance to a
house servant. While he brushed the cigar ashes from

the table the men continued their talk without heeding him.

Chauvenet and his friend had spoken from the first in French, but in addressing some directions to the servant, the blond, who assumed the rôle of host, employed a Servian dialect.

"I think we were saying that the mortality list in certain directions will have to be stimulated a trifle before we can do our young friend Francis any good. You have business in America, *carino*. That paper we filched from old Stroebel strengthens our hold on Francis; but there is still that question as to Karl and Frederick Augustus. Our dear Francis is not satisfied. He wishes to be quite sure that his dear father and brother are dead. We must reassure him, dearest Jules."

"Don't be a fool, Durand. You never seem to understand that the United States of America is a trifle larger than a barnyard. And I don't believe those fellows are over there. They're probably lying in wait here somewhere, ready to take advantage of any opportunity,—that is, if they are alive. A man can hardly fail to be impressed with the fact that so few lives stand between him and—"

"The heights—the heights!" And the young man,

whom Chauvenet called Durand, lifted his tiny glass airily.

"Yes; the heights," repeated Chauvenet a little dreamily.

"But that declaration—that document! You have never honored me with a glimpse; but you have it put safely away, I dare say."

"There is no place—but one—that I dare risk. It is always within easy reach, my dear friend."

"You will do well to destroy that document. It is better out of the way."

"Your deficiencies in the matter of wisdom are unfortunate. That paper constitutes our chief asset, my dear associate. So long as we have it we are able to keep dear Francis in order. Therefore we shall hold fast to it, remembering that we risked much in removing it from the lamented Stroebel's archives."

"Do you say 'risked much'? My valued neck, that is all!" said the other. "You and Winkelried are without gratitude."

"You will do well," said Chauvenet, "to keep an eye open in Vienna for the unknown. If you hear murmurs in Hungary one of these fine days—! Nothing has happened for some time; therefore much may happen."

He glanced at his watch.

"I have work in Paris before sailing for New York. Shall we discuss the matter of those Peruvian claims? That is business. These other affairs are more in the nature of delightful diversions, my dear comrade."

They drew nearer the table and Durand produced a box of papers over which he bent with serious attention. Armitage had heard practically all of their dialogue, and, what was of equal interest, had been able to study the faces and learn the tones of voice of the two conspirators. He was cramped from his position on the narrow balcony and wet and chilled by the rain, which was now slowly abating. He had learned much that he wished to know, and with an ease that astonished him; and he was well content to withdraw with gratitude for his good fortune.

His legs were numb and he clung close to the railing of the little ladder for support as he crept toward the area. At the second story his foot slipped on the wet iron, smooth from long use, and he stumbled down several steps before he recovered himself. He listened a moment, heard nothing but the tinkle of the rain in the spout, then continued his retreat.

As he stepped out upon the brick courtyard he was

seized from behind by a pair of strong arms that clasped him tight. In a moment he was thrown across the threshold of a door into an unlighted room, where his captor promptly sat upon him and proceeded to strike a light.

CHAPTER V

To other woods the trail leads on,
To other worlds and new,
Where they who keep the secret here
Will keep the promise too.
—*Henry A. Beers.*

The man clenched Armitage about the body with his
legs while he struck a match on a box he produced from
his pocket. The suddenness with which he had been
flung into the kitchen had knocked the breath out of
Armitage, and the huge thighs of his captor pinned his
arms tight. The match spurted fire and he looked into
the face of the servant whom he had seen in the room
above. His round head was covered with short, wire-like
hair that grew low upon his narrow forehead. Armitage
noted, too, the man's bull-like neck, small sharp eyes and
bristling mustache. The fitful flash of the match disclosed the rough furniture of a kitchen; the brick flooring and his wet inverness lay cold at Armitage's back.

64

The fellow growled an execration in Servian; then with ponderous difficulty asked a question in German. "Who are you and what do you want here?"

Armitage shook his head; and replied in English: "I do not understand."

The man struck a series of matches that he might scrutinize his captive's face, then ran his hands over Armitage's pockets to make sure he had no arms. The big fellow was clearly puzzled to find that he had caught a gentleman in water-soaked evening clothes lurking in the area, and as the matter was beyond his wits it only remained for him to communicate with his master. This, however, was not so readily accomplished. He had reasons of his own for not calling out, and there were difficulties in the way of holding the prisoner and at the same time bringing down the men who had gone to the most distant room in the house for their own security.

Several minutes passed during which the burly Servian struck his matches and took account of his prisoner; and meanwhile Armitage lay perfectly still, his arms fast numbing from the rough clasp of the stalwart servant's legs. There was nothing to be gained by a struggle in this position, and he knew that the Servian would not risk losing him in the effort to summon the

odd pair who were bent over their papers at the top of
the house. The Servian was evidently a man of action.

"Get up," he commanded, still in rough German, and
he rose in the dark and jerked Armitage after him.
There was a moment of silence in which Armitage shook
and stretched himself, and then the Servian struck another match and held it close to a revolver which he
held pointed at Armitage's head.

"I will shoot," he said again in his halting German.

"Undoubtedly you will!" and something in the fellow's manner caused Armitage to laugh. He had been
caught and he did not at once see any safe issue out of
his predicament; but his plight had its preposterous
side and the ease with which he had been taken at the
very outset of his quest touched his humor. Then he
sobered instantly and concentrated his wits upon the
immediate situation.

The Servian backed away with a match upheld in one
hand and the leveled revolver in the other, leaving Armitage in the middle of the kitchen.

"I am going to light a lamp and if you move I will
kill you," admonished the fellow, and Armitage heard
his feet scraping over the brick floor of the kitchen as he
backed toward a table that stood against the wall near
the outer door.

Armitage stood perfectly still. The neighborhood and the house itself were quiet; the two men in the third-story room were probably engrossed with the business at which Armitage had left them; and his immediate affair was with the Servian alone. The fellow continued to mumble his threats; but Armitage had resolved to play the part of an Englishman who understood no German, and he addressed the man sharply in English several times to signify that he did not understand.

The Servian half turned toward his prisoner, the revolver in his left hand, while with the fingers of his right he felt laboriously for a lamp that had been revealed by the fitful flashes of the matches. It is not an easy matter to light a lamp when you have only one hand to work with, particularly when you are obliged to keep an eye on a mysterious prisoner of whose character you are ignorant; and it was several minutes before the job was done.

"You will go to that corner;" and the Servian translated for his prisoner's benefit with a gesture of the revolver.

"Anything to please you, worthy fellow," replied Armitage, and he obeyed with amiable alacrity. The man's object was to get him as far from the inner door as pos-

sible while he called help from above, which was, of
course, the wise thing from his point of view, as Armitage recognized.

Armitage stood with his back against a rack of pots;
the table was at his left and beyond it the door opening
upon the court; a barred window was at his right; opposite him was another door that communicated with the
interior of the house and disclosed the lower steps of a
rude stairway leading upward. The Servian now closed
and locked the outer kitchen door with care.

Armitage had lost his hat in the area; his light walk-
ing-stick lay in the middle of the floor; his inverness
coat hung wet and bedraggled about him; his shirt was
crumpled and soiled. But his air of good humor and his
tame acceptance of capture seemed to increase the Servian's caution, and he backed away toward the inner
door with his revolver still pointed at Armitage's head.

He began calling lustily up the narrow stair-well in
Servian, changing in a moment to German. He made
a ludicrous figure, as he held his revolver at arm's
length, craning his neck into the passage, and howling
until he was red in the face. He paused to listen, then
renewed his cries, while Armitage, with his back against
the rack of pots, studied the room and made his plans.

Armitage stood with his back against a rack of pots   *Page 68*

"There is a thief here! I have caught a thief!" yelled the Servian, now exasperated by the silence above. Then, as he relaxed a moment and turned to make sure that his revolver still covered Armitage, there was a sudden sound of steps above and a voice bawled angrily down the stairway:

"Zmai, stop your noise and tell me what's the trouble."

It was the voice of Durand speaking in the Servian dialect; and Zmai opened his mouth to explain.

As the big fellow roared his reply Armitage snatched from the rack a heavy iron boiling-pot, swung it high by the bail with both hands and let it fly with all his might at the Servian's head, upturned in the earnestness of his bawling. On the instant the revolver roared loudly in the narrow kitchen and Armitage seized the brass lamp and flung it from him upon the hearth, where it fell with a great clatter without exploding.

It was instantly pitch dark. The Servian had gone down like a felled ox and Armitage at the threshold leaped over him into the hall past the rear stairs down which the men were stumbling, cursing volubly as they came.

Armitage had assumed the existence of a front stair-way, and now that he was launched upon an unexpected adventure, he was in a humor to prolong it for a moment, even at further risk. He crept along a dark passage to the front door, found and turned the key to provide himself with a ready exit, then, as he heard the men from above stumble over the prostrate Servian, he bounded up the front stairway, gained the second floor, then the third, and readily found by its light the room that he had observed earlier from the outside.

Below there was smothered confusion and the crackling of matches as Durand and Chauvenet sought to grasp the unexpected situation that confronted them. The big servant, Armitage knew, would hardly be able to clear matters for them at once, and he hurriedly turned over the packets of papers that lay on the table. They were claims of one kind and another against several South and Central American republics, chiefly for naval and military supplies, and he merely noted their general character. They were, on the face of it, certified accounts in the usual manner of business. On the back of each had been printed with a rubber stamp the words:

Vienna, Paris, Washington.
Chauvenet et Durand.

Armitage snatched up the coat which Chauvenet had

so carefully placed on the back of his chair, ran his hands through the pockets, found them empty, then gathered the garment tightly in his hands, laughed a little to himself to feel papers sewn into the lining, and laughed again as he tore the lining loose and drew forth a flat linen envelope brilliant with three seals of red wax.

Steps sounded below; a man was running up the back stairs; and from the kitchen rose sounds of mighty groanings and cursings in the heavy gutturals of the Servian, as he regained his wits and sought to explain his plight.

Armitage picked up a chair, ran noiselessly to the head of the back stairs, and looked down upon Chauvenet, who was hurrying up with a flaming candle held high above his head, its light showing anxiety and fear upon his face. He was half-way up the last flight, and Armitage stood in the dark, watching him with a mixture of curiosity and something, too, of humor. Then he spoke —in French—in a tone that imitated the cool irony he had noted in Durand's tone:

"A few murders more or less! But Von Stroebel was hardly a fair mark, dearest Jules!"

With this he sent the chair clattering down the steps, where it struck Jules Chauvenet's legs with a force that carried him howling lustily backward to the second landing.

Armitage turned and sped down the front stairway, hearing renewed clamor from the rear and cries of rage and pain from the second story. In fumbling for the front door he found a hat, and, having lost his own, placed it upon his head, drew his inverness about his shoulders, and went quickly out. A moment later he slipped the catch in the wall door and stepped into the boulevard.

The stars were shining among the flying clouds overhead and he drew deep breaths of the freshened air into his lungs as he walked back to the Monte Rosa. Occasionally he laughed quietly to himself, for he still grasped tightly in his hand, safe under his coat, the envelope which Chauvenet had carried so carefully concealed; and several times Armitage muttered to himself:

"A few murders, more or less!"

At the hotel he changed his clothes, threw the things from his dressing-table into a bag, and announced his departure for Paris by the night express.

As he drove to the railway station he felt for his cigarette case, and discovered that it was missing. The loss evidently gave him great concern, for he searched and researched his pockets and opened his bags at the station to see if he had by any chance overlooked it, but it was not to be found.

His annoyance at the loss was balanced—could he have known it—by the interest with which, almost before the wall door had closed upon him, two gentlemen —one of them still in his shirt sleeves and with a purple lump over his forehead—bent over a gold cigarette case in the dark house on the Boulevard Froissart. It was a pretty trinket, and contained, when found on the kitchen floor, exactly four cigarettes of excellent Turkish tobacco. On one side of it was etched, in shadings of blue and white enamel, a helmet, surmounted by a falcon, poised for flight, and, beneath, the motto *Fide non armis.* The back bore in English script, written large, the letters *F. A.*

The men stared at each other wonderingly for an instant, then both leaped to their feet.

"It isn't possible!" gasped Durand.

"It is quite possible," replied Chauvenet. "The emblem is unmistakable. Good God, look!"

The sweat had broken out on Chauvenet's face and he leaped to the chair where his coat hung, and caught up the garment with shaking hands. The silk lining fluttered loose where Armitage had roughly torn out the envelope.

"Who is he? Who is he?" whispered Durand, very white of face.

"It may be—it must be some one deeply concerned."

Chauvenet paused, drawing his hand across his forehead slowly; then the color leaped back into his face, and he caught Durand's arm so tight that the man flinched.

"There has been a man following me about; I thought he was interested in the Claibornes. He's here—I saw him at the Monte Rosa to-night. God!"

He dropped his hand from Durand's arm and struck the table fiercely with his clenched hand.

"John Armitage—John Armitage! I heard his name in Florence."

His eyes were snapping with excitement, and amazement grew in his face.

"Who is John Armitage?" demanded Durand sharply; but Chauvenet stared at him in stupefaction for a tense moment, then muttered to himself:

"Is it possible? Is it possible?" and his voice was hoarse and his hand trembled as he picked up the cigarette case.

"My dear Jules, you act as though you had seen a ghost. Who the devil is Armitage?"

Chauvenet glanced about the room cautiously, then bent forward and whispered very low, close to Durand's ear:

"Suppose he were the son of the crazy Karl! Suppose he were Frederick Augustus!"

"Bah! It is impossible! What is your man Armitage like?" asked Durand irritably.

"He is the right age. He is a big fellow and has quite an air. He seems to be without occupation."

"Clearly so," remarked Durand ironically. "But he has evidently been watching us. Quite possibly the lamented Stroebel employed him. He may have seen Stroebel here—"

Chauvenet again struck the table smartly.

"Of course he would see Stroebel! Stroebel was the Archduke's friend; Stroebel and this fellow between them—"

"Stroebel is dead. The Archduke is dead; there can be no manner of doubt of that," said Durand; but doubt was in his tone and in his eyes.

"Nothing is certain; it would be like Karl to turn up again with a son to back his claims. They may both be living. This Armitage is not the ordinary pig of a secret agent. We must find him."

"And quickly. There must be—"

"—another death added to our little list before we are quite masters of the situation in Vienna."

They gave Zmai orders to remain on guard at the house and went hurriedly out together.

CHAPTER VI

Her blue eyes sought the west afar,
For lovers love the western star.
              —*Lay of the Last Minstrel.*

Geneva is a good point from which to plan flight to
any part of the world, for there at the top of Europe
the whole continental railway system is easily within
your grasp, and you may make your choice of sailing
ports. It is, to be sure, rather out of your way to seek a
ship at Liverpool unless you expect to gain some particular advantage in doing so. Mr. John Armitage hurried thither in the most breathless haste to catch the
King Edward, whereas he might have taken the *Tou-
raine* at Cherbourg and saved himself a mad scamper;
but his satisfaction in finding himself aboard the *King
Edward* was supreme. He was and is, it may be said, a
man who salutes the passing days right amiably, no matter how somber their colors.

Shirley Claiborne and Captain Richard Claiborne, her

brother, were on deck watching the shipping in the Mersey as the big steamer swung into the channel.

"I hope," observed Dick, "that we have shaken off all your transatlantic suitors. That little Chauvenet died easier than I had expected. He never turned up after we left Florence, but I'm not wholly sure that we shan't find him at the dock in New York. And that mysterious Armitage, who spent so much railway fare following us about, and who almost bought you a watch in Geneva, really disappoints me. His persistence had actually compelled my admiration. For a glass-blower he was fairly decent, though, and better than a lot of these little toy men with imitation titles."

"Is that an American cruiser? I really believe it is the *Tecumseh*. What on earth were you talking about, Dick?"

Shirley fluttered her handkerchief in the direction of the American flag displayed by the cruiser, and Dick lifted his cap.

"I was bidding farewell to your foreign suitors, Shirley, and congratulating myself that as soon as *père et mère* get their sea legs they will resume charge of you, and let me look up two or three very presentable specimens of your sex I saw come on board. Your affairs

have annoyed me greatly and I shall be glad to be free
of the responsibility."

"Thank you, Captain."

"And if there are any titled blackguards on board—"

"You will do dreadfully wicked things to them, won't
you, little brother?"

"Humph! Thank God, I'm an American!"

"That's a worthy sentiment, Richard."

"I'd like to give out, as our newspapers say, a signed
statement throwing a challenge to all Europe. I wish
we'd get into a real war once so we could knock the conceit out of one of their so-called first-class powers. I'd
like to lead a regiment right through the most sacred
precincts of London; or take an early morning gallop
through Berlin to wake up the Dutch. All this talk
about hands across the sea and such rot makes me sick.
The English are the most benighted and the most con-
ceited and condescending race on earth; the Germans
and Austrians are stale beer-vats, and the Italians and
French are mere decadents and don't count."

"Yes, dearest," mocked Shirley. "Oh, my large
brother, I have a confession to make. Please don't in-
dulge in great oaths or stamp a hole in this sturdy deck,
but there are flowers in my state-room—"

"Probably from the Liverpool consul—he's been pestering father to help him get a transfer to a less gloomy hole."

"Then I shall intercede myself with the President when I get home. They're orchids—from London—but —with Mr. Armitage's card. Wouldn't that excite you?"

"It makes me sick!" and Dick hung heavily on the rail and glared at a passing tug.

"They are beautiful orchids. I don't remember when orchids have happened to me before, Richard—in such quantities. Now, you really didn't disapprove of him so much, did you? This is probably good-by forever, but he wasn't so bad; and he may be an American, after all."

"A common adventurer! Such fellows are always turning up, like bad pennies, or a one-eyed dog. If I should see him again—"

"Yes, Richard, if you should meet again—"

"I'd ask him to be good enough to stop following us about, and if he persisted I should muss him up."

"Yes; I'm sure you would protect me from his importunities at any hazard," mocked Shirley, turning and leaning against the rail so that she looked along the deck beyond her brother's stalwart shoulders.

"Don't be silly," observed Dick, whose eyes were upon
a trim yacht that was steaming slowly beneath them.

"I shan't, but please don't be violent! Do not murder
the poor man, Dickie, dear,"—and she took hold of his
arm entreatingly—"for there he is—as tall and mysterious as ever—and me found guilty with a few of his
orchids pinned to my jacket!"

"This is good fortune, indeed," said Armitage a moment later when they had shaken hands. "I finished my
errand at Geneva unexpectedly and here I am."

He smiled at the feebleness of his explanation, and
joined in their passing comment on the life of the harbor. He was not so dull but that he felt Dick Claiborne's
resentment of his presence on board. He knew perfectly
well that his acquaintance with the Claibornes was too
slight to be severely strained, particularly where a fellow of Dick Claiborne's high spirit was concerned. He
talked with them a few minutes longer, then took himself off; and they saw little of him the rest of the day.

Armitage did not share their distinction of a seat at
the captain's table, and Dick found him late at night in
the smoking-saloon with pipe and book. Armitage nodded and asked him to sit down.

"You are a sailor as well as a soldier, Captain. You

are fortunate; I always sit up the first night to make
sure the enemy doesn't lay hold of me in my sleep."

He tossed his book aside, had brandy and soda brought
and offered Claiborne a cigar.

"This is not the most fortunate season for crossing;
I am sure to fall to-morrow. My father and mother hate
the sea particularly and have retired for three days. My
sister is the only one of us who is perfectly immune."

"Yes; I can well image Miss Claiborne in the good
graces of the elements," replied Armitage; and they
were silent for several minutes while a big Russian, who
was talking politics in a distant corner with a very small
and solemn German, boomed out his views on the East-
ern question in a tremendous bass.

Dick Claiborne was a good deal amused at finding
himself sitting beside Armitage,—enjoying, indeed, his
fellow traveler's hospitality; but Armitage, he was forced
to admit, bore all the marks of a gentleman. He had, to
be sure, followed Shirley about, but even the young
man's manner in this was hardly a matter at which he
could cavil. And there was something altogether likable
in Armitage; his very composure was attractive to Claiborne; and the bold lines of his figure were not wasted
on the young officer. In the silence, while they smoked,

he noted the perfect taste that marked Armitage's belongings, which to him meant more, perhaps, than the
steadiness of the man's eyes or the fine lines of his face.
Unconsciously Claiborne found himself watching Armitage's strong ringless hands, and he knew that such a
hand, well kept though it appeared, had known hard
work, and that the long supple fingers were such as
might guide a tiller fearlessly or set a flag daringly upon
a fire-swept parapet.

Armitage was thinking rapidly of something he had
suddenly resolved to say to Captain Claiborne. He knew
that the Claibornes were a family of distinction; the
father was an American diplomat and lawyer of wide
reputation; the family stood for the best of which America is capable, and they were homeward bound to the
American capital where their social position and the
father's fame made them conspicuous.

Armitage put down his cigar and bent toward Claiborne, speaking with quiet directness.

"Captain Claiborne, I was introduced to you at Geneva by Mr. Singleton. You may have observed me several times previously at Venice, Rome, Florence, Paris,
Berlin. I certainly saw you! I shall not deny that I in-
tentionally followed you, nor"—John Armitage smiled,

then grew grave again—"can I make any adequate apology for doing so."

Claiborne looked at Armitage wonderingly. The man's attitude and tone were wholly serious and compelled respect. Claiborne nodded and threw away his cigar that he might give his whole attention to what Armitage might have to say.

"A man does not like to have his sister forming the acquaintances of persons who are not properly vouched for. Except for Singleton you know nothing of me; and Singleton knows very little of me, indeed."

Claiborne nodded. He felt the color creeping into his cheeks consciously as Armitage touched upon this matter.

"I speak to you as I do because it is your right to know who and what I am, for I am not on the *King Edward* by accident but by intention, and I am going to Washington because your sister lives there."

Claiborne smiled in spite of himself.

"But, my dear sir, this is most extraordinary! I don't know that I care to hear any more; by listening I seem to be encouraging you to follow us—it's altogether too unusual. It's almost preposterous!"

And Dick Claiborne frowned severely; but Armitage still met his eyes gravely.

"It's only decent for a man to give his references when it's natural for them to be required. I was educated at Trinity College, Toronto. I spent a year at the Harvard Law School. And I am not a beggar utterly. I own a ranch in Montana that actually pays and a thousand acres of the best wheat land in Nebraska. At the Bronx Loan and Trust Company in New York I have securities to a considerable amount,—I am perfectly willing that any one who is at all interested should inquire of the Trust Company officers as to my standing with them. If I were asked to state my occupation I should have to say that I am a cattle herder—what you call a cowboy. I can make my living in the practice of the business almost anywhere from New Mexico north to the Canadian line. I flatter myself that I am pretty good at it," and John Armitage smiled and took a cigarette from a box on the table and lighted it.

Dick Claiborne was greatly interested in what Armitage had said, and he struggled between an inclination to encourage further confidence and a feeling that he should, for Shirley's sake, make it clear to this young stranger that it was of no consequence to any member of the Claiborne family who he was or what might be the extent of his lands or the unimpeachable character

of his investments. But it was not so easy to turn aside
a fellow who was so big of frame and apparently so sane
and so steady of purpose as this Armitage. And there
was, too, the further consideration that while Armitage
was volunteering gratuitous information, and assuming
an interest in his affairs by the Claibornes that was
wholly unjustified, there was also the other side of the
matter: that his explanations proceeded from motives
of delicacy that were praiseworthy. Dick was puzzled,
and piqued besides, to find that his resources as a
big protecting brother were so soon exhausted. What
Armitage was asking was the right to seek his sister
Shirley's hand in marriage, and the thing was absurd.
Moreover, who was John Armitage?

The question startled Claiborne into a realization of
the fact that Armitage had volunteered considerable information without at all answering this question. Dick
Claiborne was a human being, and curious.

"Pardon me," he asked, "but are you an Englishman?"

"I am not," answered Armitage. "I have been so long
in America that I feel as much at home there as anywhere—but I am neither English nor American by
birth; I am, on the other hand—"

He hesitated for the barest second, and Claiborne was sensible of an intensification of interest; now at last there was to be a revelation that amounted to something.

"On the other hand," Armitage repeated, "I was born at Fontainebleau, where my parents lived for only a few months; but I do not consider that that fact makes me a Frenchman. My mother is dead. My father died—very recently. I have been in America enough to know that a foreigner is often under suspicion—particularly if he have a title! My distinction is that I am a foreigner without one!" John Armitage laughed.

"It is, indeed, a real merit," declared Dick, who felt that something was expected of him. In spite of himself, he found much to like in John Armitage. He particularly despised sham and pretense, and he had been won by the evident sincerity of Armitage's wish to appear well in his eyes.

"And now," said Armitage, "I assure you that I am not in the habit of talking so much about myself—and if you will overlook this offense I promise not to bore you again."

"I have been interested," remarked Dick; "and," he added, "I can not do less than thank you, Mr. Armitage."

Armitage began talking of the American army—its strength and weaknesses—with an intimate knowledge that greatly surprised and interested the young officer; and when they separated presently it was with a curious mixture of liking and mystification that Claiborne reviewed their talk.

The next day brought heavy weather, and only hardened sea-goers were abroad. Armitage, breakfasting late, was not satisfied that he had acted wisely in speaking to Captain Claiborne; but he had, at any rate, eased in some degree his own conscience, and he had every intention of seeing all that he could of Shirley Claiborne during these days of their fellow-voyaging.

CHAPTER VII

Ease, of all good gifts the best,
War and wave at last decree:
Love alone denies us rest,
Crueler than sword or sea.
William Watson.

"I am Columbus every time I cross," said Shirley. "What lies out there in the west is an undiscovered country."

"Then I shall have to take the part of the rebellious and doubting crew. There is no America, and we're sure to get into trouble if we don't turn back."

"You shall be clapped into irons and fed on bread and water, and turned over to the Indians as soon as we reach land."

"Don't starve me! Let me hang from the yard-arm at once, or walk the plank. I choose the hour immediately after dinner for my obsequies!"

"Choose a cheerfuller word!" pleaded Shirley.

"I am sorry to suggest mortality, but I was trying to

89

let my imagination play a little on the eternal novelty of travel, and you have dropped me down 'full faddom five.'"

"I'm sorry, but I have only revealed an honest tendency of character. Piracy is probably a more profitable line of business than discovery. Discoverers benefit mankind at great sacrifice and expense, and die before they can receive the royal thanks. A pirate's business is all done over the counter on a strictly cash basis."

They were silent for a moment, continuing their tramp. Fair weather was peopling the decks. Dick Claiborne was engrossed with a vivacious California girl, and Shirley saw him only at meals; but he and Armitage held night sessions in the smoking-room, with increased liking on both sides.

"Armitage isn't a bad sort," Dick admitted to Shirley. "He's either an awful liar, or he's seen a lot of the world."

"Of course, he has to travel to sell his glassware," observed Shirley. "I'm surprised at your seeming intimacy with a mere 'peddler,'—and you an officer in the finest cavalry in the world."

"Well, if he's a peddler he's a high-class one—probably the junior member of the firm that owns the works."

Armitage saw something of all the Claibornes every
day in the pleasant intimacy of ship life, and Hilton
Claiborne found the young man an interesting talker.
Judge Claiborne is, as every one knows, the best-posted
American of his time in diplomatic history; and when
they were together Armitage suggested topics that were
well calculated to awaken the old lawyer's interest.

"The glass-blower's a deep one, all right," remarked
Dick to Shirley. "He jollies me occasionally, just to
show there's no hard feeling; then he jollies the governor; and when I saw our mother footing it on his arm
this afternoon I almost fell in a faint. I wish you'd
hold on to him tight till we're docked. My little friend
from California is crazy about him—and I haven't dared
tell her he's only a drummer; such a fling would be un-
chivalrous of me—"

"It would, Richard. Be a generous foe—whether—
whether you can afford to be or not!"

"My sister—my own sister says this to me! This is
quite the unkindest. I'm going to offer myself to the
daughter of the redwoods at once."

Shirley and Armitage talked—as people will on ship-
board—of everything under the sun. Shirley's enthusi-
asms were in themselves interesting; but she was

informed in the world's larger affairs, as became the
daughter of a man who was an authority in such matters,
and found it pleasant to discuss them with Armitage.
He felt the poetic quality in her; it was that which had
first appealed to him; but he did not know that something of the same sort in himself touched her; it was
enough for those days that he was courteous and amusing, and gained a trifle in her eyes from the fact that he
had no tangible background.

Then came the evening of the fifth day. They were
taking a turn after dinner on the lighted deck. The
spring stars hung faint and far through thin clouds and
the wind was keen from the sea. A few passengers were
out; the deck stewards went about gathering up rugs
and chairs for the night.

"Time oughtn't to be reckoned at all at sea, so that
people who feel themselves getting old might sail forth
into the deep and defy the old man with the hour-glass."

"I like the idea. Such people could become fishers—
permanently, and grow very wise from so much brain
food."

"They wouldn't eat, Mr. Armitage. Brain-food forsooth! You talk like a breakfast-food advertisement.
My idea—mine, please note—is for such fortunate peo-

ple to sail in pretty little boats with orange-tinted sails
and pick up lost dreams. I got a hint of that in a pretty
poem once—

> " 'Time seemed to pause a little pace,
>   I heard a dream go by.' "

"But out here in mid-ocean a little boat with lateen
sails wouldn't have much show. And dreams passing
over—the idea is pretty, and is creditable to your imagination. But I thought your fancy was more militant.
Now, for example, you like battle pictures—" he said,
and paused inquiringly.

She looked at him quickly.

"How do you know I do?"

"You like Detaille particularly."

"Am I to defend my taste?—what's the answer, if you
don't mind?"

"Detaille is much to my liking, also; but I prefer
Flameng, as a strictly personal matter. That was a wonderful collection of military and battle pictures shown
in Paris last winter."

She half withdrew her hand from his arm, and turned
away. The sea winds did not wholly account for the
sudden color in her cheeks. She had seen Armitage in
Paris—in cafés, at the opera, but not at the great exhibi-

tion of world-famous battle pictures; yet undoubtedly
he had seen her; and she remembered with instant con-
sciousness the hours of absorption she had spent before
those canvases.

"It was a public exhibition, I believe; there was no
great harm in seeing it."

"No; there certainly was not!" He laughed, then was
serious at once. Shirley's tense, arrested figure, her
bright, eager eyes, her parted lips, as he saw her before
the battle pictures in the gallery at Paris, came up before
him and gave him pause. He could not play upon that
stolen glance or tease her curiosity in respect to it. If
this were a ship flirtation, it might be well enough; but
the very sweetness and open-heartedness of her youth
shielded her. It seemed to him in that moment a con-
temptible and unpardonable thing that he had followed
her about—and caught her, there at Paris, in an exalted
mood, to which she had been wrought by the moving incidents of war.

"I was in Paris during the exhibition," he said quietly.
"Ormsby, the American painter—the man who did the
High Tide at Gettysburg—is an acquaintance of mine."

"Oh!"

It was Ormsby's painting that had particularly captivated Shirley. She had returned to it day after day; and the thought that Armitage had taken advantage of her deep interest in Pickett's charging gray line was annoying, and she abruptly changed the subject.

Shirley had speculated much as to the meaning of Armitage's remark at the carriage door in Geneva—that he expected the slayer of the old Austrian prime minister to pass that way. Armitage had not referred to the crime in any way in his talks with her on the *King Edward;* their conversations had been pitched usually in a light and frivolous key, or if one were disposed to be serious the other responded in a note of levity.

"We're all imperialists at heart," said Shirley, referring to a talk between them earlier in the day. "We Americans are hungry for empire; we're simply waiting for the man on horseback to gallop down Broadway and up Fifth Avenue with a troop of cavalry at his heels and proclaim the new dispensation."

"And before he'd gone a block a big Irish policeman would arrest him for disorderly conduct or disturbing the peace, or for giving a show without a license, and the republic would continue to do business at the old stand."

"No; the police would have been bribed in advance,

and would deliver the keys of the city to the new emperor at the door of St. Patrick's Cathedral, and his
majesty would go to Sherry's for luncheon, and sign a
few decrees, and order the guillotine set up in Union
Square. Do you follow me, Mr. Armitage?"

"Yes; to the very steps of the guillotine, Miss Claiborne. But the looting of the temples and the plunder-
ing of banks—if the thing is bound to be—I should like
to share in the general joy. But I have an idea, Miss
Claiborne," he exclaimed, as though with inspiration.

"Yes—you have an idea—"

"Let me be the man on horseback; and you might
be—"

"Yes—the suspense is terrible!—what might I be,
your Majesty?"

"Well, we should call you—"

He hesitated, and she wondered whether he would be
bold enough to meet the issue offered by this turn of
their nonsense.

"I seem to give your Majesty difficulty; the silence
isn't flattering," she said mockingly; but she was conscious of a certain excitement as she walked the deck beside him.

"Oh, pardon me! The difficulty is only as to title—

you would, of course, occupy the dais; but whether you should be queen or empress—that's the rub! If America is to be an empire, then of course you would be an empress. So there you are answered."

They passed laughingly on to the other phases of the matter in the whimsical vein that was natural in her, and to which he responded. They watched the lights of an east-bound steamer that was passing near. The exchange of rocket signals—that pretty and graceful parley between ships that pass in the night—interested them for a moment. Then the deck lights went out so suddenly it seemed that a dark curtain had descended and shut them in with the sea.

"Accident to the dynamo—we shall have the lights on in a moment!" shouted the deck officer, who stood near, talking to a passenger.

"Shall we go in?" asked Armitage.

"Yes, it is getting cold," replied Shirley.

For a moment they were quite alone on the dark deck, though they heard voices near at hand.

They were groping their way toward the main saloon, where they had left Mr. and Mrs. Claiborne, when Shirley was aware of some one lurking near. A figure seemed to be crouching close by, and she felt its furtive

movements and knew that it had passed but remained
a few feet away. Her hand on Armitage's arm tightened.

"What is that?—there is some one following us," she
said.

At the same moment Armitage, too, became aware of
the presence of a stooping figure behind him. He
stopped abruptly and faced about.

"Stand quite still, Miss Claiborne."

He peered about, and instantly, as though waiting for
his voice, a tall figure rose not a yard from him and a
long arm shot high above his head and descended swiftly.
They were close to the rail, and a roll of the ship sent
Armitage off his feet and away from his assailant. Shirley at the same moment threw out her hands, defensively
or for support, and clutched the arm and shoulder of the
man who had assailed Armitage. He had driven a knife
at John Armitage, and was poising himself for another
attempt when Shirley seized his arm. As he drew back
a fold of his cloak still lay in Shirley's grasp, and she
gave a sharp little cry as the figure, with a quick jerk,
released the cloak and slipped away into the shadows. A
moment later the lights were restored, and she saw Armitage regarding ruefully a long slit in the left arm of
his ulster.

"Are you hurt? What has happened?" she demanded.

"It must have been a sea-serpent," he replied, laughing.

The deck officer regarded them curiously as they blinked in the glare of light, and asked whether anything was wrong. Armitage turned the matter off.

"I guess it was a sea-serpent," he said. "It bit a hole in my ulster, for which I am not grateful." Then in a lower tone to Shirley: "That was certainly a strange proceeding. I am sorry you were startled; and I am under greatest obligations to you, Miss Claiborne. Why, you actually pulled the fellow away!"

"Oh, no," she returned lightly, but still breathing hard; "it was the instinct of self-preservation. I was unsteady on my feet for a moment, and sought something to take hold of. That pirate was the nearest thing, and I caught hold of his cloak; I'm sure it was a cloak, and that makes me sure he was a human villain of some sort. He didn't feel in the least like a sea-serpent. But some one tried to injure you—it is no jesting matter—"

"Some lunatic escaped from the steerage, probably. I shall report it to the officers."

"Yes, it should be reported," said Shirley.

"It was very strange. Why, the deck of the *King Ed-*

ward is the safest place in the world; but it's something
to have had hold of a sea-serpent, or a pirate! I hope
you will forgive me for bringing you into such an encounter; but if you hadn't caught his cloak—"

Armitage was uncomfortable, and anxious to allay
her fears. The incident was by no means trivial, as he
knew. Passengers on the great transatlantic steamers
are safeguarded by every possible means; and the fact
that he had been attacked in the few minutes that the
deck lights had been out of order pointed to an espio-
nage that was both close and daring. He was greatly
surprised and more shaken than he wished Shirley to
believe. The thing was disquieting enough, and it could
not but impress her strangely that he, of all the persons
on board, should have been the object of so unusual an
assault. He was in the disagreeable plight of having
subjected her to danger, and as they entered the brilliant saloon he freed himself of the ulster with its tell-
tale gash and sought to minimize her impression of the
incident.

Shirley did not refer to the matter again, but resolved
to keep her own counsel. She felt that any one who
would accept the one chance in a thousand of striking
down an enemy on a steamer deck must be animated by

very bitter hatred. She knew that to speak of the affair
to her father or brother would be to alarm them and
prejudice them against John Armitage, about whom her
brother, at least, had entertained doubts. And it is not
reassuring as to a man of whom little or nothing is
known that he is menaced by secret enemies.

The attack had found Armitage unprepared and off
guard, but with swift reaction his wits were at work. He
at once sought the purser and scrutinized every name on
the passenger list. It was unlikely that a steerage passenger could reach the saloon deck unobserved; a second
cabin passenger might do so, however, and he sought
among the names in the second cabin list for a clue. He
did not believe that Chauvenet or Durand had boarded
the *King Edward*. He himself had made the boat only
by a quick dash, and he had left those two gentlemen at
Geneva with much to consider.

It was, however, quite within the probabilities that
they would send some one to watch him, for the two men
whom he had overheard in the dark house on the Boulevard Froissart were active and resourceful rascals, he
had no doubt. Whether they would be able to make anything of the cigarette case he had stupidly left behind
he could not conjecture; but the importance of recover-

ing the packet he had cut from Chauvenet's coat was not
a trifle that rogues of their caliber would ignore. There
was, the purser said, a sick man in the second cabin,
who had kept close to his berth. The steward believed
the man to be a continental of some sort, who spoke bad
German. He had taken the boat at Liverpool, paid for
his passage in gold, and, complaining of illness, retired,
evidently for the voyage. His name was Peter Ludovic,
and the steward described him in detail.

"Big fellow; bullet head; bristling mustache; small
eyes—"

"That will do," said Armitage, grinning at the ease
with which he identified the man.

"You understand that it is wholly irregular for us to
let such a matter pass without acting—" said the purser.

"It would serve no purpose, and might do harm. I
will take the responsibility."

And John Armitage made a memorandum in his note-
book:

"Zmai ——; travels as Peter Ludovic."

Armitage carried the envelope which he had cut from
Chauvenet's coat pinned into an inner pocket of his
waistcoat, and since boarding the *King Edward* he had

examined it twice daily to see that it was intact. The three red wax seals were in blank, replacing those of like size that had originally been affixed to the envelope; and at once after the attack on the dark deck he opened the packet and examined the papers—some half-dozen sheets of thin linen, written in a clerk's clear hand in black ink. There had been no mistake in the matter; the packet which Chauvenet had purloined from the old prime minister at Vienna had come again into Armitage's hands. He was daily tempted to destroy it and cast it in bits to the sea winds; but he was deterred by the remembrance of his last interview with the old prime minister.

"Do something for Austria—something for the Empire." These phrases repeated themselves over and over again in his mind until they rose and fell with the cadence of the high, wavering voice of the Cardinal Archbishop of Vienna as he chanted the mass of requiem for Count Ferdinand von Stroebel.

CHAPTER VIII

Low he lies, yet high and great
Looms he, lying thus in state.—
How exalted o'er ye when
Dead, my lords and gentlemen!
                    —*James Whitcomb Riley*.

John Armitage lingered in New York for a week, not to press the Claibornes too closely, then went to Washington. He wrote himself down on the register of the New American as John Armitage, Cinch Tight, Montana, and took a suite of rooms high up, with an outlook that swept Pennsylvania Avenue. It was on the evening of a bright April day that he thus established himself; and after he had unpacked his belongings he stood long at the window and watched the lights leap out of the dusk over the city. He was in Washington because Shirley Claiborne lived there, and he knew that even if he wished to do so he could no longer throw an air of inadvertence into his meetings with her. He had

104

been very lonely in those days when he first saw her abroad; the sight of her had lifted his mood of depression; and now, after those enchanted hours at sea, his coming to Washington had been inevitable.

Many things passed through his mind as he stood at the open window. His life, he felt, could never be again as it had been before, and he sighed deeply as he recalled his talk with the old prime minister at Geneva. Then he laughed quietly as he remembered Chauvenet and Durand and the dark house on the Boulevard Froissart; but the further recollection of the attack made on his life on the deck of the *King Edward* sobered him, and he turned away from the window impatiently. He had seen the sick second-cabin passenger leave the steamer at New York, but had taken no trouble either to watch or to avoid him. Very likely the man was under instructions, and had been told to follow the Claibornes home; and the thought of their identification with himself by his enemies angered him. Chauvenet was likely to appear in Washington at any time, and would undoubtedly seek the Claibornes at once. The fact that the man was a scoundrel might, in some circumstances, have afforded Armitage comfort, but here again Armitage's mood grew dark. Jules Chauvenet was undoubtedly a rascal of a shrewd and dangerous type; but who, pray, was John Armitage?

The bell in his entry rang, and he flashed on the lights and opened the door.

"Well, I like this! Setting yourself up here in gloomy splendor and never saying a word. You never deserved to have any friends, John Armitage!"

"Jim Sanderson, come in!" Armitage grasped the hands of a red-bearded giant of forty, the possessor of alert brown eyes and a big voice.

"It's my rural habit of reading the register every night in search of constituents that brings me here. They said they guessed you were in, so I just came up to see whether you were opening a poker game or had come to sneak a claim past the watch-dog of the treasury."

The caller threw himself into a chair and rolled a fat, unlighted cigar about in his mouth. "You're a peach, all right, and as offensively hale and handsome as ever. When are you going to the ranch?"

"Well, not just immediately; I want to sample the flesh-pots for a day or two."

"You're getting soft,—that's what's the matter with you! You're afraid of the spring zephyrs on the Mon-

tana range. Well, I'll admit that it's rather more diverting here."

"There is no debating that, Senator. How do you like
being a statesman? It was so sudden and all that. I
read an awful roast of you in an English paper. They
took your election to the Senate as another evidence of
the complete domination of our politics by the pluto-
crats."

Sanderson winked prodigiously.

"The papers *have* rather skinned me; but on the
whole, I'll do very well. They say it isn't respectable
to be a senator these days, but they oughtn't to hold it
up against a man that he's rich. If the Lord put silver
in the mountains of Montana and let me dig it out, it's
nothing against me, is it?"

"Decidedly not! And if you want to invest it in a
senatorship it's the Lord's hand again."

"Why sure!" and the Senator from Montana winked
once more. "But it's expensive. I've got to be elected
again next winter—I'm only filling out Billings' term—
and I'm not sure I can go up against it."

"But you are nothing if not unselfish. If the good of
the country demands it you'll not falter, if I know you."

"There's hot water heat in this hotel, so please turn

off the hot air. I saw your foreman in Helena the last time I was out there, and he was sober. I mention the fact, knowing that I'm jeopardizing my reputation for veracity, but it's the Lord's truth. Of course you spent Christmas at the old home in England—one of those yule-log and plum-pudding Christmases you read of in novels. You Englishmen—"

"My dear Sanderson, don't call me English! I've told you a dozen times that I'm not English."

"So you did; so you did! I'd forgotten that you're so damned sensitive about it;" and Sanderson's eyes regarded Armitage intently for a moment, as though he were trying to recall some previous discussion of the young man's nativity.

"I offer you free swing at the bar, Senator. May I summon a Montana cocktail? You taught me the ingredients once—three dashes orange bitters; two dashes acid phosphate; half a jigger of whisky; half a jigger of Italian vermuth. You undermined the constitutions of half Montana with that mess."

Sanderson reached for his hat with sudden dejection.

"The sprinkling cart for me! I've got a nerve specialist engaged by the year to keep me out of sanatoriums. See here, I want you to go with us to-night to the Secretary of State's push. Not many of the Montana boys get this far from home, and I want you for exhibition purposes. Say, John, when I saw Cinch Tight, Montana, written on the register down there it increased my circulation seven beats! You're all right, and I guess you're about as good an American as they make—anywhere— John Armitage!"

The function for which the senator from Montana provided an invitation for Armitage was a large affair in honor of several new ambassadors. At ten o'clock Senator Sanderson was introducing Armitage right and left as one of his representative constituents. Armitage and he owned adjoining ranches in Montana, and Sanderson called upon his neighbor to stand up boldly for their state before the minions of effete monarchies.

Mrs. Sanderson had asked Armitage to return to her for a little Montana talk, as she put it, after the first rush of their entrance was over, and as he waited in the drawing-room for an opportunity of speaking to her, he chatted with Franzel, an attaché of the Austrian embassy, to whom Sanderson had introduced him. Franzel was a gloomy young man with a monocle, and he was waiting for a particular girl, who happened to be the daughter of the Spanish Ambassador. And, this being

his object, he had chosen his position with care, near the
door of the drawing-room, and Armitage shared for the
moment the advantage that lay in the Austrian's point
of view. Armitage had half expected that the Claibornes
would be present at a function as comprehensive of the
higher official world as this, and he intended asking
Mrs. Sanderson if she knew them as soon as opportunity offered. The Austrian attaché proved tiresome, and
Armitage was about to drop him, when suddenly he
caught sight of Shirley Claiborne at the far end of the
broad hall. Her head was turned partly toward him; he
saw her for an instant through the throng; then his eyes
fell upon Chauvenet at her side, talking with liveliest
animation. He was not more than her own height, and
his profile presented the clean, sharp effect of a cameo.
The vivid outline of his dark face held Armitage's eyes;
then as Shirley passed on through an opening in the
crowd her escort turned, holding the way open for her,
and Armitage met the man's gaze.

It was with an accented gravity that Armitage nodded
his head to some declaration of the melancholy attaché
at this moment. He had known when he left Geneva
that he had not done with Jules Chauvenet; but the
man's prompt appearance surprised Armitage. He ran

over the names of the steamers by which Chauvenet
might easily have sailed from either a German or a
French port and reached Washington quite as soon as
himself. Chauvenet was in Washington, at any rate,
and not only there, but socially accepted and in the
good graces of Shirley Claiborne.

The somber attaché was speaking of the Japanese.

"They must be crushed—crushed," said Franzel. The
two had been conversing in French.

"Yes, *he* must be crushed," returned Armitage absent-mindedly, in English; then, remembering himself,
he repeated the affirmation in French, changing the pro-
noun.

Mrs. Sanderson was now free. She was a pretty, vivacious woman, much younger than her stalwart husband,
—a college graduate whom he had found teaching school
near one of his silver mines.

"Welcome once more, constituent! We're proud to
see you, I can tell you. Our host owns some marvelous
tapestries and they're hung out to-night for the world
to see." She guided Armitage toward the Secretary's
gallery on an upper floor. Their host was almost as famous as a connoisseur as for his achievements in diplo-
macy, and the gallery was a large apartment in which

every article of furniture, as well as the paintings, tapestries and specimens of pottery, was the careful choice of a thoroughly cultivated taste.

"It isn't merely an art gallery; it's the most beautiful room in America," murmured Mrs. Sanderson.

"I can well believe it. There's my favorite Vibert,—I wondered what had become of it."

"It isn't surprising that the Secretary is making a great reputation by his dealings with foreign powers. It's a poor ambassador who could not be persuaded after an hour in this splendid room. The ordinary affairs of life should not be mentioned here. A king's coronation would not be out of place,—in fact, there's a chair in the corner against that Gobelin that would serve the situation. The old gentleman by that cabinet is the Baron von Marhof, the Ambassador from Austria-Hungary. He's a brother-in-law of Count von Stroebel, who was murdered so horribly in a railway carriage a few weeks ago."

"Ah, to be sure! I haven't seen the Baron in years. He has changed little."

"Then you knew him,—in the old country?"

"Yes; I used to see him—when I was a boy," remarked Armitage.

Mrs. Sanderson glanced at Armitage sharply. She had dined at his ranch house in Montana and knew that he lived like a gentleman,—that his house, its appointments and service were unusual for a western ranchman. And she recalled, too, that she and her husband had often speculated as to Armitage's antecedents and history, without arriving at any conclusion in regard to him.

The room had slowly filled and they strolled about, dividing attention between distinguished personages and the not less celebrated works of art.

"Oh, by the way, Mr. Armitage, there's the girl I have chosen for you to marry. I suppose it would be just as well for you to meet her now, though that dark little foreigner seems to be monopolizing her."

"I am wholly agreeable," laughed Armitage. "The sooner the better, and be done with it."

"Don't be so frivolous. There—you can look safely now. She's stopped to speak to that bald and pink Justice of the Supreme Court,—the girl with the brown eyes and hair,—have a care!"

Shirley and Chauvenet left the venerable Justice, and Mrs. Sanderson intercepted them at once.

"To think of all these beautiful things in our own

America !" exclaimed Shirley. "And you, Mr. Armitage,—"

"Among the other curios, Miss Claiborne," laughed John, taking her hand.

"But I haven't introduced you yet"—began Mrs. Sanderson, puzzled.

"No; the *King Edward* did that. We crossed together. Oh, Monsieur Chauvenet, let me present Mr. Armitage," said Shirley, seeing that the men had not spoken.

The situation amused Armitage and he smiled rather more broadly than was necessary in expressing his pleasure at meeting Monsieur Chauvenet. They regarded each other with the swift intentness of men who are used to the sharp exercise of their eyes; and when Armitage turned toward Shirley and Mrs. Sanderson, he was aware that Chauvenet continued to regard him with fixed gaze.

"Miss Claiborne is a wonderful sailor; the Atlantic is a little tumultuous at times in the spring, but she reported to the captain every day."

"Miss Claiborne is nothing if not extraordinary," declared Mrs. Sanderson with frank admiration.

"The word seems to have been coined for her," said

Chauvenet, his white teeth showing under his thin black mustache.

"And still leaves the language distinguished chiefly for its poverty," added Armitage; and the men bowed to Shirley and then to Mrs. Sanderson, and again to each other. It was like a rehearsal of some trifle in a comedy.

"How charming!" laughed Mrs. Sanderson. "And this lovely room is just the place for it."

They were still talking together as Franzel, with whom Armitage had spoken below, entered hurriedly. He held a crumpled note, whose contents, it seemed, had shaken him out of his habitual melancholy composure.

"Is Baron von Marhof in the room?" he asked of Armitage, fumbling nervously at his monocle.

The Austrian Ambassador, with several ladies, and led by Senator Sanderson, was approaching.

The attaché hurried to his chief and addressed him in a low tone. The Ambassador stopped, grew very white, and stared at the messenger for a moment in blank unbelief.

The young man now repeated, in English, in a tone that could be heard in all parts of the hushed room:

"His Majesty, the Emperor Johann Wilhelm, died

suddenly to-night, in Vienna," he said, and gave his arm
to his chief.

It was a strange place for the delivery of such a message, and the strangeness of it was intensified to Shirley
by the curious glance that passed between John Armitage and Jules Chauvenet. Shirley remembered after-
ward that as the attaché's words rang out in the room,
Armitage started, clenched his hands, and caught his
breath in a manner very uncommon in men unless they
are greatly moved. The Ambassador walked directly
from the room with bowed head, and every one waited
in silent sympathy until he had gone.

The word passed swiftly through the great house, and
through the open windows the servants were heard cry-
ing loudly for Baron von Marhof's carriage in the court
below.

"The King is dead; long live the King!" murmured
Shirley.

"Long live the King!" repeated Chauvenet and Mrs.
Sanderson, in unison; and then Armitage, as though
mastering a phrase they were teaching him, raised his
head and said, with an unction that surprised them,
"Long live the Emperor and King! God save Austria!"

Then he turned to Shirley with a smile.

"It is very pleasant to see you on your own ground. I hope your family are well."

"Thank you; yes. My father and mother are here somewhere."

"And Captain Claiborne?"

"He's probably sitting up all night to defend Fort Myer from the crafts and assaults of the enemy. I hope you will come to see us, Mr. Armitage."

"Thank you; you are very kind," he said gravely. "I shall certainly give myself the pleasure very soon."

As Shirley passed on with Chauvenet Mrs. Sanderson launched upon the girl's praises, but she found him suddenly preoccupied.

"The girl has gone to your head. Why didn't you tell me you knew the Claibornes?"

"I don't remember that you gave me a chance; but I'll say now that I intend to know them better."

She bade him take her to the drawing-room. As they went down through the house they found that the announcement of the Emperor Johann Wilhelm's death had cast a pall upon the company. All the members of the diplomatic corps had withdrawn at once as a mark of respect and sympathy for Baron von Marhof, and at midnight the ball-room held all of the company that re-

mained. Armitage had not sought Shirley again. He
found a room that had been set apart for smokers, threw
himself into a chair, lighted a cigar and stared at a picture that had no interest for him whatever. He put
down his cigar after a few whiffs, and his hand went to
the pocket in which he had usually carried his cigarette
case.

"Ah, Mr. Armitage, may I offer you a cigarette?"

He turned to find Chauvenet close at his side. He
had not heard the man enter, but Chauvenet had been in
his thoughts and he started slightly at finding him so
near. Chauvenet held in his white-gloved hand a gold
cigarette case, which he opened with a deliberate care
that displayed its embellished side. The smooth golden
surface gleamed in the light, the helmet in blue, and the
white falcon flashed in Armitage's eyes. The meeting
was clearly by intention, and a slight smile played about
Chauvenet's lips in his enjoyment of the situation. Armitage smiled up at him in amiable acknowledgment of
his courtesy, and rose.

"You are very considerate, Monsieur. I was just at
the moment regretting our distinguished host's over-
sight in providing cigars alone. Allow me!"

He bent forward, took the outstretched open case

into his own hands, removed a cigarette, snapped the case shut and thrust it into his trousers pocket,—all, as it seemed, at a single stroke.

"My dear sir," began Chauvenet, white with rage.

"My dear Monsieur Chauvenet," said Armitage, striking a match, "I am indebted to you for returning a trinket that I value highly."

The flame crept half the length of the stick while they regarded each other; then Armitage raised it to the tip of his cigarette, lifted his head and blew a cloud of smoke.

"Are you able to prove your property, Mr. Armitage?" demanded Chauvenet furiously.

"My dear sir, they have a saying in this country that possession is nine points of the law. You had it—now I have it—wherefore it must be mine!"

Chauvenet's rigid figure suddenly relaxed; he leaned against a chair with a return of his habitual nonchalant air, and waved his hand carelessly.

"Between gentlemen—so small a matter!"

"To be sure—the merest trifle," laughed Armitage with entire good humor.

"And where a gentleman has the predatory habits of a burglar and housebreaker—"

"Then lesser affairs, such as picking up trinkets—"

"Come naturally—quite so!" and Chauvenet twisted his mustache with an air of immense satisfaction.

"But the genial art of assassination—there's a business that requires a calculating hand, my dear Monsieur Chauvenet!"

Chauvenet's hand went again to his lip.

"To be sure!" he ejaculated with zest.

"But alone—alone one can do little. For larger operations one requires—I should say—courageous associates. Now in my affairs—would you believe me?—I am obliged to manage quite alone."

"How melancholy!" exclaimed Chauvenet.

"It is indeed very sad!" and Armitage sighed, tossed his cigarette into the smoldering grate and bade Chauvenet a ceremonious good night.

"Ah, we shall meet again, I dare say!"

"The thought does credit to a generous nature!" responded Armitage, and passed out into the house.

CHAPTER IX

"THIS IS AMERICA, MR. ARMITAGE"

Lo! as I came to the crest of the hill, the sun on the heights
    had arisen,
The dew on the grass was shining, and white was the mist
    on the vale;
Like a lark on the wing of the dawn I sang; like a guiltless
    one freed from his prison,
As backward I gazed through the valley, and saw no one on
    my trail.
                        —*L. Frank Tooker.*

Spring, planting green and gold banners on old Virginia battle-fields, crossed the Potomac and occupied
Washington.

Shirley Claiborne called for her horse and rode forth
to greet the conqueror. The afternoon was keen and
sunny, and she had turned impatiently from a tea, to
which she was committed, to seek the open. The call of
the outdoor gods sang in her blood. Daffodils and
crocuses lifted yellow flames and ruddy torches from
every dooryard. She had pinned a spray of arbutus to
the lapel of her tan riding-coat; it spoke to her of the

blue horizons of the near Virginia hills. The young
buds in the maples hovered like a mist in the tree-tops.
Towering over all, the incomparable gray obelisk
climbed to the blue arch and brought it nearer earth.
Washington, the center of man's hope, is also, in spring,
the capital of the land of heart's desire.

With a groom trailing after her, Shirley rode toward
Rock Creek,—that rippling, murmuring, singing trifle
of water that laughs day and night at the margin of
the beautiful city, as though politics and statesmanship
were the hugest joke in the world. The flag on the
Austro-Hungarian embassy hung at half-mast and sym-
bols of mourning fluttered from the entire front of the
house. Shirley lifted her eyes gravely as she passed.
Her thoughts flew at once to the scene at the house of
the Secretary of State a week before, when Baron von
Marhof had learned of the death of his sovereign; and
by association she thought, too, of Armitage, and of his
look and voice as he said:

"Long live the Emperor and King! God save Austria!"

Emperors and kings! They were as impossible to-
day as a snowstorm. The grave ambassadors as they
appeared at great Washington functions, wearing their

decorations, always struck her as being particularly distinguished. It just now occurred to her that they were all linked to the crown and scepter; but she dismissed the whole matter and bowed to two dark ladies in a passing victoria with the quick little nod and bright smile that were the same for these titled members of the Spanish Ambassador's household as for the young daughters of a western senator, who democratically waved their hands to her from a doorstep.

Armitage came again to her mind. He had called at the Claiborne house twice since the Secretary's ball, and she had been surprised to find how fully she accepted him as an American, now that he was on her own soil. He derived, too, a certain stability from the fact that the Sandersons knew him; he was, indeed, an entirely different person since the Montana Senator definitely connected him with an American landscape. She had kept her own counsel touching the scene on the dark deck of the *King Edward,* but it was not a thing lightly to be forgotten. She was half angry with herself this mellow afternoon to find how persistently Armitage came into her thoughts, and how the knife-thrust on the steamer deck kept recurring in her mind and quickening her sympathy for a man of whom she knew so little; and she touched her horse impatiently with the crop and rode into the park at a gait that roused the groom to attention.

At a bend of the road Chauvenet and Franzel, the attaché, swung into view, mounted, and as they met, Chauvenet turned his horse and rode beside her.

"Ah, these American airs! This spring! Is it not good to be alive, Miss Claiborne?"

"It is all of that!" she replied. It seemed to her that the day had not needed Chauvenet's praise.

"I had hoped to see you later at the Wallingford tea!" he continued.

"No teas for me on a day like this! The thought of being indoors is tragic!"

She wished that he would leave her, for she had ridden out into the spring sunshine to be alone. He somehow did not appear to advantage in his riding-coat,— his belongings were too perfect. She had really enjoyed his talk when they had met here and there abroad; but she was in no mood for him now; and she wondered what he had lost by the transfer to America. He ran on airily in French, speaking of the rush of great and small social affairs that marked the end of the season.

"Poor Franzel is indeed *triste*. He is taking the death of Johann Wilhelm quite hard. But here in America the death of an emperor seems less important. A king or a peasant, what does it matter!"

"Better ask the robin in yonder budding chestnut tree, Monsieur. This is not an hour for hard questions!"

"Ah, you are very cruel! You drive me back to poor, melancholy Franzel, who is indeed a funeral in himself."

"That is very sad, Monsieur,"—and she smiled at him with mischief in her eyes. "My heart goes out to any one who is left to mourn—alone."

He gathered his reins and drew up his horse, lifting his hat with a perfect gesture.

"There are sadder blows than losing one's sovereign, Mademoiselle!" and he shook his bared head mournfully and rode back to find his friend.

She sought now her favorite bridle-paths and her heart was light with the sweetness and peace of the spring as she heard the rush and splash of the creek, saw the flash of wings and felt the mystery of awakened life throbbing about her. The heart of a girl in spring is the home of dreams, and Shirley's heart overflowed

with them, until her pulse thrilled and sang in quickening cadences. The wistfulness of April, the dream of
unfathomable things, shone in her brown eyes; and a
girl with dreams in her eyes is the divinest work of the
gods. Into this twentieth century, into the iron heart of
cities, she still comes, and the clear, high stars of April
nights and the pensive moon of September are glad because of her.

The groom marveled at the sudden changes of gait,
the gallops that fell abruptly to a walk with the altera-
tions of mood in the girl's heart, the pauses that marked
a moment of meditation as she watched some green
curving bank, or a plunge of the mad little creek that
sent a glory of spray whitely into the sunlight. It
grew late and the shadows of waning afternoon crept
through the park. The crowd had hurried home to
escape the chill of the spring dusk, but she lingered on,
reluctant to leave, and presently left her horse with the
groom that she might walk alone beside the creek in a
place that was beautifully wild. About her lay a narrow
strip of young maples and beyond this the wide park
road wound at the foot of a steep wooded cliff. The
place was perfectly quiet save for the splash and babble
of the creek.

Several minutes passed. Once she heard her groom speak to the horses, though she could not see him, but the charm of the place held her. She raised her eyes from the tumbling water before her and looked off through the maple tangle. Then she drew back quickly, and clasped her riding-crop tightly. Some one had paused at the farther edge of the maple brake and dismounted, as she had, for a more intimate enjoyment of the place. It was John Armitage, tapping his riding-boot idly with his crop as he leaned against a tree and viewed the miniature valley.

He was a little below her, so that she saw him quite distinctly, and caught a glimpse of his horse pawing, with arched neck, in the bridle-path behind him. She had no wish to meet him there and turned to steal back to her horse when a movement in the maples below caught her eye. She paused, fascinated and alarmed by the cautious stir of the undergrowth. The air was perfectly quiet; the disturbance was not caused by the wind. Then the head and shoulders of a man were disclosed as he crouched on hands and knees, watching Armitage. His small head and big body as he crept forward suggested to Shirley some fantastic monster of legend, and her heart beat fast with terror as a knife

flashed in his hand. He moved more rapidly toward the
silent figure by the tree, and still Shirley watched wide-
eyed, her figure tense and trembling, the hand that held
the crop half raised to her lips, while the dark form
rose and poised for a spring.

Then she cried out, her voice ringing clear and high
across the little vale and sounding back from the cliff.

"Oh! Oh!" and Armitage leaped forward and turned.
His crop fell first upon the raised hand, knocking the
knife far into the trees, then upon the face and shoulders of the Servian. The fellow turned and fled through
the maple tangle, Armitage after him, and Shirley ran
back toward the bridge where she had left her groom
and met him half-way hurrying toward her.

"What is it, Miss? Did you call?"

"No; it was nothing, Thomas—nothing at all," and
she mounted and turned toward home.

Her heart was still pounding with excitement and
she walked her horse to gain composure. Twice, in
circumstances most unusual and disquieting, she had
witnessed an attack on John Armitage by an unknown
enemy. She recalled now a certain pathos of his figure
as she first saw him leaning against the tree watching
the turbulent little stream, and she was impatient to

find how her sympathy went out to him. It made no difference who John Armitage was; his enemy was a coward, and the horror of such a menace to a man's life appalled her. She passed a mounted policeman, who recognized her and raised his hand in salute, but the idea of reporting the strange affair in the strip of woodland occurred to her only to be dismissed. She felt that here was an ugly business that was not within the grasp of a park patrolman, and, moreover, John Armitage was entitled to pursue his own course in matters that touched his life so closely. The thought of him reassured her; he was no simple boy to suffer such attacks to pass unchallenged; and so, dismissing him, she raised her head and saw him gallop forth from a by-path and rein his horse beside her.

"Miss Claiborne!"

The suppressed feeling in his tone made the moment tense and she saw that his lips trembled. It was a situation that must have its quick relief, so she said instantly, in a mockery of his own tone:

"Mr. Armitage!" She laughed. "I am almost caught in the dark. The blandishments of spring have beguiled me."

He looked at her with a quick scrutiny. It did not

seem possible that this could be the girl who had called to him in warning scarce five minutes before; but he knew it had been she,—he would have known her voice anywhere in the world. They rode silent beside the creek, which was like a laughing companion seeking to mock them into a cheerier mood. At an opening through the hills they saw the western horizon aglow in tints of lemon deepening into gold and purple. Save for the riot of the brook the world was at peace. She met his eyes for an instant, and their gravity, and the firm lines in which his lips were set, showed that the shock of his encounter had not yet passed.

"You must think me a strange person, Miss Claiborne. It seems inexplicable that a man's life should be so menaced in a place like this. If you had not called to me—"

"Please don't speak of that! It was so terrible!"

"But I must speak of it! Once before the same attempt was made—that night on the *King Edward.*"

"Yes; I have not forgotten."

"And to-day I have reason to believe that the same man watched his chance, for I have ridden here every day since I came, and he must have kept track of me."

"But this is America, Mr. Armitage!"

"That does not help me with you. You have every reason to resent my bringing you into such dangers,— it is unpardonable—indefensible!"

She saw that he was greatly troubled.

"But you couldn't help my being in the park to-day! I have often stopped just there before. It's a favorite place for meditations. If you know the man—"

"I know the man."

"Then the law will certainly protect you, as you know very well. He was a dreadful-looking person. The police can undoubtedly find and lock him up."

She was seeking to minimize the matter,—to pass it off as a commonplace affair of every day. They were walking their horses; the groom followed stolidly behind.

Armitage was silent, a look of great perplexity on his face. When he spoke he was quite calm.

"Miss Claiborne, I must tell you that this is an affair in which I can't ask help in the usual channels. You will pardon me if I seem to make a mystery of what should be ordinarily a bit of business between myself and the police; but to give publicity to these attempts to injure me just now would be a mistake. I could have caught that man there in the wood; but I let him go,

for the reason—for the reason that I want the men back
of him to show themselves before I act. But if it isn't
presuming—"

He was quite himself again. His voice was steady and
deep with the ease and assurance that she liked in him.
She had marked to-day in his earnestness, more than at
any other time, a slight, an almost indistinguishable
trace of another tongue in his English.

"How am I to know whether it would be presuming?"
she asked.

"But I was going to say—"

"When rudely interrupted!" She was trying to make
it easy for him to say whatever he wished.

"—that these troubles of mine are really personal.
I have committed no crime and am not fleeing from justice."

She laughed and urged her horse into a gallop for a
last stretch of road near the park limits.

"How uninteresting! We expect a Montana ranchman to have a spectacular past."

"But not to carry it, I hope, to Washington. On the
range I might become a lawless bandit in the interest
of picturesqueness; but here—"

"Here in the world of frock-coated statesmen nothing really interesting is to be expected."

She walked her horse again. It occurred to her that he might wish an assurance of silence from her. What she had seen would make a capital bit of gossip, to say nothing of being material for the newspapers, and her conscience, as she reflected, grew uneasy at the thought of shielding him. She knew that her father and mother, and, even more strictly, her brother, would close their doors on a man whose enemies followed him over seas and lay in wait for him in a peaceful park; but here she tested him. A man of breeding would not ask protection of a woman on whom he had no claim, and it was certainly not for her to establish an understanding with him in so strange and grave a matter.

"It must be fun having a ranch with cattle on a thousand hills. I always wished my father would go in for a western place, but he can't travel so far from home. Our ranch is in Virginia."

"You have a Virginia farm? That is very interesting."

"Yes; at Storm Springs. It's really beautiful down there," she said simply.

It was on his tongue to tell her that he, too, owned a

bit of Virginia soil, but he had just established himself
as a Montana ranchman, and it seemed best not to mul-
tiply his places of residence. He had, moreover, forgotten the name of the county in which his preserve lay.
He said, with truth:

"I know nothing of Virginia or the South; but I have
viewed the landscape from Arlington and some day I
hope to go adventuring in the Virginia hills."

"Then you should not overlook our valley. I am sure
there must be adventures waiting for somebody down
there. You can tell our place by the spring lamb on
the hillside. There's a huge inn that offers the long-
distance telephone and market reports and golf links
and very good horses, and lots of people stop there as a
matter of course in their flight between Florida and
Newport. They go up and down the coast like the mercury in a thermometer—up when it's warm, down when
it's cold. There's the secret of our mercurial temperament."

A passing automobile frightened her horse, and he
watched her perfect coolness in quieting the animal with
rein and voice.

"He's just up from the farm and doesn't like town

very much. But he shall go home again soon," she said as they rode on.

"Oh, you go down to shepherd those spring lambs!" he exclaimed, with misgiving in his heart. He had followed her across the sea and now she was about to take flight again!

"Yes; and to escape from the tiresome business of trying to remember people's names."

"Then you reverse the usual fashionable process—you go south to meet the rising mercury."

"I hadn't thought of it, but that is so. I dearly love a hillside, with pines and cedars, and sloping meadows with sheep—and rides over mountain roads to the gate of dreams, where Spottswood's golden horseshoe knights ride out at you with a grand sweep of their plumed hats. Now what have you to say to that?"

"Nothing, but my entire approval," he said.

He dimly understood, as he left her in this gay mood, at the Claiborne house, that she had sought to make him forget the lurking figure in the park thicket and the dark deed thwarted there. It was her way of conveying to him her dismissal of the incident, and it implied a greater kindness than any pledge of secrecy. He rode away with grave eyes, and a new hope filled his heart.

CHAPTER X

Afoot and light-hearted I take to the open road,
Healthy, free, the world before me,
The long brown path before me leading wherever I choose.
—*Walt Whitman.*

Armitage dined alone that evening and left the hotel at nine o'clock for a walk. He unaffectedly enjoyed paved ground and the sights and ways of cities, and he walked aimlessly about the lighted thoroughfares of the capital with conscious pleasure in the movement and color of life. He let his eyes follow the Washington Monument's gray line starward; and he stopped to enjoy the high-poised equestrian statue of Sherman, to which the starry dusk gave something of legendary and Old World charm.

Coming out upon Pennsylvania Avenue he strolled past the White House, and, at the wide-flung gates, paused while a carriage swept by him at the driveway. He saw within the grim face of Baron von Marhof and

136

unconsciously lifted his hat, though the Ambassador was deep in thought and did not see him. Armitage struck the pavement smartly with his stick as he walked slowly on, pondering; but he was conscious a moment later that some one was loitering persistently in his wake. Armitage was at once on the alert with all his faculties sharpened. He turned and gradually slackened his pace, and the person behind him immediately did likewise.

The sensation of being followed is at first annoying; then a pleasant zest creeps into it, and in Armitage's case the reaction was immediate. He was even amused to reflect that the shadow had chosen for his exploit what is probably the most conspicuous and the best-guarded spot in America. It was not yet ten o'clock, but the streets were comparatively free of people. He slackened his pace gradually, and threw open his overcoat, for the night was warm, to give an impression of ease, and when he had reached the somber façade of the Treasury Building he paused and studied it in the glare of the electric lights, as though he were a chance traveler taking a preliminary view of the sights of the capital. A man still lingered behind him, drawing nearer now, at a moment when they had the sidewalk comparatively free to themselves. The fellow was short,

but of soldierly erectness, and even in his loitering pace
lifted his feet with the quick precision of the drilled
man. Armitage walked to the corner of Pennsylvania
Avenue and Fifteenth Street, then turned and retraced
his steps slowly past the Treasury Building. The man
who had been following faced about and walked slowly
in the opposite direction, and Armitage, quickening his
own pace, amused himself by dogging the fellow's steps
closely for twenty yards, then passed him.

When he had gained the advantage of a few feet,
Armitage stopped suddenly and spoke to the man in
the casual tone he might have used in addressing a
passing acquaintance.

"My friend," he said, "there are two policemen across
the street; if you continue to follow me I shall call their
attention to you."

"Pardon me—"

"You are watching me; and the thing won't do."

"Yes, I'm watching you; but—"

"But the thing won't do! If you are hired—"

"*Nein! Nein!* You do me a wrong, sir."

"Then if you are not hired you are your own master,
and you serve yourself ill when you take the trouble to
follow me. Now I'm going to finish my walk, and I beg

you to keep out of my way. This is not a place where liberties may be infringed with impunity. Good evening, sir."

Armitage wheeled about sharply, and as his face came into the full light of the street lamps the stranger stared at him intently.

Armitage was fumbling in his pocket for a coin, but this impertinence caused him to change his mind. Two policemen were walking slowly toward them, and Armitage, annoyed by the whole incident, walked quickly away.

He was not wholly at ease over the meeting. The fact that Chauvenet had so promptly put a spy as well as the Servian assassin on his trail quickened his pulse with anger for an instant and then sobered him.

He continued his walk, and paused presently before an array of books in a shop window. Then some one stopped at his side and he looked up to find the same man he had accosted at the Treasury Building lifting his hat,—an American soldier's campaign hat. The fellow was an extreme blond, with a smooth-shaven, weather-beaten face, blue eyes and light hair.

"Pardon me! You are mistaken; I am not a spy. But it is wonderful; it is quite wonderful—"

The man's face was alight with discovery, with an alert pleasure that awaited recognition.

"My dear fellow, you really become annoying," and Armitage again thrust his hand into his trousers pocket. "I should hate awfully to appeal to the police; but you must not crowd me too far."

The man seemed moved by deep feeling, and his eyes were bright with excitement. His hands clasped tightly the railing that protected the glass window of the book shop. As Armitage turned away impatiently the man ejaculated huskily, as though some over-mastering influence wrung the words from him:

"Don't you know me? I am Oscar—don't you remember me, and the great forest, where I taught you to shoot and fish? You are—"

He bent toward Armitage with a fierce insistence, his eyes blazing in his eagerness to be understood.

John Armitage turned again to the window, leaned lightly upon the iron railing and studied the title of a book attentively. He was silently absorbed for a full minute, in which the man who had followed him waited. Taking his cue from Armitage's manner he appeared to be deeply interested in the bookseller's display; but the excitement still glittered in his eyes.

Armitage was thinking swiftly, and his thoughts covered a very wide range of time and place as he stood there. Then he spoke very deliberately and coolly, but with a certain peremptory sharpness.

"Go ahead of me to the New American and wait in the office until I come."

The man's hand went to his hat.

"None of that!"

Armitage arrested him with a gesture. "My name is Armitage,—John Armitage," he said. "I advise you to remember it. Now go!"

The man hurried away, and Armitage slowly followed.

It occurred to him that the man might be of use, and with this in mind he returned to the New American, got his key from the office, nodded to his acquaintance of the street and led the way to the elevator.

Armitage put aside his coat and hat, locked the hall door, and then, when the two stood face to face in his little sitting-room, he surveyed the man carefully.

"What do you want?" he demanded bluntly.

He took a cigarette from a box on the table, lighted it, and then, with an air of finality, fixed his gaze upon the man, who eyed him with a kind of stupefied won-

der. Then there flashed into the fellow's bronzed face
something of dignity and resentment. He stood perfectly erect with his felt hat clasped in his hand. His
clothes were cheap, but clean, and his short coat was
buttoned trimly about him.

"I want nothing, Mr. Armitage," he replied humbly,
speaking slowly and with a marked German accent.

"Then you will be easily satisfied," said Armitage.
"You said your name was— ?"

"Oscar—Oscar Breunig."

Armitage sat down and scrutinized the man again
without relaxing his severity.

"You think you have seen me somewhere, so you
have followed me in the streets to make sure. When did
this idea first occur to you ?"

"I saw you at Fort Myer at the drill last Friday. I
have been looking for you since, and saw you leave your
horse at the hotel this afternoon. You ride at Rock
Creek—yes ?"

"What do you do for a living, Mr. Breunig ?" asked
Armitage.

"I was in the army, but served out my time and was
discharged a few months ago and came to Washington
to see where they make the government—yes ? I am

going to South America. Is it Peru? Yes; there will
be a revolution."

He paused, and Armitage met his eyes; they were
very blue and kind,—eyes that spoke of sincerity and
fidelity, such eyes as a leader of forlorn hopes would
like to know were behind him when he gave the order
to charge. Then a curious thing happened. It may have
been the contact of eye with eye that awoke question and
response between them; it may have been a need in one
that touched a chord of helplessness in the other; but
suddenly Armitage leaped to his feet and grasped the
outstretched hands of the little soldier.

"Oscar!" he said; and repeated, very softly, "Oscar!"

The man was deeply moved and the tears sprang into
his eyes. Armitage laughed, holding him at arm's
length.

"None of that nonsense! Sit down!" He turned to
the door, opened it, and peered into the hall, locked the
door again, then motioned the man to a chair.

"So you deserted your mother country, did you, and
have borne arms for the glorious republic?"

"I served in the Philippines,—yes?"

"Rank, titles, emoluments, Oscar?"

"I was a sergeant; and the surgeon could not find the bullet after Big Bend, Luzon; so they were sorry and gave me a certificate and two dollars a month to my pay," said the man, so succinctly and colorlessly that Armitage laughed.

"You have done well, Oscar; honor me by accepting a cigar."

The man took a cigar from the box which Armitage extended, but would not light it. He held it rather absent-mindedly in his hand and continued to stare.

"You are not dead,—Mr.—Armitage; but your father— ?"

"My father is dead, Oscar."

"He was a good man," said the soldier.

"Yes; he was a good man," repeated Armitage gravely. "I am alive, and yet I am dead, Oscar; do you grasp the idea? You were a good friend when we were lads together in the great forest. If I should want you to help me now—"

The man jumped to his feet and stood at attention so gravely that Armitage laughed and slapped his knee.

"You are well taught, Sergeant Oscar! Sit down. I am going to trust you. My affairs just now are not without their trifling dangers."

"There are enemies—yes?" and Oscar nodded his head solemnly in acceptance of the situation.

"I am going to trust you absolutely. You have no confidants—you are not married?"

"How should a man be married who is a soldier? I have no friends; they are unprofitable," declared Oscar solemnly.

"I fear you are a pessimist, Oscar; but a pessimist who keeps his mouth shut is a good ally. Now, if you are not afraid of being shot or struck with a knife, and if you are willing to obey my orders for a few weeks we may be able to do some business. First, remember that I am Mr. Armitage; you must learn that now, and remember it for all time. And if any one should ever suggest anything else—"

The man nodded his comprehension.

"That will be the time for Oscar to be dumb. I understand, Mr. Armitage."

Armitage smiled. The man presented so vigorous a picture of health, his simple character was so transparently reflected in his eyes and face that he did not in the least question him.

"You are an intelligent person, Sergeant. If you are

equally discreet—able to be deaf when troublesome questions are asked, then I think we shall get on."

"You should remember—" began Oscar.

"I remember nothing," observed Armitage sharply; and Oscar was quite humble again. Armitage opened a trunk and took out an envelope from which he drew several papers and a small map, which he unfolded and spread on the table. He marked a spot with his lead-pencil and passed the map to Oscar.

"Do you think you could find that place?"

The man breathed hard over it for several minutes.

"Yes; it would be easy," and he nodded his head several times as he named the railroad stations nearest the point indicated by Armitage. The place was in one of the mountainous counties of Virginia, fifteen miles from an east and west railway line. Armitage opened a duly recorded deed which conveyed to himself the title to two thousand acres of land; also a curiously complicated abstract of title showing the successive transfers of ownership from colonial days down through the years of Virginia's splendor to the dread time when battle shook the world. The title had passed from the receiver of a defunct shooting-club to Armitage, who had been charmed by the description of the property as set forth

in an advertisement, and lured, moreover, by the amazingly small price at which the preserve was offered.

"It is a farm—yes?"

"It is a wilderness, I fancy," said Armitage. "I have
never seen it; I may never see it, for that matter; but
you will find your way there—going first to this town,
Lamar, studying the country, keeping your mouth shut,
and seeing what the improvements on the ground
amount to. There's some sort of a bungalow there, built
by the shooting-club. Here's a description of the place,
on the strength of which I bought it. You may take
these papers along to judge the size of the swindle."

"Yes, sir."

"And a couple of good horses; plenty of commissary
stores—plain military necessities, you understand—and
some bedding should be provided. I want you to take
full charge of this matter and get to work as quickly as
possible. It may be a trifle lonesome down there among
the hills, but if you serve me well you shall not regret
it."

"Yes, I am quite satisfied with the job," said Oscar.

"And after you have reached the place and settled
yourself you will tell the postmaster and telegraph operator who you are and where you may be found, so that

messages may reach you promptly. If you get an un-
signed message advising you of—let me consider—a
shipment of steers, you may expect me any hour. On
the other hand, you may not see me at all. We'll consider that our agreement lasts until the first snow flies
next winter. You are a soldier. There need be no further discussion of this matter, Oscar."

The man nodded gravely.

"And it is well for you not to reappear in this hotel.
If you should be questioned on leaving here—"

"I have not been here—is it not?"

"It is," replied Armitage, smiling. "You read and
write English?"

"Yes; one must, to serve in the army."

"If you should see a big Servian with a neck like a
bull and a head the size of a pea, who speaks very bad
German, you will do well to keep out of his way,—unless
you find a good place to tie him up. I advise you not to
commit murder without special orders,—do you understand?"

"It is the custom of the country," assented Oscar, in
a tone of deep regret.

"To be sure," laughed Armitage; "and now I am go-

ing to give you money enough to carry out the project
I have indicated."

He took from his trunk a long bill-book, counted out
twenty new one-hundred-dollar bills and threw them on
the table.

"It is much money," observed Oscar, counting the
bills laboriously.

"It will be enough for your purposes. You can't spend
much money up there if you try. Bacon—perhaps eggs;
a cow may be necessary,—who can tell without trying
it? Don't write me any letters or telegrams, and forget
that you have seen me if you don't hear from me again."

He went to the elevator and rode down to the office
with Oscar and dismissed him carelessly. Then John
Armitage bought an armful of magazines and newspapers and returned to his room, quite like any traveler
taking the comforts of his inn.

CHAPTER XI

THE TOSS OF A NAPKIN

As music and splendor
    Survive not the lamp and the lute,
The heart's echoes render
    No song when the spirit is mute—
No songs but sad dirges,
    Like the wind through a ruined cell,
Or the mournful surges
    That ring the dead seaman's knell.
                                    —*Shelley.*

Captain Richard Claiborne gave a supper at the Army
and Navy Club for ten men in honor of the newly-ar-
rived military attaché of the Spanish legation. He had
drawn his guests largely from his foreign acquaintances
in Washington because the Spaniard spoke little English; and Dick knew Washington well enough to understand that while a girl and a man who speak different
languages may sit comfortably together at table, men in
like predicament grow morose and are likely to quarrel

with their eyes before the cigars are passed. It was
Friday, and the whole party had witnessed the drill at
Fort Myer that afternoon, with nine girls to listen to
their explanation of the manœuvers and the earliest
spring bride for chaperon. Shirley had been of the
party, and somewhat the heroine of it, too, for it was
Dick who sat on his horse out in the tanbark with the
little whistle to his lips and manipulated the troop.

"Here's a confusion of tongues; I may need you to
interpret," laughed Dick, indicating a chair at his left;
and when Armitage sat down he faced Chauvenet across
the round table.

With the first filling of glasses it was found that every
one could speak French, and the talk went forward
spiritedly. The discussion of military matters naturally
occupied first place, and all were anxious to steer clear
of anything that might be offensive to the Spaniard,
who had lost a brother at San Juan. Claiborne thought
it wisest to discuss nations that were not represented at
the table, and this made it very simple for all to unite
in rejecting the impertinent claims of Japan to be
reckoned among world powers, and to declare, for the
benefit of the Russian attaché, that Slav and Saxon must
ultimately contend for the earth's dominion.

Then they fell to talking about individuals, chiefly men in the public eye; and as the Austro-Hungarian embassy was in mourning and unrepresented at the table, the new Emperor-king was discussed with considerable frankness.

"He has not old Stroebel's right hand to hold him up," remarked a young German officer.

"Thereby hangs a dark tale," remarked Claiborne. "Somebody stuck a knife into Count von Stroebel at a singularly inopportune moment. I saw him in Geneva two days before he was assassinated, and he was very feeble and seemed harassed. It gives a man the shudders to think of what might happen if his Majesty, Charles Louis, should go by the board. His only child died a year ago—after him his cousin Francis, and then the deluge."

"Bah! Francis is not as dark as he's painted. He's the most lied-about prince in Europe," remarked Chauvenet. "He would most certainly be an improvement on Charles Louis. But alas! Charles Louis will undoubtedly live on forever, like his lamented father. The King is dead: long live the King!"

"Nothing can happen," remarked the German sadly. "I have lost much money betting on upheavals in that direction. If there were a man in Hungary it would be different; but riots are not revolutions."

"That is quite true," said Armitage quietly.

"But," observed the Spaniard, "if the Archduke Karl had not gone out of his head and died in two or three dozen places, so that no one is sure he is dead at all, things at Vienna might be rather more interesting. Karl took a son with him into exile. Suppose one or the other of them should reappear, stir up strife and incite rebellion—?"

"Such speculations are quite idle," commented Chauvenet. "There is no doubt whatever that Karl is dead, or we should hear of him."

"Of course," said the German. "If he were not, the death of the old Emperor would have brought him to life again."

"The same applies to the boy he carried away with him—undoubtedly dead—or we should hear of him. Karl disappeared soon after his son Francis was born. It was said— "

"A pretty tale it is !" commented the German—"that the child wasn't exactly Karl's own. He took it quite hard—went away to hide his shame in exile, taking his son Frederick Augustus with him."

"He was surely mad," remarked Chauvenet, sipping a cordial. "He is much better dead and out of the way for the good of Austria. Francis, as I say, is a good fellow. We have hunted together, and I know him well."

They fell to talking about the lost sons of royal houses—and a goodly number there have been, even in these later centuries—and then of the latest marriages between American women and titled foreigners. Chauvenet was now leading the conversation; it might even have seemed to a critical listener that he was guiding it with a certain intention.

He laughed as though at the remembrance of something amusing, and held the little company while he bent over a candle to light a cigar.

"With all due respect to our American host, I must say that a title in America goes further than anywhere else in the world. I was at Bar Harbor three years ago when the Baron von Kissel devastated that region. He made sad havoc among the ladies that summer; the rest of us simply had no place to stand. You remember, gentlemen,"—and Chauvenet looked slowly around the listening circle,—"that the unexpected arrival of the excellent Ambassador of Austria-Hungary caused the Baron to leave Bar Harbor between dark and daylight. The story was that he got off in a sail-boat; and the next we heard of him he was masquerading under some title in San Francisco, where he proved to be a dangerous forger. You all remember that the papers were full of his performances for a while, but he was a lucky rascal, and always disappeared at the proper psychological moment. He had, as you may say, the cosmopolitan accent, and was the most plausible fellow alive."

Chauvenet held his audience well in hand, for nearly every one remembered the brilliant exploits of the fraudulent baron, and all were interested in what promised to be some new information about him. Armitage, listening intently to Chauvenet's recital, felt his blood quicken, and his face flushed for a moment. His cigarette case lay upon the edge of the table, and he snapped it shut and fingered it nervously as he listened.

"It's my experience," continued Chauvenet, "that we never meet a person once only—there's always a second meeting somewhere; and I was not at all surprised when I ran upon my old friend the baron in Germany last fall."

"At his old tricks, I suppose," observed some one.

"No; that was the strangest part of it. He's struck a deeper game—though I'm blessed if I can make it out—

he's dropped the title altogether, and now calls himself
Mister—I've forgotten for the moment the rest of it,
but it is an English name. He's made a stake somehow,
and travels about in decent comfort. He passes now as
an American—his English is excellent—and he hints at
large American interests."

"He probably has forged securities to sell," commented the German. "I know those fellows. The business is best done quietly."

"I dare say," returned Chauvenet.

"Of course, you greeted him as a long-lost friend," remarked Claiborne leadingly.

"No; I wanted to make sure of him; and, strangely
enough, he assisted me in a very curious way."

All felt that they were now to hear the dénouement
of the story, and several men bent forward in their
absorption with their elbows on the table. Chauvenet
smiled and resumed, with a little shrug of his shoulders.

"Well, I must go back a moment to say that the man
I knew at Bar Harbor had a real crest—the ladies to
whom he wrote notes treasured them, I dare say, because of the pretty insignium. He had it engraved on
his cigarette case, a bird of some kind tiptoeing on a
helmet, and beneath there was a motto, *Fide non armis.*"

"The devil!" exclaimed the young German. "Why, that's very like—"

"Very like the device of the Austrian Schomburgs. Well, I remembered the cigarette case, and one night at a concert—in Berlin, you know—I chanced to sit with some friends at a table quite near where he sat alone; I had my eye on him, trying to assure myself of his identity, when, in closing his cigarette case, it fell almost at my feet, and I bumped heads with a waiter as I picked it up—I wanted to make sure—and handed it to him, the imitation baron."

"That was your chance to startle him a trifle, I should say," remarked the German.

"He was the man, beyond doubt. There was no mistaking the cigarette case. What I said was,"—continued Chauvenet,— " 'Allow me, Baron!' "

"Well spoken!" exclaimed the Spanish officer.

"Not so well, either," laughed Chauvenet. "He had the best of it—he's a clever man, I am obliged to admit! He said—" and Chauvenet's mirth stifled him for a moment.

"Yes; what was it?" demanded the German impatiently.

"He said: 'Thank you, waiter!' and put the cigarette case back into his pocket!"

They all laughed. Then Captain Claiborne's eyes fell upon the table and rested idly on John Armitage's cigarette case—on the smoothly-worn gold of the surface, on the snowy falcon and the silver helmet on which the bird poised. He started slightly, then tossed his napkin carelessly on the table so that it covered the gold trinket completely.

"Gentlemen," he said, "if we are going to show ourselves at the Darlington ball we'll have to run along."

Below, in the coat room, Claiborne was fastening the frogs of his military overcoat when Armitage, who had waited for the opportunity, spoke to him.

"That story is a lie, Claiborne. That man never saw me or my cigarette case in Berlin; and moreover, I was never at Bar Harbor in my life. I gave you some account of myself on the *King Edward*—every word of it is true."

"You should face him—you must have it out with him!" exclaimed Claiborne, and Armitage saw the conflict and uncertainty in the officer's eyes.

"But the time hasn't come for that—"

"Then if there is something between you,"—began Claiborne, the doubt now clearly dominant.

"There is undoubtedly a great deal between us, and there will be more before we reach the end."

Dick Claiborne was a perfectly frank, outspoken fellow, and this hint of mystery by a man whose character had just been boldly assailed angered him.

"Good God, man! I know as much about Chauvenet as I do about you. This thing is ugly, as you must see. I don't like it, I tell you! You've got to do more than deny a circumstantial story like that by a fellow whose standing here is as good as yours! If you don't offer some better explanation of this by to-morrow night I shall have to ask you to cut my acquaintance—and the acquaintance of my family!"

Armitage's face was grave, but he smiled as he took his hat and stick.

"I shall not be able to satisfy you of my respectability by to-morrow night, Captain Claiborne. My own affairs must wait on larger matters."

"Then you need never take the trouble!"

"In my own time you shall be quite fully satisfied," said Armitage quietly, and turned away.

He was not among the others of the Claiborne party

when they got into their carriages to go to the ball. He went, in fact, to the telegraph office and sent a message to Oscar Breunig, Lamar, Virginia, giving notice of a shipment of steers.

Then he returned to the New American and packed his belongings.

CHAPTER XII

—Who climbed the blue Virginia hills
  Against embattled foes;
And planted there, in valleys fair,
  The lily and the rose;
Whose fragrance lives in many lands,
  Whose beauty stars the earth,
And lights the hearths of happy homes
  With loveliness and worth.
                    —*Francis O. Ticknor.*

The study of maps and time-tables is a far more profit-able business than appears. John Armitage possessed a great store of geographical knowledge as interpreted in such literature. He could tell you, without leaving his room, and probably without opening his trunk, the quickest way out of Tokio, or St. Petersburg, or Calcutta, or Cinch Tight, Montana, if you suddenly received a cablegram calling you to Vienna or Paris or Washington from one of those places.

Such being the case, it was remarkable that he should have started for a point in the Virginia hills by way of

Boston, thence to Norfolk by coastwise steamer, and on
to Lamar by lines of railroad whose schedules would
have been the despair of unhardened travelers. He had
expressed his trunks direct, and traveled with two suit-
cases and an umbrella. His journey, since his boat
swung out into Massachusetts Bay, had been spent in
gloomy speculations, and two young women booked for
Baltimore wrongly attributed his reticence and aloof-
ness to a grievous disappointment in love.

He had wanted time to think—to ponder his affairs—
to devise some way out of his difficulties, and to con-
trive the defeat of Chauvenet. Moreover, his relations
to the Claibornes were in an ugly tangle: Chauvenet had
dealt him a telling blow in a quarter where he particularly wished to appear to advantage.

He jumped out of the day coach in which he had accomplished the last stage of his journey to Lamar, just
at dawn, and found Oscar with two horses waiting.

"Good morning," said Oscar, saluting.

"You are prompt, Sergeant," and Armitage shook
hands with him.

As the train roared on through the valley, Armitage
opened one of the suit-cases and took out a pair of leather
leggings, which he strapped on. Then Oscar tied the

cases together with a rope and hung them across his saddle-bow.

"The place—what of it?" asked Armitage.

"There may be worse—I have not decided."

Armitage laughed aloud.

"Is it as bad as that?"

The man was busy tightening the saddle girths, and he answered Armitage's further questions with soldier-like brevity.

"You have been here—"

"Two weeks, sir."

"And nothing has happened? It is a good report."

"It is good for the soul to stand on mountains and look at the world. You will like that animal—yes? He is lighter than a cavalry horse. Mine, you will notice, is a trifle heavier. I bought them at a stock farm in another valley, and rode them up to the place."

The train sent back loud echoes. A girl in a pink sunbonnet rode up on a mule and carried off the mail pouch. The station agent was busy inside at his telegraph instruments and paid no heed to the horsemen. Save for a few huts clustered on the hillside, there were no signs of human habitation in sight. The lights in a switch target showed yellow against the growing dawn.

"I am quite ready, sir," reported Oscar, touching his hat. "There is nothing here but the station; the settlement is farther on our way."

"Then let us be off," said Armitage, swinging into the saddle.

Oscar led the way in silence along a narrow road that clung close to the base of a great pine-covered hill. The morning was sharp and the horses stepped smartly, the breath of their nostrils showing white on the air. The far roar and whistle of the train came back more and more faintly, and when it had quite ceased Armitage sighed, pushed his soft felt hat from his face, and settled himself more firmly in his saddle. The keen air was as stimulating as wine, and he put his horse to the gallop and rode ahead to shake up his blood.

"It is good," said the stolid cavalryman, as Armitage wheeled again into line with him.

"Yes, it is good," repeated Armitage.

A peace descended upon him that he had not known in many days. The light grew as the sun rose higher, blazing upon them like a brazen target through deep clefts in the mountains. The morning mists retreated before them to farther ridges and peaks, and the beautiful gray-blue of the Virginia hills delighted Armitage's eyes. The region was very wild. Here and there from some mountaineer's cabin a light penciling of smoke stole upward. They once passed a boy driving a yoke of steers. After several miles the road, that had hung midway of the rough hill, dipped down sharply, and they came out into another and broader valley, where there were tilled farms, and a little settlement, with a blacksmith shop and a country store, post-office and inn combined. The storekeeper stood in the door, smoking a cob pipe. Seeing Oscar, he went inside and brought out some letters and newspapers, which he delivered in silence.

"This is Lamar post-office," announced Oscar.

"There must be some mail here for me," said Armitage.

Oscar handed him several long envelopes—they bore the name of the Bronx Loan and Trust Company, whose office in New York was his permanent address, and he opened and read a number of letters and cablegrams that had been forwarded. Their contents evidently gave him satisfaction, for he whistled cheerfully as he thrust them into his pocket.

"You keep in touch with the world, do you, Oscar? It is commendable."

"I take a Washington paper—it relieves the monot-
ony, and I can see where the regiments are moving, and
whether my old captain is yet out of the hospital, and
what happened to my lieutenant in his court-martial
about the pay accounts. One must observe the world—
yes? At the post-office back there"—he jerked his head
to indicate—"it is against the law to sell whisky in a
post-office, so that storekeeper with the red nose and
small yellow eyes keeps it in a brown jug in the back
room."

"To be sure," laughed Armitage. "I hope it is a good
article."

"It is vile," replied Oscar. "His brother makes it up
in the hills, and it is as strong as wood lye."

"Moonshine! I have heard of it. We must have some
for rainy days."

It was a new world to John Armitage, and his heart
was as light as the morning air as he followed Oscar
along the ruddy mountain road. He was in Virginia,
and somewhere on this soil, perhaps in some valley like
the one through which he rode, Shirley Claiborne had
gazed upon blue distances, with ridge rising against
ridge, and dark pine-covered slopes like these he saw
for the first time. He had left his affairs in Washing-

ton in a sorry muddle; but he faced the new day with a buoyant spirit, and did not trouble himself to look very far ahead. He had a definite business before him; his cablegrams were reassuring on that point. The fact that he was, in a sense, a fugitive did not trouble him in the least. He had no intention of allowing Jules Chauvenet's assassins to kill him, or of being locked up in a Washington jail as the false Baron von Kissel. If he admitted that he was not John Armitage, it would be difficult to prove that he was anybody else—a fact touching human testimony which Jules Chauvenet probably knew perfectly well.

On the whole he was satisfied that he had followed the wisest course thus far. The broad panorama of the morning hills communicated to his spirit a growing elation. He began singing in German a ballad that recited the sorrows of a pale maiden prisoner in a dark tower on the Rhine, whence her true knight rescued her, after many and fearsome adventures. On the last stave he ceased abruptly, and an exclamation of wonder broke from him.

They had been riding along a narrow trail that afforded, as Oscar said, a short cut across a long timbered ridge that lay between them and Armitage's property.

The path was rough and steep, and the low-hanging pine boughs and heavy underbrush increased the difficulties of ascent. Straining to the top, a new valley, hidden until now, was disclosed in long and beautiful vistas.

Armitage dropped the reins upon the neck of his panting horse.

"It is a fine valley—yes?" asked Oscar.

"It is a possession worthy of the noblest gods!" replied Armitage. "There is a white building with colonnades away over there—is it the house of the reigning deity?"

"It is not, sir," answered Oscar, who spoke English with a kind of dogged precision, giving equal value to all words. "It is a vast hotel where the rich spend much money. That place at the foot of the hills—do you see? —it is there they play a foolish game with sticks and little balls—"

"Golf? Is it possible!"

"There is no doubt of it, sir. I have seen the fools myself—men and women. The place is called Storm Valley."

Armitage slapped his thigh sharply, so that his horse started.

"Yes; you are probably right, Oscar. I have heard of

the place. And those houses that lie beyond there in the valley belong to gentlemen of taste and leisure who drink the waters and ride horses and play the foolish game you describe with little white balls."

"I could not tell it better," responded Oscar, who had dismounted, like a good trooper, to rest his horse.

"And our place—is it below there?" demanded Armitage.

"It is not, sir. It lies to the west. But a man may come here when he is lonesome, and look at the people and the gentlemen's houses. At night it is a pleasure to see the lights, and sometimes, when the wind is right, there is music of bands."

"Poor Oscar!" laughed Armitage.

His mood had not often in his life been so high.

On his flight northward from Washington and southward down the Atlantic capes, the thought that Shirley Claiborne and her family must now believe him an ignoble scoundrel had wrought misgivings and pain in his heart; but at least he would soon be near her—even now she might be somewhere below in the lovely valley, and he drew off his hat and stared down upon what was glorified and enchanted ground.

"Let us go," he said presently.

Oscar saluted, standing bridle in hand.

"You will find it easier to walk," he said, and, lead-ing their horses, they retraced their steps for several hundred yards along the ridge, then mounted and pro-ceeded slowly down again until they came to a mountain road. Presently a high wire fence followed at their right, where the descent was sharply arrested, and they came to a barred wooden gate, and beside it a small cabin, evidently designed for a lodge.

"This is the place, sir," and Oscar dismounted and threw open the gate.

The road within followed the rough contour of the hillside, that still turned downward until it broadened into a wooded plateau. The flutter of wings in the un-derbrush, the scamper of squirrels, the mad lope of a fox, kept the eye busy. A deer broke out of a hazel thicket, stared at the horsemen in wide-eyed amazement, then plunged into the wood and disappeared.

"There are deer, and of foxes a great plenty," re-marked Oscar.

He turned toward Armitage and added with lowered voice:

"It is different from our old hills and forests—yes? but sometimes I have been homesick."

"But this is not so bad, Oscar; and some day you shall go back!"

"Here," said the soldier, as they swung out of the wood and into the open, "is what they call the Port of Missing Men."

There was a broad park-like area that tended downward almost imperceptibly to a deep defile. They dismounted and walked to the edge and looked down the steep sides. A little creek flowed out of the wood and emptied itself with a silvery rush into the vale, caught its breath below, and became a creek again. A slight suspension bridge flung across the defile had once afforded a short cut to Storm Springs, but it was now in disrepair, and at either end was posted "No Thoroughfare." Armitage stepped upon the loose planking and felt the frail thing vibrate under his weight.

"It is a bad place," remarked Oscar, as the bridge creaked and swung, and Armitage laughed and jumped back to solid ground.

The surface of this harbor of the hills was rough with outcropping rock. In some great stress of nature the trees had been destroyed utterly, and only a scant growth of weeds and wild flowers remained. The place suggested a battle-ground for the winds, where they might meet and struggle in wild combat; or more practically, it was large enough for the evolutions of a squadron of cavalry.

"Why the name?" asked Armitage.

"There were gray soldiers of many battles—yes?— who fought the long fight against the blue soldiers in the Valley of Virginia; and after the war was over some of them would not surrender—no; but they marched here, and stayed a long time, and kept their last flag, and so the place was called the Port of Missing Men. They built that stone wall over there beyond the patch of cedars, and camped. And a few died, and their graves are there by the cedars. Yes; they had brave hearts," and Oscar lifted his hat as though he were saluting the lost legion.

They turned again to the road and went forward at a gallop, until, half a mile from the gate, they came upon a clearing and a low, red-roofed bungalow.

"Your house, sir," and Oscar swung himself down at the steps of a broad veranda. He led the horses away to a barn beyond the house, while Armitage surveyed the landscape. The bungalow stood on a rough knoll, and was so placed as to afford a splendid view of a wide region. Armitage traversed the long veranda, studying the landscape, and delighting in the far-stretching pine-covered barricade of hills. He was aroused by Oscar, who appeared carrying the suit-cases.

"There shall be breakfast," said the man.

He threw open the doors and they entered a wide, bare hall, with a fireplace, into which Oscar dropped a match.

"All one floor—plenty of sleeping-rooms, sir—a place to eat here—a kitchen beyond—a fair barracks for a common soldier; that is all."

"It is enough. Throw these bags into the nearest bed-room, if there is no choice, and camp will be established."

"This is yours—the baggage that came by express is there. A wagon goes with the place, and I brought the things up yesterday. There is a shower-bath beyond the rear veranda. The mountain water is off the ice, but—you will require hot water for shaving—is it not so?"

"You oppress me with luxuries, Oscar. Wind up the clock, and nothing will be wanting."

Oscar unstrapped the trunks and then stood at attention in the door. He had expected Armitage to condemn the place in bitter language, but the proprietor of the abandoned hunting preserve was in excellent spirits, and whistled blithely as he drew out his keys.

"The place was built by fools," declared Oscar gloomily.

"Undoubtedly! There is a saying that fools build
houses and wise men live in them—you see where that
leaves us, Oscar. Let us be cheerful!"

He tried the shower and changed his raiment, while
Oscar prepared coffee and laid a cloth on the long table
before the fire. When Armitage appeared, coffee steamed
in the tin pot in which it had been made. Bacon, eggs
and toast were further offered.

"You have done excellently well, Oscar. Go get your
own breakfast." Armitage dropped a lump of sugar into
his coffee cup and surveyed the room.

A large map of Virginia and a series of hunting prints
hung on the untinted walls, and there were racks for
guns, and a work-bench at one end of the room, where
guns might be taken apart and cleaned. A few novels,
several three-year-old magazines and a variety of pipes
remained on the shelf above the fireplace. The house
offered possibilities of meager comfort, and that was
about all. Armitage remembered what the agent through
whom he had made the purchase had said—that the
place had proved too isolated for even a hunting preserve, and that its only value was in the timber. He was

satisfied with his bargain, and would not set up a lumber mill yet a while. He lighted a cigar and settled himself in an easy chair before the fire, glad of the luxury
of peace and quiet after his circuitous journey and the
tumult of doubt and question that had shaken him.

He slit the wrapper of the Washington newspaper
that Oscar had brought from the mountain post-office
and scanned the head-lines. He read with care a despatch from London that purported to reflect the sentiment of the continental capitals toward Charles Louis,
the new Emperor-king of Austria-Hungary, and the
paper dropped upon his knees and he stared into the
fire. Then he picked up a paper of earlier date and read
all the foreign despatches and the news of Washington.
He was about to toss the paper aside, when his eyes fell
upon a boldly-headlined article that caused his heart to
throb fiercely. It recited the sudden reappearance of the
fraudulent Baron von Kissel in Washington, and described in detail the baron's escapades at Bar Harbor
and his later career in California and elsewhere. Then
followed a story, veiled in careful phrases, but based, so
the article recited, upon information furnished by a
gentleman of extensive acquaintance on both sides of
the Atlantic, that Baron von Kissel, under a new pseu-

donym, and with even more daring effrontery, had with•
in a fortnight sought to intrench himself in the most ex-
clusive circles of Washington.

Armitage's cigar slipped from his fingers and fell
upon the brick hearth as he read:

"The boldness of this clever adventurer is said to have
reached a climax in this city within a few days. He had,
under the name of Armitage, palmed himself off upon
members of one of the most distinguished families of
the capital, whom he had met abroad during the winter.
A young gentleman of this family, who, it will suffice to
say, bears a commission and title from the American
government, entertained a small company of friends at
a Washington club only a few nights ago, and this plausible adventurer was among the guests. He was recognized at once by one of the foreigners present, who, out
of consideration for the host and fellow guests, held his
tongue; but it is understood that this gentleman sought
Armitage privately and warned him to leave Washington, which accounts for the fact that the sumptuous
apartments at the New American in which Mr. John Armitage, alias Baron von Kissel, had established himself
were vacated immediately. None of those present at the
supper will talk of the matter, but it has been the subject of lively gossip for several days, and the German
embassy is said to have laid before the Washington po-

lice all the information in its archives relating to the American adventures of this impudent scoundrel."

Armitage rose, dropped the paper into the fire, and, with his elbow resting on the mantel-shelf, watched it burn. He laughed suddenly and faced about, his back to the flames. Oscar stood at attention in the middle of the room.

"Shall we unpack—yes?"

"It is a capital idea," said John Armitage.

"I was striker for my captain also, who had fourteen pairs of boots and a bad disposition—and his uniforms —yes? He was very pretty to look at on a horse."

"The ideal is high, Oscar, but I shall do my best. That one first, please."

The contents of the two trunks were disposed of deftly by Oscar as Armitage directed. One of the bedrooms was utilized as a closet, and garments for every imaginable occasion were brought forth. There were stout English tweeds for the heaviest weather, two dress suits, and Norfolk jackets in corduroy. The owner's taste ran to grays and browns, it seemed, and he whimsically ordered his raiment grouped by colors as he lounged about with a pipe in his mouth.

"You may hang those scarfs on the string provided by my predecessor, Sergeant. They will help our color scheme. That pale blue doesn't blend well in our rainbow—put it in your pocket and wear it, with my compliments; and those tan shoes are not bad for the Virginia mud—drop them here. Those gray campaign hats are comfortable—give the oldest to me. And there is a riding-cloak I had forgotten I ever owned—I gave gold for it to a Madrid tailor. The mountain nights are cool, and the thing may serve me well," he added whimsically.

He clapped on the hat and flung the cloak upon his shoulders. It fell to his heels, and he gathered it together with one hand at the waist and strutted out into the hall, whither Oscar followed, staring, as Armitage began to declaim:

> " 'Give me my robe; put on my crown; I have
> Immortal longings in me!'

" 'Tis an inky cloak, as dark as Hamlet's mind; I will go forth upon a bloody business, and who hinders me shall know the bitter taste of death. Oscar, by the faith of my body, you shall be the Horatio of the tragedy. Set me right afore the world if treason be my undoing, and while we await the trumpets, cast that silly pair of trousers as rubbish to the void, and choose of mine own raiment as thou wouldst, knave! And now—

> —" 'Nothing can we call our own but death,
> And that small model of the barren earth
> Which serves as paste and cover to our bones.
> For God's sake, let us sit upon the ground
> And tell sad stories of the death of kings.' "

Then he grew serious, tossed the cloak and hat upon a bench that ran round the room, and refilled and lighted his pipe. Oscar, soberly unpacking, saw Armitage pace the hall floor for an hour, deep in thought.

"Oscar," he called abruptly, "how far is it down to Storm Springs?"

"A forced march, and you are there in an hour and a half, sir."

CHAPTER XIII

April, April,
Laugh thy girlish laughter;
Then, the moment after,
Weep thy girlish tears!
April, that mine ears
Like a lover greetest,
If I tell thee, sweetest,
All my hopes and fears,
April, April,
Laugh thy golden laughter,
But, the moment after,
Weep thy golden tears!
                                —*William Watson.*

A few photographs of foreign scenes tacked on the
walls; a Roman blanket hung as a tapestry over the
mantel; a portfolio and traveler's writing materials distributed about a table produced for the purpose, and
additions to the meager book-shelf—a line of Baedekers,
a pocket atlas, a comprehensive American railway guide,
several volumes of German and French poetry—and the
place was not so bad. Armitage slept for an hour after

180

a simple luncheon had been prepared by Oscar, studied
his letters and cablegrams—made, in fact, some notes in
regard to them—and wrote replies. Then, at four
o'clock, he told Oscar to saddle the horses.

"It is spring, and in April a man's blood will not be
quiet. We shall go forth and taste the air."

He had studied the map of Lamar County with care,
and led the way out of his own preserve by the road over
which they had entered in the morning. Oscar and his
horses were a credit to the training of the American
army, and would have passed inspection anywhere. Armitage watched his adjutant with approval. The man
served without question, and, quicker of wit than of
speech, his buff-gauntleted hand went to his hat-brim
whenever Armitage addressed him.

They sought again the spot whence Armitage had first
looked down upon Storm Valley, and he opened his
pocket map, the better to clarify his ideas of the region.

"We shall go down into the valley, Oscar," he said;
and thereafter it was he that led.

They struck presently into an old road that had been
an early highway across the mountains. Above and below the forest hung gloomily, and passing clouds darkened the slopes and occasionally spilled rain. Armitage

drew on his cloak and Oscar enveloped himself in a
slicker as they rode through a sharp shower. At a lower
level they came into fair weather again, and, crossing a
bridge, rode down into Storm Valley. The road at once
bore marks of care; and they passed a number of traps
that spoke unmistakably of cities, and riders whose
mounts knew well the bridle-paths of Central Park. The
hotel loomed massively before them, and beyond were
handsome estates and ambitious mansions scattered
through the valley and on the lower slopes.

Armitage paused in a clump of trees and dismounted.

"You will stay here until I come back. And remember that we don't know any one; and at our time of life,
Oscar, one should be wary of making new acquaintances."

He tossed his cloak over the saddle and walked toward
the inn. The size of the place and the great number of
people going and coming surprised him, but in the num-
bers he saw his own security, and he walked boldly up
the steps of the main hotel entrance. He stepped into
the long corridor of the inn, where many people lounged
about, and heard with keen satisfaction and relief the
click of a telegraph instrument that seemed at once to
bring him into contact with the remote world. He

filed his telegrams and walked the length of the broad
hall, his riding-crop under his arm. The gay banter
and laughter of a group of young men and women just
returned from a drive gave him a touch of heartache,
for there was a girl somewhere in the valley whom he
had followed across the sea, and these people were of
her own world—they undoubtedly knew her; very likely
she came often to this huge caravansary and mingled
with them.

At the entrance he passed Baron von Marhof, who, by
reason of the death of his royal chief, had taken a cottage at the Springs to emphasize his abstention from the
life of the capital. The Ambassador lifted his eyes and
bowed to Armitage, as he bowed to a great many young
men whose names he never remembered; but, oddly
enough, the Baron paused, stared after Armitage for a
moment, then shook his head and walked on with knit
brows. Armitage had lifted his hat and passed out, tapping his leg with his crop.

He walked toward the private houses that lay scattered over the valley and along the gradual slope of the
hills as though carelessly flung from a dice box. Many
of the places were handsome estates, with imposing
houses set amid beautiful gardens. Half a mile from

the hotel he stopped a passing negro to ask who owned
a large house that stood well back from the road. The
man answered; he seemed anxious to impart further information, and Armitage availed himself of the opportunity.

"How near is Judge Claiborne's place?" he asked.

The man pointed. It was the next house, on the right-
hand side; and Armitage smiled to himself and strolled
on.

He looked down in a moment upon a pretty estate,
distinguished by its formal garden, but with the broad
acres of a practical farm stretching far out into the valley. The lawn terraces were green, broken only by plots
of spring flowers; the walks were walled in box and
privet; the house, of the pillared colonial type, crowned
a series of terraces. A long pergola, with pillars topped
by red urns, curved gradually through the garden toward the mansion. Armitage followed a side road along
the brick partition wall and contemplated the inner
landscape. The sharp snap of a gardener's shears far up
the slope was the only sound that reached him. It was
a charming place, and he yielded to a temptation to explore it. He dropped over the wall and strolled away
through the garden, the smell of warm earth, moist from

the day's light showers, and the faint odor of green
things growing, sweet in his nostrils. He walked to the
far end of the pergola, sat down on a wooden bench, and
gave himself up to reverie. He had been denounced as an
impostor; he was on Claiborne soil; and the situation
required thought.

It was while he thus pondered his affairs that Shirley,
walking over the soft lawn from a neighboring estate,
came suddenly upon him.

Her head went up with surprise and—he was sure—
with disdain. She stopped abruptly as he jumped to his
feet.

"I am caught—*in flagrante delicto!* I can only plead
guilty and pray for mercy."

"They said—they said you had gone to Mexico?" said
Shirley questioningly.

"Plague take the newspapers! How dare they so mis-
represent me!" he laughed.

"Yes, I read those newspaper articles with a good deal
of interest. And my brother—"

"Yes, your brother—he is the best fellow in the
world!"

She mused, but a smile of real mirth now played over
her face and lighted her eyes.

"Those are generous words, Mr. Armitage. My brother warned me against you in quite unequivocal language. He told me about your match-box—"

"Oh, the cigarette case!" and he held it up. "It's really mine—and I'm going to keep it. It was very damaging evidence. It would argue strongly against me in any court of law."

"Yes, I believe that is true." And she looked at the trinket with frank interest.

"But I particularly do not wish to have to meet that charge in any court of law, Miss Claiborne."

She met his gaze very steadily, and her eyes were grave. Then she asked, in much the same tone that she would have used if they had been very old friends and he had excused himself for not riding that day, or for not going upon a hunt, or to the theater:

"Why?"

"Because I have a pledge to keep and a work to do, and if I were forced to defend myself from the charge of being the false Baron von Kissel, everything would be spoiled. You see, unfortunately—most unfortunately —I am not quite without responsibilities, and I have come down into the mountains, where I hope not to be shot and tossed over a precipice until I have had time to watch certain people and certain events a little while. I tried to say as much to Captain Claiborne, but I saw that my story did not impress him. And now I have said the same thing to you—"

He waited, gravely watching her, hat in hand.

"And I have stood here and listened to you, and done exactly what Captain Claiborne would not wish me to do under any circumstances," said Shirley.

"You are infinitely kind and generous—"

"No. I do not wish you to think me either of those things—of course not!"

Her conclusion was abrupt and pointed.

"Then—"

"Then I will tell you—what I have not told any one else—that I know very well that you are not the person who appeared at Bar Harbor three years ago and palmed himself off as the Baron von Kissel."

"You know it—you are quite sure of it?" he asked blankly.

"Certainly. I saw that person—at Bar Harbor. I had gone up from Newport for a week—I was even at a tea where he was quite the lion, and I am sure you are not the same person."

Her direct manner of speech, her decisive tone, in

which she placed the matter of his identity on a purely
practical and unsentimental plane, gave him a new impression of her character.

"But Captain Claiborne—"

He ceased suddenly and she anticipated the question
at which he had faltered, and answered, a little icily:

"I do not consider it any of my business to meddle in
your affairs with my brother. He undoubtedly believes
you are the impostor who palmed himself off at Bar
Harbor as the Baron von Kissel. He was told so—"

"By Monsieur Chauvenet."

"So he said."

"And of course he is a capital witness. There is no
doubt of Chauvenet's entire credibility," declared Armitage, a little airily.

"I should say not," said Shirley unresponsively. "I
am quite as sure that he was not the false baron as I am
that you were not."

Armitage laughed.

"That is a little pointed."

"It was meant to be," said Shirley sternly. "It is"—
she weighed the word—"ridiculous that both of you
should be here."

"Thank you, for my half! I didn't know he was here!

But I am not exactly *here*—I have a much safer place,"
—he swept the blue-hilled horizon with his hand. "Monsieur Chauvenet and I will not shoot at each other in the
hotel dining-room. But I am really relieved that he has
come. We have an interesting fashion of running into
each other; it would positively grieve me to be obliged
to wait long for him."

He smiled and thrust his hat under his arm. The sun
was dropping behind the great western barricade, and a
chill wind crept sharply over the valley.

He started to walk beside her as she turned away, but
she paused abruptly.

"Oh, this won't do at all! I can't be seen with you,
even in the shadow of my own house. I must trouble you
to take the side gate,"—and she indicated it by a nod of
her head.

"Not if I know myself! I am not a fraudulent member of the German nobility—you have told me so yourself. Your conscience is clear—I assure you mine is
equally so! And I am not a person, Miss Claiborne, to
sneak out by side gates—particularly when I came over
the fence! It's a long way around anyhow—and I have
a horse over there somewhere by the inn."

"My brother—"

"Is at Fort Myer, of course. At about this hour they are having dress parade, and he is thoroughly occupied."

"But—there is Monsieur Chauvenet. He has nothing to do but amuse himself."

They had reached the veranda steps, and she ran to the top and turned for a moment to look at him. He still carried his hat and crop in one hand, and had dropped the other into the side pocket of his coat. He was wholly at ease, and the wind ruffled his hair and gave him a boyish look that Shirley liked. But she had no wish to be found with him, and she instantly nodded his dismissal and half turned away to go into the house, when he detained her for a moment.

"I am perfectly willing to afford Monsieur Chauvenet all imaginable entertainment. We are bound to have many meetings. I am afraid he reached this charming valley before me; but—as a rule—I prefer to be a little ahead of him; it's a whim—the merest whim, I assure you."

He laughed, thinking little of what he said, but delighting in the picture she made, the tall pillars of the veranda framing her against the white wall of the house, and the architrave high above speaking, so he thought, for the amplitude, the breadth of her nature. Her green

He delighted in the picture she made   *Page 190*

cloth gown afforded the happiest possible contrast with
the white background; and her hat—(for a gown, let us
remember, may express the dressmaker, but a hat ex-
presses the woman who wears it)—her hat, Armitage
was aware, was a trifle of black velvet caught up at one
side with snowy plumes well calculated to shock the
sensibilities of the Audubon Society. Yet the bird, if
he knew, doubtless rejoiced in his fate! Shirley's hand,
thrice laid down, and there you have the length of that
velvet cap, plume and all. Her profile, as she half turned
away, must awaken regret that Reynolds and Gains-
borough paint no more; yet let us be practical: Sargent,
in this particular, could not serve us ill.

Her annoyance at finding herself lingering to listen
to him was marked in an almost imperceptible gathering
of her brows. It was all the matter of an instant. His
heart beat fast in his joy at the sight of her, and the
tongue that years of practice had skilled in reserve and
evasion was possessed by a reckless spirit.

She nodded carelessly, but said nothing, waiting for
him to go on.

"But when I wait for people they always come—even
in a strange pergola!" he added daringly. "Now, in
Geneva, not long ago—"

He lost the profile and gained her face as he liked it best, though her head was lifted a little high in resentment against her own yielding curiosity. He was speaking rapidly, and the slight hint of some other tongue than his usually fluent English arrested her ear now, as it had at other times.

"In Geneva, when I told a young lady that I was waiting for a very wicked man to appear—it was really the oddest thing in the world that almost immediately Monsieur Jules Chauvenet arrived at mine own inn! It is inevitable; it is always sure to be my fate," he concluded mournfully.

He bowed low, restored the shabby hat to his head with the least bit of a flourish and strolled away through the garden by a broad walk that led to the front gate.

He would have been interested to know that when he was out of sight Shirley walked to the veranda rail and bent forward, listening to his steps on the gravel, after the hedge and shrubbery had hidden him. And she stood thus until the faint click of the gate told her that he had gone.

She did not know that as the gate closed upon him he met Chauvenet face to face.

CHAPTER XIV,

En garde, Messieurs! And if my hand is hard,
Remember I've been buffeting at will;
I am a whit impatient, and 'tis ill
To cross a hungry dog. *Messieurs, en garde.*
                                        —*W. Lindsey.*

"Monsieur Chauvenet!"

Armitage uncovered smilingly. Chauvenet stared mutely as Armitage paused with his back to the Claiborne gate. Chauvenet was dressed with his usual care, and wore the latest carnation in the lapel of his top-coat. He struck the ground with his stick, his look of astonishment passed, and he smiled pleasantly as he returned Armitage's salutation.

"My dear Armitage!" he murmured.

"I didn't go to Mexico after all, my good Chauvenet. The place is full of fevers; I couldn't take the risk."

"He is indeed a wise man who safeguards his health," replied the other.

193

"You are quite right. And when one has had many narrow escapes, one may be excused for exercising rather particular care. Do you not find it so?" mocked Armitage.

"My dear fellow, my life is one long fight against ennui. Danger, excitement, the hazard of my precious life—such pleasures of late have been denied me."

"But you are young and of intrepid spirit, Monsieur. It would be quite surprising if some perilous adventure did not overtake you before the silver gets in your hair."

"Ah! I assure you the speculation interests me; but I must trouble you to let me pass," continued Chauvenet, in the same tone. "I shall quite forget that I set out to make a call if I linger longer in your charming society."

"But I must ask you to delay your call for the present. I shall greatly value your company down the road a little way. It is a trifling favor, and you are a man of delightful courtesy."

Chauvenet twisted his mustache reflectively. His mind had been busy seeking means of turning the meeting to his own advantage. He had met Armitage at quite the least imaginable spot in the world for an encounter between them; and he was not a man who enjoyed

surprises. He had taken care that the exposure of
Armitage at Washington should be telegraphed to every
part of the country, and put upon the cables. He had
expected Armitage to leave Washington, but he had no
idea that he would turn up at a fashionable resort
greatly affected by Washingtonians and only a comparatively short distance from the capital. He was at a
great disadvantage in not knowing Armitage's plans
and strategy; his own mind was curiously cunning, and
his reasoning powers traversed oblique lines. He was
thus prone to impute similar mental processes to other
people; simplicity and directness he did not understand
at all. He had underrated Armitage's courage and daring; he wished to make no further mistakes, and he
walked back toward the hotel with apparent good grace.
Armitage spoke now in a very different key, and the
change displeased Chauvenet, for he much affected ironical raillery, and his companion's sterner tones discon-
certed him.

"I take this opportunity to give you a solemn warning,
Monsieur Jules Chauvenet, alias Rambaud, and thereby
render you a greater service than you know. You have
undertaken a deep and dangerous game—it is spectacular—it is picturesque—it is immense! It is so stupen-

dous that the taking of a few lives seems trifling in
comparison with the end to be attained. Now look about
you for a moment, Monsieur Jules Chauvenet! In this
mountain air a man may grow very sane and see matters very clearly. London, Paris, Berlin, Vienna—they
are a long way off, and the things they stand for lose
their splendor when a man sits among these American
mountains and reflects upon the pettiness and sordidness of man's common ambitions."

"Is this exordium or peroration, my dear fellow?"

"It is both," replied Armitage succinctly, and
Chauvenet was sorry he had spoken, for Armitage
stopped short in a lonely stretch of the highway and continued in a disagreeable, incisive tone:

"I ran away from Washington after you told that
story at Claiborne's supper-table, not because I was
afraid of your accusation, but because I wanted to
watch your plans a little in security. The only man
who could have helped me immediately was Senator
Sanderson, and I knew that he was in Montana."

Chauvenet smiled with a return of assurance.

"Of course. The hour was chosen well!"

"More wisely, in fact, than your choice of that big
assassin of yours. He's a clumsy fellow, with more

brawn than brains. I had no trouble in shaking him off in Boston, where you probably advised him I should be taking the Montreal express."

Chauvenet blinked. This was precisely what he had told Zmai to expect. He shifted from one foot to another, and wondered just how he was to escape from Armitage. He had gone to Storm Springs to be near Shirley Claiborne, and he deeply resented having business thrust upon him.

"He is a wise man who wields the knife himself, Monsieur Chauvenet. In the taking of poor Count von Stroebel's life so deftly and secretly, you prove my philosophy. It was a clever job, Monsieur!"

Chauvenet's gloved fingers caught at his mustache.

"That is almost insulting, Monsieur Armitage. A distinguished statesman is killed—therefore I must have murdered him. You forget that there's a difference between us—you are an unknown adventurer, carried on the books of the police as a fugitive from justice, and I can walk to the hotel and get twenty reputable men to vouch for me. I advise you to be careful not to mention my name in connection with Count von Stroebel's death."

He had begun jauntily, but closed in heat, and when

he finished Armitage nodded to signify that he understood perfectly.

"A few more deaths and you would be in a position
to command tribute from a high quarter, Monsieur."

"Your mind seems to turn upon assassination. If
you know so much about Stroebel's death, it's unfortunate that you left Europe at a time when you might
have rendered important aid in finding the murderer.
It's a bit suspicious, Monsieur Armitage! It is known
at the Hotel Monte Rosa in Geneva that you were the
last person to enjoy an interview with the venerable
statesman—you see I am not dull, Monsieur Armitage!"

"You are not dull, Chauvenet; you are only short-
sighted. The same witnesses know that John Armitage
was at the Hotel Monte Rosa for twenty-four hours
following the Count's departure. Meanwhile, where were
you, Jules Chauvenet?"

Chauvenet's hand again went to his face, which
whitened, though he sought refuge again in flippant
irony.

"To be sure! Where was I, Monsieur? Undoubtedly
you know all my movements, so that it is unnecessary
for me to have any opinions in the matter."

"Quite so! Your opinions are not of great value to

me, for I employed agents to trace every move you made during the month in which Count von Stroebel was stabbed to death in his railway carriage. It is so interesting that I have committed the record to memory. If the story would interest you—"

The hand that again sought the slight mustache trembled slightly; but Chauvenet smiled.

"You should write the memoirs of your very interesting career, my dear fellow. I can not listen to your babble longer."

"I do not intend that you shall; but your whereabouts on Monday night, March eighteenth, of this year, may need explanation, Monsieur Chauvenet."

"If it should, I shall call upon you, my dear fellow!"

"Save yourself the trouble! The bureau I employed to investigate the matter could assist you much better. All I could offer would be copies of its very thorough reports. The number of cups of coffee your friend Durand drank for breakfast this morning at his lodgings in Vienna will reach me in due course!"

"You are really a devil of a fellow, John Armitage! So much knowledge! So acute an intellect! You are too wise to throw away your life futilely."

"You have been most generous in sparing it thus

far!" laughed Armitage, and Chauvenet took instant advantage of his change of humor.

"Perhaps—perhaps—I have pledged my faith in the wrong quarter, Monsieur. If I may say it, we are both fairly clever men; together we could achieve much!"

"So you would sell out, would you?" laughed Armitage. "You miserable little blackguard, I should like to join forces with you! Your knack of getting the poison into the right cup every time would be a valuable asset! But we are not made for each other in this world. In the next—who knows?"

"As you will! I dare say you would be an exacting partner."

"All of that, Chauvenet! You do best to stick to your present employer. He needs you and the like of you—I don't! But remember—if there's a sudden death in Vienna, in a certain high quarter, you will not live to reap the benefits. Charles Louis rules Austria-Hungary; his cousin, your friend Francis, is not of kingly proportions. I advise you to cable the amiable Durand of a dissolution of partnership. It is now too late for you to call at Judge Claiborne's, and I shall trouble you to walk on down the road for ten minutes. If you look round or follow me, I shall certainly turn you into something less attractive than a pillar of salt. You do well to consult your watch—forward!"

Armitage pointed down the road with his riding-crop. As Chauvenet walked slowly away, swinging his stick, Armitage turned toward the hotel. The shadow of night was enfolding the hills, and it was quite dark when he found Oscar and the horses.

He mounted, and they rode through the deepening April dusk, up the winding trail that led out of Storm Valley.

CHAPTER XV

Nightingales warble about it
  All night under blossom and star;
The wild swan is dying without it,
  And the eagle crieth afar;
The sun, he doth mount but to find it
  Searching the green earth o'er;
But more doth a man's heart mind it—
  O more, more, more!

—*G. E. Woodberry.*

Shirley Claiborne was dressed for a ride, and while waiting for her horse she re-read her brother's letter; and the postscript, which follows, she read twice:

"I shall never live down my acquaintance with the delectable Armitage. My brother officers insist on rubbing it in. I even hear, *ma chérie,* that you have gone into retreat by reason of the exposure. I'll admit, for your consolation, that he really took me in; and, further, I really wonder who the devil he is,—or *was!* Our last interview at the Club, after Chauvenet told his story, lingers with me disagreeably. I was naturally pretty hot to find him playing the darkly mysterious,

202

which never did go with me,—after eating my bird and drinking my bottle. As a precaution I have looked up Chauvenet to the best of my ability. At the Austro-Hungarian Embassy they speak well of him. He's over here to collect the price of a few cruisers or some such rubbish from one of our sister republics below the Gulf. But bad luck to all foreigners! Me for America every time!"

"Dear old Dick!" and she dropped the letter into a drawer and went out into the sunshine, mounted her horse and turned toward the hills.

She had spent the intermediate seasons of the year at Storm Springs ever since she could remember, and had climbed the surrounding hills and dipped into the valleys with a boy's zest and freedom. The Virginia mountains were linked in her mind to the dreams of her youth, to her earliest hopes and aspirations, and to the books she had read, and she galloped happily out of the valley to the tune of an old ballad. She rode as a woman should, astride her horse and not madly clinging to it in the preposterous ancient fashion. She had known horses from early years, in which she had tumbled from her pony's back in the stable-yard, and she knew how to train a horse to a gait and how to master a beast's fear; and even some of the tricks of the troopers in the Fort Myer drill she had surreptitiously practised in the meadow back of the Claiborne stable.

It was on Tuesday that John Armitage had appeared before her in the pergola. It was now Thursday afternoon, and Chauvenet had been to see her twice since, and she had met him the night before at a dance at one of the cottages.

Judge Claiborne was distinguished for his acute and sinewy mind; but he had, too, a strong feeling for art in all its expressions, and it was his gift of imagination,—the ability to forecast the enemy's strategy and then strike his weakest point,—that had made him a great lawyer and diplomat. Shirley had played chess with her father until she had learned to see around corners as he did, and she liked a problem, a test of wit, a contest of powers. She knew how to wait and ponder in silence, and therein lay the joy of the saddle, when she could ride alone with no groom to bother her, and watch enchantments unfold on the hilltops.

Once free of the settlement she rode far and fast, until she was quite beyond the usual routes of the Springs excursionists; then in mountain byways she enjoyed the luxury of leisure and dismounted now and then to delight in the green of the laurel and question the rhododendrons.

Jules Chauvenet had scoured the hills all day and explored many mountain paths and inquired cautiously of the natives. The telegraph operator at the Storm Springs inn was a woman, and the despatch and receipt by Jules Chauvenet of long messages, many of them in cipher, piqued her curiosity. No member of the Washington diplomatic circle who came to the Springs,—not even the shrewd and secretive Russian Ambassador,—received longer or more cryptic cables. With the social diversions of the Springs and the necessity for making a show of having some legitimate business in America, Jules Chauvenet was pretty well occupied; and now the presence of John Armitage in Virginia added to his burdens.

He was tired and perplexed, and it was with unaffected pleasure that he rode out of an obscure hill-path into a bit of open wood overhanging a curious defile and came upon Shirley Claiborne.

The soil was soft and his horse carried him quite near before she heard him. A broad sheet of water flashed down the farther side of the narrow pass, sending up a pretty spurt of spray wherever it struck the jutting rock.

As Shirley turned toward him he urged his horse over
the springy turf.

"A pity to disturb the picture, Miss Claiborne! A
thousand pardons! But I really wished to see whether
the figure could come out of the canvas. Now that I
have dared to make the test, pray do not send me away."

Her horse turned restlessly and brought her face to
face with Chauvenet.

"Steady, Fanny! Don't come near her, please——"
this last to Chauvenet, who had leaped down and put
out his hand to her horse's bridle. She had the true
horsewoman's pride in caring for herself and her eyes
flashed angrily for a moment at Chauvenet's proffered
aid. A man might open a door for her or pick up her
handkerchief, but to touch her horse was an altogether
different business. The pretty, graceful mare was calm
in a moment and arched her neck contentedly under the
stroke of Shirley's hand.

"Beautiful! The picture is even more perfect, Mademoiselle!"

"Fanny is best in action, and splendid when she runs
away. She hasn't run away to-day, but I think she is
likely to before I get home."

She was thinking of the long ride which she had no

intention of taking in Chauvenet's company. He stood uncovered beside her, holding his horse.

"But the danger, Mademoiselle! You should not hazard your life with a runaway horse on these roads. It is not fair to your friends."

"You are a conservative, Monsieur. I should be ashamed to have a runaway in a city park, but what does one come to the country for?"

"What, indeed, but for excitement? You are not of those tame young women across the sea who come out into the world from a convent, frightened at all they see and whisper 'Yes, Sister,' 'No, Sister,' to everything they hear."

"Yes; we Americans are deficient in shyness and humility. I have often heard it remarked, Monsieur Chauvenet."

"No! No! You misunderstand! Those deficiencies, as you term them, are delightful; they are what give the charm to the American woman. I hope you would not believe me capable of speaking in disparagement, Mademoiselle,—you must know—"

The water tumbled down the rock into the vale; the soft air was sweet with the scent of pines. An eagle cruised high against the blue overhead. Shirley's hand

tightened on the rein, and Fanny lifted her head ex-
pectantly.

Chauvenet went on rapidly in French:

"You must know why I am here—why I have crossed
the sea to seek you in your own home. I have loved you,
Mademoiselle, from the moment I first saw you in Flor-
ence. Here, with only the mountains, the sky, the wood,
I must speak. You must hear—you must believe, that
I love you! I offer you my life, my poor attainments—"

"Monsieur, you do me a great honor, but I can not
listen. What you ask is impossible, quite impossible.
But, Monsieur—"

Her eyes had fallen upon a thicket behind him where
something had stirred. She thought at first that it was
an animal of some sort; but she saw now quite distinctly
a man's shabby felt hat that rose slowly until the bearded
face of its wearer was disclosed.

"Monsieur!" cried Shirley in a low tone; "look behind you and be careful what you say or do. Leave the
man to me."

Chauvenet turned and faced a scowling mountaineer
who held a rifle and drew it to his shoulder as Chauvenet threw out his arms, dropped them to his thighs and
laughed carelessly.

"What is it, my dear fellow—my watch—my purse—my horse?" he said in English.

"He wants none of those things," said Shirley, urging her horse a few steps toward the man. "The mountain people are not robbers. What can we do for you?" she asked pleasantly.

"You cain't do nothin' for me," drawled the man. "Go on away, Miss. I want to see this little fella'. I got a little business with him."

"He is a foreigner—he knows little of our language. You will do best to let me stay," said Shirley.

She had not the remotest idea of what the man wanted, but she had known the mountain folk from childhood and well understood that familiarity with their ways and tact were necessary in dealing with them.

"Miss, I have seen you befo', and I reckon we ain't got no cause for trouble with you; but this little fella' ain't no business up hy'eh. Them hotel people has their own places to ride and drive, and it's all right for you, Miss; but what's yo' frien' ridin' the hills for at night? He's lookin' for some un', and I reckon as how that some un' air me!"

He spoke drawlingly with a lazy good humor in his tones, and Shirley's wits took advantage of his deliberation to consider the situation from several points of view. Chauvenet stood looking from Shirley to the man and back again. He was by no means a coward, and he did not in the least relish the thought of owing his safety to a woman. But the confidence with which Shirley addressed the man, and her apparent familiarity with the peculiarities of the mountaineers impressed him. He spoke to her rapidly in French.

"Assure the man that I never heard of him before in my life—that the idea of seeking him never occurred to me."

The rifle—a repeater of the newest type—went to the man's shoulder in a flash and the blue barrel pointed at Chauvenet's head.

"None o' that! I reckon the American language air good enough for these 'ere negotiations."

Chauvenet shrugged his shoulders; but he gazed into the muzzle of the rifle unflinchingly.

"The gentleman was merely explaining that you are mistaken; that he does not know you and never heard of you before, and that he has not been looking for you in the mountains or anywhere else."

As Shirley spoke these words very slowly and distinctly she questioned for the first time Chauvenet's position. Perhaps, after all, the mountaineer had a real cause of grievance. It seemed wholly unlikely, but while she listened to the man's reply she weighed the matter judicially. They were in an unfrequented part of the mountains, which cottagers and hotel guests rarely explored. The mountaineer was saying:

"Mountain folks air slow, and we don't know much, but a stranger don't ride through these hills more than once for the scenery; the second time he's got to tell why; and the third time—well, Miss, you kin tell the little fella' that there ain't no third time."

Chauvenet flushed and he ejaculated hotly:

"I have never been here before in my life."

The man dropped the rifle into his arm without taking his eyes from Chauvenet. He said succinctly, but still with his drawl:

"You air a liar, seh!"

Chauvenet took a step forward, looked again into the rifle barrel, and stopped short. Fanny, bored by the prolonged interview, bent her neck and nibbled at a weed.

"This gentleman has been in America only a few weeks; you are certainly mistaken, friend," said Shirley boldly. Then the color flashed into her face, as an explanation of the mountaineer's interest in a stranger riding the hills occurred to her.

"My friend," she said, "I am Miss Claiborne. You may know my father's house down in the valley. We have been coming here as far back as I can remember."

The mountaineer listened to her gravely, and at her last words he unconsciously nodded his head. Shirley, seeing that he was interested, seized her advantage.

"I have no reason for misleading you. This gentleman is not a revenue man. He probably never heard of a— still, do you call it?—in his life—" and she smiled upon him sweetly. "But if you will let him go I promise to satisfy you entirely in the matter."

Chauvenet started to speak, but Shirley arrested him with a gesture, and spoke again to the mountaineer in her most engaging tone:

"We are both mountaineers, you and I, and we don't want any of our people to be carried off to jail. Isn't that so? Now let this gentleman ride away, and I shall stay here until I have quite assured you that you are mistaken about him."

She signaled Chauvenet to mount, holding the mystified and reluctant mountaineer with her eyes. Her heart was thumping fast and her hand shook a little as she

" You air a liar, seh !" *Page 211*

tightened her grasp on the rein. She addressed Chauvenet in English as a mark of good faith to their captor.

"Ride on, Monsieur; do not wait for me."

"But it is growing dark—I can not leave you alone, Mademoiselle. You have rendered me a great service, when it is I who should have extricated you—"

"Pray do not mention it! It is a mere chance that I am able to help. I shall be perfectly safe with this gentleman."

The mountaineer took off his hat.

"Thank ye, Miss," he said; and then to Chauvenet: "Get out!"

"Don't trouble about me in the least, Monsieur Chauvenet," and Shirley affirmed the last word with a nod as Chauvenet jumped into his saddle and rode off. When the swift gallop of his horse had carried him out of sight and sound down the road, Shirley faced the mountaineer.

"What is your name?"

"Tom Selfridge."

"Whom did you take that man to be, Mr. Selfridge?" asked Shirley, and in her eagerness she bent down above the mountaineer's bared tangle of tow.

"The name you called him ain't it. It's a queer name I never heerd tell on befo'—it's—it's like the a'my—"

"Is it Armitage?" asked Shirley quickly.

"That's it, Miss! The postmaster over at Lamar told me to look out fer 'im. He's moved up hy'eh, and it ain't fer no good. The word's out that a city man's lookin' for some*thing* or some*body* in these hills. And the man's stayin'—"

"Where?"

"At the huntin' club where folks don't go no more. I ain't seen him, but th' word's passed. He's a city man and a stranger, and got a little fella' that's been a soldier into th' army stayin' with 'im. I thought yo' furriner was him, Miss, honest to God I did."

The incident amused Shirley and she laughed aloud. She had undoubtedly gained information that Chauvenet had gone forth to seek; she had—and the thing was funny—served Chauvenet well in explaining away his presence in the mountains and getting him out of the clutches of the mountaineer, while at the same time she was learning for herself the fact of Armitage's where-abouts and keeping it from Chauvenet. It was a curious adventure, and she gave her hand smilingly to the mysti-fied and still doubting mountaineer.

"I give you my word of honor that neither man is a government officer and neither one has the slightest interest in you—will you believe me?"

"I reckon I got to, Miss."

"Good; and now, Mr. Selfridge, it is growing dark and I want you to walk down this trail with me until we come to the Storm Springs road."

"I'll do it gladly, Miss."

"Thank you; now let us be off."

She made him turn back when they reached a point from which they could look upon the electric lights of the Springs colony, and where the big hotel and its piazzas shone like a steamship at night. A moment later Chauvenet, who had waited impatiently, joined her, and they rode down together. She referred at once to the affair with the mountaineer in her most frivolous key.

"They are an odd and suspicious people, but they're as loyal as the stars. And please let us never mention the matter again—not to any one, if you please, Monsieur!"

CHAPTER XVI

NARROW MARGINS

The black-caps pipe among the reeds,
   And there'll be rain to follow;
There is a murmur as of wind
   In every coign and hollow;
The wrens do chatter of their fears
While swinging on the barley-ears.
                              —*Amélie Rives.*

The Judge and Mrs. Claiborne were dining with some old friends in the valley, and Shirley, left alone, carried to the table several letters that had come in the late mail. The events of the afternoon filled her mind, and she was not sorry to be alone. It occurred to her that she was building up a formidable tower of strange secrets, and she wondered whether, having begun by keeping her own counsel as to the attempts she had witnessed against John Armitage's life, she ought now to unfold all she knew to her father or to Dick. In the twentieth century homicide was not a common practice among men she knew or was likely to know; and the feeling of culpa-

bility for her silence crossed lances with a deepening
sympathy for Armitage. She had learned where he was
hiding, and she smiled at the recollection of the trifling
bit of strategy she had practised upon Chauvenet.

The maid who served Shirley noted with surprise the
long pauses in which her young mistress sat staring
across the table lost in reverie. A pretty picture was
Shirley in these intervals: one hand raised to her cheek,
bright from the sting of the spring wind in the hills.
Her forearm, white and firm and strong, was circled by
a band of Roman gold, the only ornament she wore, and
when she lifted her hand with its quick deft gesture, the
trinket flashed away from her wrist and clasped the
warm flesh as though in joy of the closer intimacy. Her
hair was swept up high from her brow; her nose,
straight, like her father's, was saved from arrogance by
a sensitive mouth, all eloquent of kindness and wholesome mirth—but we take unfair advantage! A girl dining in candle-light with only her dreams for company
should be safe from impertinent eyes.

She had kept Dick's letter till the last. He wrote often
and in the key of his talk. She dropped a lump of sugar
into her coffee-cup and read his hurried scrawl:

"What do you think has happened now? I have four-

teen dollars' worth of telegrams from Sanderson—wiring
from some God-forsaken hole in Montana, that it's all
rot about Armitage being that fake Baron von Kissel.
The newspaper accounts of the *exposé* at my supper
party had just reached him, and he says Armitage was
on his (Armitage's) ranch all that summer the noble
baron was devastating our northern sea-coast. Where,
may I ask, does this leave me? And what cad gave that
story to the papers? And where and *who* is John Armitage? Keep this mum for the present—even from the
governor. If Sanderson is right, Armitage will undoubtedly turn up again—he has a weakness for turning up in
your neighborhood!—and sooner or later he's bound to
settle accounts with Chauvenet. Now that I think of it,
who in the devil is *he!* And why didn't Armitage call
him down there at the club? As I think over the whole
business my mind grows addled, and I feel as though I
had been kicked by a horse."

Shirley laughed softly, keeping the note open before
her and referring to it musingly as she stirred her coffee.
She could not answer any of Dick's questions, but her
interest in the contest between Armitage and Chauvenet
was intensified by this latest turn in the affair. She read
for an hour in the library, but the air was close, and she
threw aside her book, drew on a light coat and went out

upon the veranda. A storm was stealing down from the hills, and the fitful wind tasted of rain. She walked the length of the veranda several times, then paused at the farther end of it, where steps led out into the pergola. There was still a mist of starlight, and she looked out upon the vague outlines of the garden with thoughts of its needs and the gardener's work for the morrow. Then she was aware of a light step far out in the pergola, and listened carelessly to mark it, thinking it one of the house servants returning from a neighbor's; but the sound was furtive, and as she waited it ceased abruptly. She was about to turn into the house to summon help when she heard a stir in the shrubbery in quite another part of the garden, and in a moment the stooping figure of a man moved swiftly toward the pergola.

Shirley stood quite still, watching and listening. The sound of steps in the pergola reached her again, then the rush of flight, and out in the garden a flying figure darted in and out among the walks. For several minutes two dark figures played at vigorous hide-and-seek. Occasionally gravel crunched underfoot and shrubbery snapped back with a sharp swish where it was caught and held for support at corners. Pursued and pursuer were alike silent; the scene was like a pantomime.

Then the tables seemed to be turned; the bulkier figure of the pursuer was now in flight; and Shirley lost
both for a moment, but immediately a dark form rose at
the wall; she heard the scratch of feet upon the brick
surface as a man gained the top, turned and lifted his
arm as though aiming a weapon.

Then a dark object, hurled through the air, struck him
squarely in the face and he tumbled over the wall, and
Shirley heard him crash through the hedge of the neighboring estate, then all was quiet again.

The game of hide-and-seek in the garden and the
scramble over the wall had consumed only two or three
minutes, and Shirley now waited, her eyes bent upon the
darkly-outlined pergola for some manifestation from the
remaining intruder. A man now walked rapidly toward
the veranda, carrying a cloak on his arm. She recognized Armitage instantly. He doffed his hat and bowed.
The lights of the house lamps shone full upon him, and
she saw that he was laughing a little breathlessly.

"This is really fortunate, Miss Claiborne. I owe your
house an apology, and if you will grant me audience I
will offer it to you."

He threw the cloak over his shoulder and fanned himself with his hat.

"You are a most informal person, Mr. Armitage," said Shirley coldly.

"I'm afraid I am! The most amazing ill luck follows me! I had dropped in to enjoy the quiet and charm of your garden, but the tranquil life is not for me. There was another gentleman, equally bent on enjoying the pergola. We engaged in a pretty running match, and because I was fleeter of foot he grew ugly and tried to put me out of commission."

He was still laughing, but Shirley felt that he was again trying to make light of a serious situation, and a further tie of secrecy with Armitage was not to her liking. As he walked boldly to the veranda steps, she stepped back from him.

"No! No! This is impossible—it will not do at all, Mr. Armitage. It is not kind of you to come here in this strange fashion."

"In this way forsooth! How could I send in my card when I was being chased all over the estate! I didn't mean to apologize for coming"—and he laughed again, with a sincere mirth that shook her resolution to deal harshly with him. "But," he went on, "it was the flower-pot! He was mad because I beat him in the foot-race and wanted to shoot me from the wall, and I tossed him

a potted geranium—geraniums are splendid for the purpose—and it caught him square in the head. I have the
knack of it! Once before I handed him a boiling-pot!"

"It must have hurt him," said Shirley; and he laughed
at her tone that was meant to be severe.

"I certainly hope so; I most devoutly hope he felt it!
He was most tenderly solicitous for my health; and if
he had really shot me there in the garden it would have
had an ugly look. Armitage, the false baron, would have
been identified as a daring burglar, shot while trying to
burglarize the Claiborne mansion! But I wouldn't take
the Claiborne plate for anything, I assure you!"

"I suppose you didn't think of us—all of us, and the
unpleasant consequences to my father and brother if
something disagreeable happened here!"

There was real anxiety in her tone, and he saw that he
was going too far with his light treatment of the affair.
His tone changed instantly.

"Please forgive me! I would not cause embarrassment
or annoyance to any member of your family for kingdoms. I didn't know I was being followed—I had come
here to see you. That is the truth of it."

"You mustn't try to see me! You mustn't come here
at all unless you come with the knowledge of my father.

And the very fact that your life is sought so persistently
—at most unusual times and in impossible places, leaves
very much to explain."

"I know that! I realize all that!"

"Then you must not come! You must leave instantly."

She walked away toward the front door; but he followed, and at the door she turned to him again. They
were in the full glare of the door lamps, and she saw that
his face was very earnest, and as he began to speak he
flinched and shifted the cloak awkwardly.

"You have been hurt—why did you not tell me that?"

"It is nothing—the fellow had a knife, and he—but
it's only a trifle in the shoulder. I must be off!"

The lightning had several times leaped sharply
out of the hills; the wind was threshing the garden
foliage, and now the rain roared on the tin roof of the
veranda.

As he spoke a carriage rolled into the grounds and
came rapidly toward the porte-cochère.

"I'm off—please believe in me—a little."

"You must not go if you are hurt—and you can't run
away now—my father and mother are at the door."

There was an instant's respite while the carriage drew

up to the veranda steps. She heard the stable-boy running out to help with the horses.

"You can't go now; come in and wait."

There was no time for debate. She flung open the door
and swept him past her with a gesture—through the library and beyond, into a smaller room used by Judge
Claiborne as an office. Armitage sank down on a leather
couch as Shirley flung the portières together with a
sharp rattle of the rod rings.

She walked toward the hall door as her father and
mother entered from the veranda.

"Ah, Miss Claiborne! Your father and mother picked
me up and brought me in out of the rain. Your Storm
Valley is giving us a taste of its powers."

And Shirley went forward to greet Baron von Marhof.

CHAPTER XVII

Oh, sweetly fall the April days!
　My love was made of frost and light,
　Of light to warm and frost to blight
The sweet, strange April of her ways.
Eyes like a dream of changing skies,
And every frown and blush I prize.
　With cloud and flush the spring comes in,
　With frown and blush maids' loves begin;
For love is rare like April days.
—L. Frank Tooker.

Mrs. Claiborne excused herself shortly, and Shirley, her father and the Ambassador talked to the accompaniment of the shower that drove in great sheets against the house. Shirley was wholly uncomfortable over the turn of affairs. The Ambassador would not leave until the storm abated, and meanwhile Armitage must remain where he was. If by any chance he should be discovered in the house no ordinary excuses would explain away his presence, and as she pondered the matter, it was Armitage's plight—his injuries and the dangers that beset him—that was uppermost in her mind. The embarrassment that lay in the affair for herself if Armitage should be found concealed in the house troubled her little. Her heart beat wildly as she realized this; and the look in his eyes and the quick pain that twitched his face at the door haunted her.

The two men were talking of the new order of things in Vienna.

"The trouble is," said the Ambassador, "that Austria-Hungary is not a nation, but what Metternich called Italy—a geographical expression. Where there are so many loose ends a strong grasp is necessary to hold them together."

"And a weak hand," suggested Judge Claiborne, "might easily lose or scatter them."

"Precisely. And a man of character and spirit could topple down the card-house to-morrow, pick out what he liked, and create for himself a new edifice—and a stronger one. I speak frankly. Von Stroebel is out of the way; the new Emperor-king is a weakling, and if he should die to-night or to-morrow—"

The Ambassador lifted his hands and snapped his fingers.

"Yes; after him, what?"

"After him his scoundrelly cousin Francis; and then a stronger than Von Stroebel might easily fail to hold the *disjecta membra* of the Empire together."

"But there are shadows on the screen," remarked Judge Claiborne. "There was Karl—the mad prince."

"Humph! There was some red blood in him; but he was impossible; he had a taint of democracy, treason, rebellion."

Judge Claiborne laughed.

"I don't like the combination of terms. If treason and rebellion are synonyms of democracy, we Americans are in danger."

"No; you are a miracle—that is the only explanation," replied Marhof.

"But a man like Karl—what if he were to reappear in the world! A little democracy might solve your problem."

"No, thank God! he is out of the way. He was sane enough to take himself off and die."

"But his ghost walks. Not a year ago we heard of him; and he had a son who chose his father's exile. What if Charles Louis, who is without heirs, should die and Karl or his son—"

"In the providence of God they are dead. Impostors

gain a little brief notoriety by pretending to be the lost
Karl or his son Frederick Augustus; but Von Stroebel
satisfied himself that Karl was dead. I am quite sure of
it. You know dear Stroebel had a genius for gaining information."

"I have heard as much," and Shirley and the Baron
smiled at Judge Claiborne's tone.

The storm was diminishing and Shirley grew more
tranquil. Soon the Ambassador would leave and she
would send Armitage away; but the mention of Stroebel's name rang oddly in her ears, and the curious way
in which Armitage and Chauvenet had come into her
life awoke new and anxious questions.

"Count von Stroebel was not a democrat, at any rate,"
she said. "He believed in the divine right and all that."

"So do I, Miss Claiborne. It's all we've got to stand
on!"

"But suppose a democratic prince were to fall heir to
one of the European thrones, insist on giving his crown
to the poor and taking his oath in a frock coat, upsetting
the old order entirely—"

"He would be a fool, and the people would drag him
to the block in a week," declared the Baron vigorously.

They pursued the subject in lighter vein a few min-

utes longer, then the Baron rose. Judge Claiborne summoned the waiting carriage from the stable, and the
Baron drove home.

"I ought to work for an hour on that Danish claims
matter," remarked the Judge, glancing toward his cur-
tained den.

"You will do nothing of the kind! Night work is not
permitted in the valley."

"Thank you! I hoped you would say that, Shirley. I
believe I am tired; and now if you will find a magazine
for me, I'll go to bed. Ring for Thomas to close the
house."

"I have a few notes to write; they'll take only a minute, and I'll write them here."

She heard her father's door close, listened to be quite
sure that the house was quiet, and threw back the curtains. Armitage stepped out into the library.

"You must go—you must go!" she whispered with
deep tensity.

"Yes; I must go. You have been kind—you are most
generous—"

But she went before him to the hall, waited, listened,
for one instant; then threw open the outer door and
bade him go. The rain dripped heavily from the eaves,

and the cool breath of the freshened air was sweet and stimulating. She was immensely relieved to have him out of the house, but he lingered on the veranda, staring helplessly about.

"I shall go home," he said, but so unsteadily that she looked at him quickly. He carried the cloak flung over his shoulder and in readjusting it dropped it to the floor, and she saw in the light of the door lamps that his arm hung limp at his side and the gray cloth of his sleeve was heavy and dark with blood. With a quick gesture she stooped and picked up the cloak.

"Come! Come! This is all very dreadful—you must go to a physician at once."

"My man and horse are waiting for me; the injury is nothing." But she threw the cloak over his shoulders and led the way, across the veranda, and out upon the walk.

"I do not need the doctor—not now. My man will care for me."

He started through the dark toward the outer wall, as though confused, and she went before him toward the side entrance. He was aware of her quick light step, of the soft rustle of her skirts, of a wish to send her back, which his tongue could not voice; but he knew that it was sweet to follow her leading. At the gate he took his bearings with a new assurance and strength.

"It seems that I always appear to you in some miserable fashion—it is preposterous for me to ask forgiveness. To thank you—"

"Please say nothing at all—but go! Your enemies must not find you here again—you must leave the valley!"

"I have a work to do! But it must not touch your life. Your happiness is too much, too sweet to me."

"You must leave the bungalow—I found out to-day where you are staying. There is a new danger there—the mountain people think you are a revenue officer. I told one of them—"

"Yes?"

"—that you are not! That is enough. Now hurry away. You must find your horse and go."

He bent and kissed her hand.

"You trust me; that is the dearest thing in the world." His voice faltered and broke in a sob, for he was worn and weak, and the mystery of the night and the dark silent garden wove a spell upon him and his heart leaped at the touch of his lips upon her fingers. Their figures were only blurs in the dark, and their low tones died instantly, muffled by the night. She opened the gate as he began to promise not to appear before her again in any way to bring her trouble; but her low whisper arrested him.

"Do not let them hurt you again—" she said; and he felt her hand seek his, felt its cool furtive pressure for a moment; and then she was gone. He heard the house door close a moment later, and gazing across the garden, saw the lights on the veranda flash out.

Then with a smile on his face he strode away to find Oscar and the horses.

CHAPTER XVIII

AN EXCHANGE OF MESSAGES

When youth was lord of my unchallenged fate,
  And time seemed but the vassal of my will,
I entertainéd certain guests of state—
  The great of older days, who, faithful still,
Have kept with me the pact my youth had made.
                            —*S. Weir Mitchell.*

"Who am I?" asked John Armitage soberly.

He tossed the stick of a match into the fireplace, where a pine-knot smoldered, drew his pipe into a glow and watched Oscar screw the top on a box of ointment which he had applied to Armitage's arm. The little soldier turned and stood sharply at attention.

"You are Mr. John Armitage, sir. A man's name is what he says it is. It is the rule of the country."

"Thank you, Oscar. Your words reassure me. There have been times lately when I have been in doubt myself. You are a pretty good doctor."

"First aid to the injured; I learned the trick from a hospital steward. If you are not poisoned, and do not die, you will recover—yes?"

233

"Thank you, Sergeant. You are a consoling spirit; but I assure you on my honor as a gentleman that if I die I shall certainly haunt you. This is the fourth day. To-morrow I shall throw away the bandage and be quite ready for more trouble."

"It would be better on the fifth—"

"The matter is settled. You will now go for the mail; and do take care that no one pots you on the way. Your death would be a positive loss to me, Oscar. And if any one asks how My Majesty is—mark, My Majesty—pray say that I am quite well and equal to ruling over many kingdoms."

"Yes, sire."

And Armitage roared with laughter, as the little man, pausing as he buckled a cartridge belt under his coat, bowed with a fine mockery of reverence.

"If a man were king he could have a devilish fine time of it, Oscar."

"He could review many troops and they would fire salutes until the powder cost much money."

"You are mighty right, as we say in Montana; and I'll tell you quite confidentially, Sergeant, that if I were out of work and money and needed a job the thought of being king might tempt me. These gentlemen who are trying to stick knives into me think highly of my chances. They may force me into the business—" and Armitage rose and kicked the flaring knot.

Oscar drew on his gauntlet with a jerk.

"They killed the great prime minister—yes?"

"They undoubtedly did, Oscar."

"He was a good man—he was a very great man," said Oscar slowly, and went quickly out and closed the door softly after him.

The life of the two men in the bungalow was established in a definite routine. Oscar was drilled in habits of observation and attention and he realized without being told that some serious business was afoot; he knew that Armitage's life had been attempted, and that the receipt and despatch of telegrams was a part of whatever errand had brought his master to the Virginia hills. His occupations were wholly to his liking; there was simple food to eat; there were horses to tend; and his errands abroad were of the nature of scouting and in keeping with one's dignity who had been a soldier. He rose often at night to look abroad, and sometimes he found Armitage walking the veranda or returning from a tramp through the wood. Armitage spent much time studying papers; and once, the day after Armitage submitted his wounded arm to Oscar's care, he had seemed upon the verge of a confidence.

"To save life; to prevent disaster; to do a little good in the world—to do something for Austria—such things are to the soul's credit, Oscar," and then Armitage's mood changed and he had begun chaffing in a fashion that was beyond Oscar's comprehension.

The little soldier rode over the hills to Lamar Station in the waning spring twilight, asked at the telegraph office for messages, stuffed Armitage's mail into his pockets at the post-office, and turned home as the moonlight poured down the slopes and flooded the valleys. The Virginia roads have been cursed by larger armies than any that ever marched in Flanders, but Oscar was not a swearing man. He paused to rest his beast occasionally and to observe the landscape with the eye of a strategist. Moonlight, he remembered, was a useful accessory of the assassin's trade, and the faint sounds of the spring night were all promptly traced to their causes as they reached his alert ears.

At the gate of the hunting-park grounds he bent forward in the saddle to lift the chain that held it; urged his horse inside, bent down to refasten it, and as his fingers clutched the iron a man rose in the shadow of the little lodge and clasped him about the middle. The iron chain swung free and rattled against the post, and the horse snorted with fright, then, at a word from Oscar, was still. There was the barest second of waiting, in which the long arms tightened, and the great body of his assailant hung heavily about him; then he dug spurs into the horse's flanks and the animal leaped forward with a snort of rage, jumped out of the path and tore away through the woods.

Oscar's whole strength was taxed to hold his seat as the burly figure thumped against the horse's flanks. He had hoped to shake the man off, but the great arms still clasped him. The situation could not last. Oscar took advantage of the moonlight to choose a spot in which to terminate it. He had his bearings now, and as they crossed an opening in the wood he suddenly loosened his grip on the horse and flung himself backward. His assailant, no longer supported, rolled to the ground with Oscar on top of him, and the freed horse galloped away toward the stable.

A rough and tumble fight now followed. Oscar's lithe, vigorous body writhed in the grasp of his antagonist, now free, now clasped by giant arms. They saw each other's faces plainly in the clear moonlight, and at breathless pauses in the struggle their eyes maintained the state of war. At one instant, when both men lay with arms interlocked, half-lying on their thighs, Oscar hissed in the giant's ear:

"You are a Servian: it is an ugly race."

And the Servian cursed him in a fierce growl.

"We expected you; you are a bad hand with the knife," grunted Oscar, and feeling the bellows-like chest beside him expand, as though in preparation for a renewal of the fight, he suddenly wrenched himself free of the Servian's grasp, leaped away a dozen paces to the shelter of a great pine, and turned, revolver in hand.

"Throw up your hands," he yelled.

The Servian fired without pausing for aim, the shot ringing out sharply through the wood. Then Oscar discharged his revolver three times in quick succession, and while the discharges were still keen on the air he drew quickly back to a clump of underbrush, and crept away a dozen yards to watch events. The Servian, with his eyes fixed upon the tree behind which his adversary had sought shelter, grew anxious, and thrust his head forward warily.

Then he heard a sound as of some one running

through the wood to the left and behind him, but still
the man he had grappled on the horse made no sign. It
dawned upon him that the three shots fired in front of
him had been a signal, and in alarm he turned toward
the gate, but a voice near at hand called loudly, "Oscar!"
and repeated the name several times.

Behind the Servian the little soldier answered sharply
in English:

"All steady, sir!"

The use of a strange tongue added to the Servian's
bewilderment, and he fled toward the gate, with Oscar
hard after him. Then Armitage suddenly leaped out of
the shadows directly in his path and stopped him with a
leveled revolver.

"Easy work, Oscar! Take the gentleman's gun and be
sure to find his knife."

The task was to Oscar's taste, and he made quick
work of the Servian's pockets.

"Your horse was a good despatch bearer. You are all
sound, Oscar?"

"Never better, sir. A revolver and two knives—" the
weapons flashed in the moonlight as he held them up.

"Good! Now start your friend toward the bungalow."

They set off at a quick pace, soon found the rough

driveway, and trudged along silently, the Servian between his captors.

When they reached the house Armitage flung open the
door and followed Oscar and the prisoner into the long
sitting-room.

Armitage lighted a pipe at the mantel, readjusted the
bandage on his arm, and laughed aloud as he looked
upon the huge figure of the Servian standing beside the
sober little cavalryman.

"Oscar, there are certainly giants in these days, and
we have caught one. You will please see that the cylin-
der of your revolver is in good order and prepare to act
as clerk of our court-martial. If the prisoner moves,
shoot him."

He spoke these last words very deliberately in German,
and the Servian's small eyes blinked his comprehension.
Armitage sat down on the writing-table, with his own
revolver and the prisoner's knives and pistol within
reach of his available hand. A smile of amusement
played over his face as he scrutinized the big body and
its small, bullet-like head.

"He is a large devil," commented Oscar.

"He is large, certainly," remarked Armitage. "Give
him a chair. Now," he said to the man in deliberate

German, "I shall say a few things to you which I
am very anxious for you to understand. You are a
Servian."

The man nodded.

"Your name is Zmai Miletich."

The man shifted his great bulk uneasily in his chair
and fastened his lusterless little eyes upon Armitage.

"Your name," repeated Armitage, "is Zmai Miletich;
your home is, or was, in the village of Toplica, where
you were a blacksmith until you became a thief. You
are employed as an assassin by two gentlemen known as
Chauvenet and Durand—do you follow me?"

The man was indeed following him with deep engross-
ment. His narrow forehead was drawn into minute
wrinkles; his small eyes seemed to recede into his head;
his great body turned uneasily.

"I ask you again," repeated Armitage, "whether you
follow me. There must be no mistake."

Oscar, anxious to take his own part in the conversation, prodded Zmai in the ribs with a pistol barrel, and
the big fellow growled and nodded his head.

"There is a house in the outskirts of Vienna where
you have been employed at times as gardener, and another house in Geneva where you wait for orders. At this

latter place it was my great pleasure to smash you in the head with a boiling-pot on a certain evening in March."

The man scowled and ejaculated an oath with so much venom that Armitage laughed.

"Your conspirators are engaged upon a succession of murders, and when they have removed the last obstacle they will establish a new Emperor-king in Vienna and you will receive a substantial reward for what you have done—"

The blood suffused the man's dark face, and he half rose, a great roar of angry denial breaking from him.

"That will do. You tried to kill me on the *King Edward;* you tried your knife on me again down there in Judge Claiborne's garden; and you came up here to-night with a plan to kill my man and then take your time to me. Give me the mail, Oscar."

He opened the letters which Oscar had brought and scanned several that bore a Paris postmark, and when he had pondered their contents a moment he laughed and jumped from the table. He brought a portfolio from his bedroom and sat down to write.

"Don't shoot the gentleman as long as he is quiet. You may even give him a glass of whisky to soothe his feelings."

Armitage wrote:

"MONSIEUR:

"Your assassin is a clumsy fellow and you will do well to send him back to the blacksmith shop at Toplica. I learn that Monsieur Durand, distressed by the delay in affairs in America, will soon join you—is even now aboard the *Tacoma,* bound for New York. I am profoundly grateful for this, dear Monsieur, as it gives me an opportunity to conclude our interesting business in republican territory without prejudice to any of the parties chiefly concerned.

"You are a clever and daring rogue, yet at times you strike me as immensely dull, Monsieur. Ponder this: should it seem expedient for me to establish my identity —which I am sure interests you greatly—before Baron von Marhof, and, we will add, the American Secretary of State, be quite sure that I shall not do so until I have taken precautions against your departure in any unseemly haste. I, myself, dear friend, am not without a certain facility in setting traps."

Armitage threw down the pen and read what he had written with care. Then he wrote as signature the initials F. A., inclosed the note in an envelope and addressed it, pondered again, laughed and slapped his knee and went into his room, where he rummaged about

until he found a small seal beautifully wrought in bronze
and a bit of wax. Returning to the table he lighted a
candle, and deftly sealed the letter. He held the red
scar on the back of the envelope to the lamp and examined it with interest. The lines of the seal were deep
cut, and the impression was perfectly distinct, of F. A.
in English script, linked together by the bar of the F.

"Oscar, what do you recommend that we do with the
prisoner?"

"He should be tied to a tree and shot; or, perhaps, it
would be better to hang him to the rafters in the kitchen.
Yet he is heavy and might pull down the roof."

"You are a bloodthirsty wretch, and there is no mercy
in you. Private executions are not allowed in this country; you would have us before a Virginia grand jury and
our own necks stretched. No; we shall send him back to
his master."

"It is a mistake. If your Excellency would go away
for an hour he should never know where the buzzards
found this large carcass."

"Tush! I would not trust his valuable life to you.
Get up!" he commanded, and Oscar jerked Zmai to his
feet.

"You deserve nothing at my hands, but I need a discreet messenger, and you shall not die to-night, as my worthy adjutant recommends. To-morrow night, however, or the following night—or any other old night, as we say in America—if you show yourself in these hills, my chief of staff shall have his way with you—buzzard meat!"

"The orders are understood," said Oscar, thrusting the revolver into the giant's ribs.

"Now, Zmai, blacksmith of Toplica, and assassin at large, here is a letter for Monsieur Chauvenet. It is still early. When you have delivered it, bring me back the envelope with Monsieur's receipt written right here, under the seal. Do you understand?"

It had begun to dawn upon Zmai that his life was not in immediate danger, and the light of intelligence kindled again in his strange little eyes. Lest he might not fully grasp the errand with which Armitage intrusted him, Oscar repeated what Armitage had said in somewhat coarser terms.

Again through the moonlight strode the three—out of Armitage's land to the valley road and to the same point to which Shirley Claiborne had only a few days before been escorted by the mountaineer.

There they sent the Servian forward to the Springs,

and Armitage went home, leaving Oscar to wait for the return of the receipt.

It was after midnight when Oscar placed it in Armitage's hands at the bungalow.

"Oscar, it would be a dreadful thing to kill a man," Armitage declared, holding the empty envelope to the light and reading the line scrawled beneath the unbroken wax. It was in French:

"You are young to die, Monsieur."

"A man more or less!" and Oscar shrugged his shoulders.

"You are not a good churchman. It is a grievous sin to do murder."

"One may repent; it is so written. The people of your house are Catholics also."

"That is quite true, though I may seem to forget it. Our work will be done soon, please God, and we shall ask the blessed sacrament somewhere in these hills."

Oscar crossed himself and fell to cleaning his rifle.

CHAPTER XIX

When he came where the trees were thin,
The moon sat waiting there to see;
On her worn palm she laid her chin,
And laughed awhile in sober glee
To think how strong this knight had been.
            —*William Vaughn Moody.*

In some mystification Captain Richard Claiborne
packed a suit-case in his quarters at Fort Myer. Being a
soldier, he obeyed orders; but being human, he was also
possessed of a degree of curiosity. He did not know just
the series of incidents and conferences that preceded his
summons to Washington, but they may be summarized
thus:

Baron von Marhof was a cautious man. When the
young gentlemen of his legation spoke to him in awed
whispers of a cigarette case bearing an extraordinary
device that had been seen in Washington he laughed
them away; then, possessing a curious and thorough
mind, he read all the press clippings relating to the

247

false Baron von Kissel, and studied the heraldic em-
blems of the Schomburgs. As he pondered, he regretted
the death of his eminent brother-in-law, Count Ferdinand von Stroebel, who was not a man to stumble over
so negligible a trifle as a cigarette case. But Von Marhof himself was not without resources. He told the gentlemen of his suite that he had satisfied himself that
there was nothing in the Armitage mystery; then he
cabled Vienna discreetly for a few days, and finally consulted Hilton Claiborne, the embassy's counsel, at the
Claiborne home at Storm Springs.

They had both gone hurriedly to Washington, where
they held a long conference with the Secretary of State.
Then the state department called the war department by
telephone, and quickly down the line to the commanding
officer at Fort Myer went a special assignment for Captain Claiborne to report to the Secretary of State. A
great deal of perfectly sound red tape was reduced to
minute particles in these manipulations; but Baron von
Marhof's business was urgent; it was also of a private
and wholly confidential character. Therefore, he returned to his cottage at Storm Springs, and the Washington papers stated that he was ill and had gone back
to Virginia to take the waters.

The Claiborne house was the pleasantest place in Storm Valley, and the library a comfortable place for a conference. Dick Claiborne caught the gravity of the older men as they unfolded to him the task for which they had asked his services. The Baron stated the case in these words:

"You know and have talked with this man Armitage; you saw the device on the cigarette case; and asked an explanation, which he refused; and you know also Chauvenet, whom we suspect of complicity with the conspirators at home. Armitage is not the false Baron von Kissel—we have established that from Senator Sanderson beyond question. But Sanderson's knowledge of the man is of comparatively recent date—going back about five years to the time Armitage purchased his Montana ranch. Whoever Armitage may be, he pays his bills; he conducts himself like a gentleman; he travels at will, and people who meet him say a good word for him."

"He is an agreeable man and remarkably well posted in European politics," said Judge Claiborne. "I talked with him a number of times on the *King Edward* and must say that I liked him."

"Chauvenet evidently knows him; there was undoubtedly something back of that little trick at my supper party at the Army and Navy," said Dick.

"It might be explained—" began the Baron; then he paused and looked from father to son. "Pardon me, but they both manifest some interest in Miss Claiborne."

"We met them abroad," said Dick; "and they both turned up again in Washington."

"One of them is here, or has been here in the valley —why not the other?" asked Judge Claiborne.

"But, of course, Shirley knows nothing of Armitage's whereabouts," Dick protested.

"Certainly not," declared his father.

"How did you make Armitage's acquaintance?" asked the Ambassador. "Some one must have been responsible for introducing him—if you can remember."

Dick laughed.

"It was in the Monte Rosa, at Geneva. Shirley and I had been chaffing each other about the persistence with which Armitage seemed to follow us. He was taking *déjeûner* at the same hour, and he passed us going out. Old Arthur Singleton—the ubiquitous—was talking to us, and he nailed Armitage with his customary zeal and introduced him to us in quite the usual American fashion. Later I asked Singleton who he was and he knew nothing about him. Then Armitage turned up on the steamer, where he made himself most agreeable. Next, Senator Sanderson vouched for him as one of his Montana constituents. You know the rest of the story. I swallowed him whole; he called at our house on several occasions, and came to the post, and I asked him to my supper for the Spanish attaché."

"And now, Dick, we want you to find him and get him into a room with ourselves, where we can ask him some questions," declared Judge Claiborne.

They discussed the matter in detail. It was agreed that Dick should remain at the Springs for a few days to watch Chauvenet; then, if he got no clue to Armitage's whereabouts, he was to go to Montana, to see if anything could be learned there.

"We must find him—there must be no mistake about it," said the Ambassador to Judge Claiborne, when they were alone. "They are almost panic-stricken in Vienna. What with the match burning close to the powder in Hungary and clever heads plotting in Vienna this American end of the game has dangerous possibilities."

"And when we have young Armitage—" the Judge began.

"Then we shall know the truth."

"But suppose—suppose," and Judge Claiborne glanced at the door, "suppose Charles Louis, Emperor-king of Austria-Hungary, should die—to-night—to-morrow—"

"We will assume nothing of the kind!" ejaculated the Ambassador sharply. "It is impossible." Then to Captain Claiborne: "You must pardon me if I do not explain further. I wish to find Armitage; it is of the greatest importance. It would not aid you if I told you why I must see and talk with him."

And as though to escape from the thing of which his counsel had hinted, Baron von Marhof took his departure at once.

Shirley met her brother on the veranda. His arrival had been unheralded and she was frankly astonished to see him.

"Well, Captain Claiborne, you are a man of mystery. You will undoubtedly be court-martialed for deserting —and after a long leave, too."

"I am on duty. Don't forget that you are the daughter of a diplomat."

"Humph! It doesn't follow, necessarily, that I should be stupid!"

"You couldn't be that, Shirley, dear."

"Thank you, Captain."

They discussed family matters for a few minutes; then she said, with elaborate irrelevance:

"Well, we must hope that your appearance will cause no battles to be fought in our garden. There was enough fighting about here in old times."

"Take heart, little sister, I shall protect you. Oh, it's rather decent of Armitage to have kept away from you, Shirley, after all that fuss about the bogus baron."

"Which he wasn't—"

"Well, Sanderson says he couldn't have been, and the rogues' gallery pictures don't resemble our friend at all."

"Ugh; don't speak of it!" and Shirley shrugged her shoulders. She suffered her eyes to climb the slopes of the far hills. Then she looked steadily at her brother and laughed.

"What do you and father and Baron von Marhof want with Mr. John Armitage?" she asked.

"Guess again!" exclaimed Dick hurriedly. "Has that been the undercurrent of your conversation? As I may have said before in this connection, you disappoint me, Shirley. You seem unable to forget that fellow."

He paused, grew very serious, and bent forward in his wicker chair.

"Have you seen John Armitage since I saw him?"

"Impertinent! How dare you?"

"But Shirley, the question is fair!"

"Is it, Richard?"

"And I want you to answer me."

"That's different."

He rose and took several steps toward her. She stood against the railing with her hands behind her back.

"Shirley, you are the finest girl in the world, but you wouldn't do *this*—"

"This what, Dick?"

"You know what I mean. I ask you again—have you or have you not seen Armitage since you came to the Springs?"

He spoke impatiently, his eyes upon hers. A wave of color swept her face, and then her anger passed and she was her usual good-natured self.

"Baron von Marhof is a charming old gentleman, isn't he?"

"He's a regular old brick," declared Dick solemnly.

"It's a great privilege for a young man like you to know him, Dick, and to have private talks with him and the governor—about subjects of deep importance. The governor is a good deal of a man himself."

"I am proud to be his son," declared Dick, meeting Shirley's eyes unflinchingly.

Shirley was silent for a moment, while Dick whistled a few bars from the latest waltz.

"A captain—a mere captain of the line—is not often plucked out of his post when in good health and standing—after a long leave for foreign travel—and sent away to visit his parents—and help entertain a distinguished Ambassador."

"Thanks for the 'mere captain,' dearest. You needn't rub it in."

"I wouldn't. But you are fair game—for your sister only! And you're better known than you were before that little supper for the Spanish attaché. It rather directed attention to you, didn't it, Dick?"

Dick colored.

"It certainly did."

"And if you should meet Monsieur Chauvenet, who caused the trouble—"

"I have every intention of meeting him!"

"Oh!"

"Of course, I shall meet him—some time, somewhere. He's at the Springs, isn't he?"

"Am I a hotel register that I should know? I haven't seen him for several days."

"What I should like to see," said Dick, "is a meeting between Armitage and Chauvenet. That would really be entertaining. No doubt Chauvenet could whip your mysterious suitor."

He looked away, with an air of unconcern, at the deepening shadows on the mountains.

"Dear Dick, I am quite sure that if you have been chosen out of all the United States army to find Mr. John Armitage, you will succeed without any help from me."

"That doesn't answer my question. You don't know what you are doing. What if father knew that you were seeing this adventurer—"

"Oh, of course, if you should tell father! I haven't said that I had seen Mr. Armitage; and you haven't exactly told me that you have a warrant for his arrest; so we are quits, Captain. You had better look in at the hotel dance to-night. There are girls there and to spare."

"When I find Mr. Armitage—"

"You seem hopeful, Captain. He may be on the high seas."

"I shall find him there—or here!"

"Good luck to you, Captain!"

There was the least flash of antagonism in the glance that passed between them, and Captain Claiborne clapped his hands together impatiently and went into the house.

CHAPTER XX

THE FIRST RIDE TOGETHER

My mistress bent that brow of hers;
Those deep dark eyes where pride demurs
When pity would be softening through,
Fixed me a breathing-while or two
　　With life or death in the balance: right!
The blood replenished me again;
My last thought was at least not vain:
I and my mistress, side by side
Shall be together, breathe and ride,
So, one day more am I deified.
　　Who knows but the world may end to-night?
　　　　　　　　　　—R. Browning.

"We shall be leaving soon," said Armitage, half to himself and partly to Oscar. "It is not safe to wait much longer."

He tossed a copy of the *Neue Freie Presse* on the table. Oscar had been down to the Springs to explore, and brought back news, gained from the stablemen at the hotel, that Chauvenet had left the hotel, presumably for Washington. It was now Wednesday in the third week in April.

258

"Oscar, you were a clever boy and knew more than you were told. You have asked me no questions. There may be an ugly row before I get out of these hills. I should not think hard of you if you preferred to leave."

"I enlisted for the campaign—yes?—I shall wait until I am discharged." And the little man buttoned his coat.

"Thank you, Oscar. In a few days more we shall probably be through with this business. There's another man coming to get into the game—he reached Washington yesterday, and we shall doubtless hear of him shortly. Very likely they are both in the hills to-night. And, Oscar, listen carefully to what I say."

The soldier drew nearer to Armitage, who sat swinging his legs on the table in the bungalow.

"If I should die unshriven during the next week, here's a key that opens a safety-vault box at the Bronx Loan and Trust Company, in New York. In case I am disabled, go at once with the key to Baron von Marhof, Ambassador of Austria-Hungary, and tell him—tell him—"

He had paused for a moment as though pondering his words with care; then he laughed and went on.

"—tell him, Oscar, that there's a message in that safety box from a gentleman who might have been King."

Oscar stared at Armitage blankly.

"That is the truth, Sergeant. The message once in the good Baron's hands will undoubtedly give him a severe shock. You will do well to go to bed. I shall take a walk before I turn in."

"You should not go out alone—"

"Don't trouble about me; I shan't go far. I think we are safe until two gentlemen have met in Washington, discussed their affairs, and come down into the mountains again. The large brute we caught the other night is undoubtedly on watch near by; but he is harmless. Only a few days more and we shall perform a real service in the world, Sergeant,—I feel it in my bones."

He took his hat from a bench by the door and went out upon the veranda. The moon had already slipped down behind the mountains, but the stars trooped brightly across the heavens. He drank deep breaths of the cool air of the mountain night, and felt the dark wooing him with its calm and peace. He returned for his cloak and walked into the wood. He followed the road to the gate, and then turned toward the Port of

Missing Men. He had formed quite definite plans of what he should do in certain emergencies, and he felt a new strength in his confidence that he should succeed in the business that had brought him into the hills.

At the abandoned bridge he threw himself down and gazed off through a narrow cut that afforded a glimpse of the Springs, where the electric lights gleamed as one lamp. Shirley Claiborne was there in the valley and he smiled with the thought of her; for soon—perhaps in a few hours—he would be free to go to her, his work done; and no mystery or dangerous task would henceforth lie between them.

He saw march before him across the night great hosts of armed men, singing hymns of war; and again he looked upon cities besieged; still again upon armies in long alignment waiting for the word that would bring the final shock of battle. The faint roar of water far below added an under-note of reality to his dream; and still he saw, as upon a tapestry held in his hand, the struggles of kingdoms, the rise and fall of empires. Upon the wide seas smoke floated from the guns of giant ships that strove mightily in battle. He was thrilled by drum-beats and the cry of trumpets. Then his mood changed and the mountains and calm stars spoke an heroic language that was of newer and nobler things; and he shook his head impatiently and gathered his cloak about him and rose.

"God said, 'I am tired of kings,'" he muttered. "But I shall keep my pledge; I shall do Austria a service," he said; and then laughed a little to himself. "To think that it may be for me to say!" And with this he walked quite to the brink of the chasm and laid his hand upon the iron cable from which swung the bridge.

"I shall soon be free," he said with a deep sigh; and looked across the starlighted hills.

Then the cable under his hand vibrated slightly; at first he thought it the night wind stealing through the vale and swaying the bridge above the sheer depth. But still he felt the tingle of the iron rope in his clasp, and his hold tightened and he bent forward to listen. The whole bridge now audibly shook with the pulsation of a step—a soft, furtive step, as of one cautiously groping a way over the unsubstantial flooring. Then through the starlight he distinguished a woman's figure, and drew back. A loose plank in the bridge floor rattled, and as she passed it freed itself and he heard it strike the rocks faintly far below; but the figure stole swiftly on, and he bent forward with a cry of warning on his lips, and snatched away the light barricade that had been nailed across the opening.

When he looked up, his words of rebuke, that had waited only for the woman's security, died on his lips.

"Shirley!" he cried; and put forth both hands and lifted her to firm ground.

A little sigh of relief broke from her. The bridge still swayed from her weight; and the cables hummed like the wires of a harp; near at hand the waterfall tumbled down through the mystical starlight.

"I did not know that dreams really came true," he said, with an awe in his voice that the passing fear had left behind.

She began abruptly, not heeding his words.

"You must go away—at once—I came to tell you that you can not stay here."

"But it is unfair to accept any warning from you! You are too generous, too kind,"—he began.

"It is not generosity or kindness, but this danger that follows you—it is an evil thing and it must not find you here. It is impossible that such a thing can be in America. But you must go—you must seek the law's aid—"

"How do you know I dare—"

"I don't know—that you dare!"

"I know that you have a great heart and that I love you," he said.

She turned quickly toward the bridge as though to retrace her steps.

"I can't be paid for a slight, a very slight service by fair words, Mr. Armitage. If you knew why I came—"

"If I dared think or believe or hope—"

"You will dare nothing of the kind, Mr. Armitage!" she replied; "but I will tell you, that I came out of ordinary Christian humanity. The idea of friends, of even slight acquaintances, being assassinated in these Virginia hills does not please me."

"How do you classify me, please—with friends or acquaintances?"

He laughed; then the gravity of what she was doing changed his tone.

"I am John Armitage. That is all you know, and yet you hazard your life to warn me that I am in danger?"

"If you called yourself John Smith I should do exactly the same thing. It makes not the slightest difference to me who or what you are."

"You are explicit!" he laughed. "I don't hesitate to tell you that I value your life much higher than you do."

"That is quite unnecessary. It may amuse you to know that, as I am a person of little curiosity, I am not the least concerned in the solution of—of—what might be called the Armitage riddle."

"Oh; I'm a riddle, am I?"

"Not to me, I assure you! You are only the object of some one's enmity, and there's something about murder that is—that isn't exactly nice! It's positively unesthetic."

She had begun seriously, but laughed at the absurdity of her last words.

"You are amazingly impersonal. You would save a man's life without caring in the least what manner of man he may be."

"You put it rather flatly, but that's about the truth of the matter. Do you know, I am almost afraid—"

"Not of me, I hope—"

"Certainly not. But it has occurred to me that you may have the conceit of your own mystery, that you may take rather too much pleasure in mystifying people as to your identity."

"That is unkind,—that is unkind," and he spoke without resentment, but softly, with a falling cadence.

He suddenly threw down the hat he had held in his hand, and extended his arms toward her.

"You are not unkind or unjust. You have a right to know who I am and what I am doing here. It seems an impertinence to thrust my affairs upon you; but if you will listen I should like to tell you—it will take but a moment—why and what—"

"Please do not! As I told you, I have no curiosity in the matter. I can't allow you to tell me; I really don't want to know!"

"I am willing that every one should know—to-morrow—or the day after—not later."

She lifted her head, as though with the earnestness of some new thought.

"The day after may be too late. Whatever it is that you have done—"

"I have done nothing to be ashamed of,—I swear I have not!"

"Whatever it is,—and I don't care what it is,"—she said deliberately, "—it is something quite serious, Mr. Armitage. My brother—"

She hesitated for a moment, then spoke rapidly.

"My brother has been detailed to help in the search for you. He is at Storm Springs now."

"But *he* doesn't understand—"

"My brother is a soldier and it is not necessary for him to understand."

"And you have done this—you have come to warn me—"

"It does look pretty bad," she said, changing her tone and laughing a little. "But my brother and I—we always had very different ideas about you, Mr. Armitage. We hold briefs for different sides of the case."

"Oh, I'm a case, am I?" and he caught gladly at the suggestion of lightness in her tone. "But I'd really like to know what he has to do with my affairs."

"Then you will have to ask him."

"To be sure. But the government can hardly have assigned Captain Claiborne to special duty at Monsieur Chauvenet's request. I swear to you that I'm as much in the dark as you are."

"I'm quite sure an officer of the line would not be taken from his duties and sent into the country on any frivolous errand. But perhaps an Ambassador from a great power made the request,—perhaps, for example, it was Baron von Marhof."

"Good Lord!"

Armitage laughed aloud.

"I beg your pardon! I really beg your pardon! But is the Ambassador looking for me?"

"I don't know, Mr. Armitage. You forget that I'm only a traitor and not a spy."

"You are the noblest woman in the world," he said boldly, and his heart leaped in him and he spoke on with a fierce haste. "You have made sacrifices for me that no woman ever made before for a man—for a man she did not know! And my life—whatever it is worth, every hour and second of it, I lay down before you, and it is yours to keep or throw away. I followed you half-way round the world and I shall follow you again and as long as I live. And to-morrow—or the day after —I shall justify these great kindnesses—this generous confidence; but to-night I have a work to do!"

As they stood on the verge of the defile, by the bridge that swung out from the cliff like a fairy structure, they heard far and faint the whistle and low rumble of the night train south-bound from Washington; and to both of them the sound urged the very real and practical world from which for a little time they had stolen away.

"I must go back," said Shirley, and turned to the bridge and put her hand on its slight iron frame; but he seized her wrists and held them tight.

"You have risked much for me, but you shall not risk your life again in my cause. You can not venture across that bridge again."

She yielded without further parley and he dropped her wrists at once.

"Please say no more. You must not make me sorry I came. I must go,—I should have gone back instantly."

"But not across that spider's web. You must go by the long road. I will give you a horse and ride with you into the valley."

"It is much nearer by the bridge,—and I have my horse over there."

"We shall get the horse without trouble," he said, and she walked beside him through the starlighted wood. As they crossed the open tract she said:

"This is the Port of Missing Men."

"Yes, here the lost legion made its last stand. There lie the graves of some of them. It's a pretty story; I hope some day to know more of it from some such authority as yourself."

"I used to ride here on my pony when I was a little girl, and dream about the gray soldiers who would not surrender. It was as beautiful as an old ballad. I'll wait here. Fetch the horse," she said, "and hurry, please."

"If there are explanations to make," he began, looking at her gravely.

"I am not a person who makes explanations, Mr. Armitage. You may meet me at the gate."

As he ran toward the house he met Oscar, who had become alarmed at his absence and was setting forth in search of him.

"Come; saddle both the horses, Oscar," Armitage commanded.

They went together to the barn and quickly brought out the horses.

"You are not to come with me, Oscar."

"A captain does not go alone; it should be the sergeant who is sent—yes?"

"It is not an affair of war, Oscar, but quite another matter. There is a saddled horse hitched to the other side of our abandoned bridge. Get it and ride it to Judge Claiborne's stables; and ask and answer no questions."

A moment later he was riding toward the gate, the led-horse following.

He flung himself down, adjusting the stirrups and

gave her a hand into the saddle. They turned silently into the mountain road.

"The bridge would have been simpler and quicker," said Shirley; "as it is, I shall be late to the ball."

"I am contrite enough; but you don't make explanations."

"No; I don't explain; and you are to come back as soon as we strike the valley. I always send gentlemen back at that point," she laughed, and went ahead of him into the narrow road. She guided the strange horse with the ease of long practice, skilfully testing his paces, and when they came to a stretch of smooth road sent him flying at a gallop over the trail. He had given her his own horse, a hunter of famous strain, and she at once defined and maintained a distance between them that made talk impossible.

Her short covert riding-coat, buttoned close, marked clearly in the starlight her erect figure; light wisps of loosened hair broke free under her soft felt hat, and when she turned her head the wind caught the brim and pressed it back from her face, giving a new charm to her profile.

He called after her once or twice at the start, but she did not pause or reply; and he could not know what

mood possessed her; or that once in flight, in the security the horse gave her, she was for the first time afraid
of him. He had declared his love for her, and had offered to break down the veil of mystery that made him
a strange and perplexing figure. His affairs, whatever
their nature, were now at a crisis, he had said; quite
possibly she should never see him again after this ride.
As she waited at the gate she had known a moment of
contrition and doubt as to what she had done. It was not
fair to her brother thus to give away his secret to the
enemy; but as the horse flew down the rough road her
blood leaped with the sense of adventure, and her pulse
sang with the joy of flight. Her thoughts were free, wild
things; and she exulted in the great starry vault and the
cool heights over which she rode. Who was John Armitage? She did not know or care, now that she had performed for him her last service. Quite likely he would
fade away on the morrow like a mountain shadow before
the sun; and the song in her heart to-night was not love
or anything akin to it, but only the joy of living.

Where the road grew difficult as it dipped sharply
down into the valley she suffered him perforce to ride
beside her.

"You ride wonderfully," he said.

"The horse is a joy. He's a Pendragon—I know
them in the dark. He must have come from this valley
somewhere. We own some of his cousins, I'm sure."

"You are quite right. He's a Virginia horse. You
are incomparable—no other woman alive could have
kept that pace. It's a brave woman who isn't a slave
to her hair-pins—I don't believe you spilled one."

She drew rein at the cross-roads.

"We part here. How shall I return Bucephalus?"

"Let me go to your own gate, please!"

"Not at all!" she said with decision.

"Then Oscar will pick him up. If you don't see him,
turn the horse loose. But my thanks—for oh, so many
things!" he pleaded.

"To-morrow—or the day after—or never!"

She laughed and put out her hand; and when he tried
to detain her she spoke to the horse and flashed away
toward home. He listened, marking her flight until the
shadows of the valley stole sound and sight from him;
then he turned back into the hills.

Near her father's estate Shirley came upon a man who
saluted in the manner of a soldier.

It was Oscar, who had crossed the bridge and ridden
down by the nearer road.

"It is my captain's horse—yes?" he said, as the slim, graceful animal whinnied and pawed the ground. "I found a horse at the broken bridge and took it to your stable—yes?"

A moment later Shirley walked rapidly through the garden to the veranda of her father's house, where her brother Dick paced back and forth impatiently.

"Where have you been, Shirley?"

"Walking."

"But you went for a ride—the stable-men told me."

"I believe that is true, Captain."

"And your horse was brought home half an hour ago by a strange fellow who saluted like a soldier when I spoke to him, but refused to understand my English."

"Well, they do say English isn't very well taught at West Point, Captain," she replied, pulling off her gloves. "You oughtn't to blame the polite stranger for his courtesy."

"I believe you have been up to some mischief, Shirley. If you are seeing that man Armitage—"

"Captain!"

"Bah! What are you going to do now?"

"I'm going to the ball with you as soon as I can

change my gown. I suppose father and mother have gone."

"They have—for which you should be grateful!"

Captain Claiborne lighted a cigar and waited.

CHAPTER XXI

THE COMEDY OF A SHEEPFOLD

A glance, a word—and joy or pain
  Befalls; what was no more shall be.
How slight the links are in the chain
  That binds us to our destiny!
                              —*T. B. Aldrich.*

Oscar's eye, roaming the landscape as he left Shirley
Claiborne and started for the bungalow, swept the upland Claiborne acres and rested upon a moving shadow.
He drew rein under a clump of wild cherry-trees at the
roadside and waited. Several hundred yards away lay
the Claiborne sheepfold, with a broad pasture rising beyond. A shadow is not a thing to be ignored by a man
trained in the niceties of scouting. Oscar, satisfying
himself that substance lay behind the shadow, dismounted and tied his horse. Then he bent low over the stone
wall and watched.

"It is the big fellow—yes? He is a stealer of sheep,
as I might have known."

Zmai was only a dim figure against the dark meadow, which he was slowly crossing from the side farthest from the Claiborne house. He stopped several times as though uncertain of his whereabouts, and then clambered over a stone wall that formed one side of the sheepfold, passed it and strode on toward Oscar and the road.

"It is mischief that brings him from the hills— yes?" Oscar reflected, glancing up and down the highway. Faintly—very softly through the night he heard the orchestra at the hotel, playing for the dance. The little soldier unbuttoned his coat, drew the revolver from his belt, and thrust it into his coat pocket. Zmai was drawing nearer, advancing rapidly, now that he had gained his bearings. At the wall Oscar rose suddenly and greeted him in mockingly-courteous tones:

"Good evening, my friend; it's a fine evening for a walk."

Zmai drew back and growled.

"Let me pass," he said in his difficult German.

"It is a long wall; there should be no difficulty in passing. This country is much freer than Servia— yes?" and Oscar's tone was pleasantly conversational.

Zmai put his hand on the wall and prepared to vault.

"A moment only, comrade. You seem to be in a hurry; it must be a business that brings you from the mountains—yes?"

"I have no time for you," snarled the Servian. "Be gone!" and he shook himself impatiently and again put his hand on the wall.

"One should not be in too much haste, comrade;" and Oscar thrust Zmai back with his finger-tips.

The man yielded and ran a few steps out of the clump of trees and sought to escape there. It was clear to Oscar that Zmai was not anxious to penetrate closer to the Claiborne house, whose garden extended quite near. He met Zmai promptly and again thrust him back.

"It is a message—yes?" asked Oscar.

"It is my affair," blurted the big fellow. "I mean no harm to you."

"It was you that tried the knife on my body. It is much quieter than shooting. You have the knife—yes?"

The little soldier whipped out his revolver.

"In which pocket is the business carried? A letter undoubtedly. They do not trust swine to carry words—Ah!"

Oscar dropped below the wall as Zmai struck at him;

when he looked up a moment later the Servian was running back over the meadow toward the sheepfold. Oscar, angry at the ease with which the Servian had evaded him, leaped the wall and set off after the big fellow. He was quite sure that the man bore a written message, and equally sure that it must be of importance to his employer. He clutched his revolver tight, brought up his elbows for greater ease in running, and sped after Zmai, now a blur on the starlighted sheep pasture.

The slope was gradual and a pretty feature of the landscape by day; but it afforded a toilsome path for runners. Zmai already realized that he had blundered in not forcing the wall; he was running uphill, with a group of sheds, another wall, and a still steeper and rougher field beyond. His bulk told against him; and behind him he heard the quick thump of Oscar's feet on the turf. The starlight grew dimmer through tracts of white scud; the surface of the pasture was rougher to the feet than it appeared to the eye. A hound in the Claiborne stable-yard bayed suddenly and the sound echoed from the surrounding houses and drifted off toward the sheepfold. Then a noble music rose from the kennels.

Captain Claiborne, waiting for his sister on the veranda, looked toward the stables, listening.

Zmai approached the sheep-sheds rapidly, with still a hundred yards to traverse beyond them before he should reach the pasture wall. His rage at thus being driven by a small man for whom he had great contempt did not help his wind or stimulate the flight of his heavy legs, and he saw now that he would lessen the narrowing margin between himself and his pursuer if he swerved to the right to clear the sheds. He suddenly slackened his pace, and with a vicious tug settled his wool hat more firmly upon his small skull. He went now at a dog trot and Oscar was closing upon him rapidly; then, quite near the sheds, Zmai wheeled about and charged his pursuer headlong. At the moment he turned, Oscar's revolver bit keenly into the night. Captain Claiborne, looking toward the slope, saw the flash before the hounds at the stables answered the report.

At the shot Zmai cried aloud in his curiously small voice and clapped his hands to his head.

"Stop; I want the letter!" shouted Oscar in German. The man turned slowly, as though dazed, and, with a hand still clutching his head, half-stumbled and half-ran toward the sheds, with Oscar at his heels.

Claiborne called to the negro stable-men to quiet the dogs, snatched a lantern, and ran away through the pergola to the end of the garden and thence into the . pasture beyond. Meanwhile Oscar, thinking Zmai badly hurt, did not fire again, but flung himself upon the fellow's broad shoulders and down they crashed against the door of the nearest pen. Zmai swerved and shook himself free while he fiercely cursed his foe. Oscar's hands slipped on the fellow's hot blood that ran from a long crease in the side of his head.

As they fell the pen door snapped free, and out into the starry pasture thronged the frightened sheep.

"The letter—give me the letter!" commanded Oscar, his face close to the Servian's. He did not know how badly the man was injured, but he was anxious to complete his business and be off. Still the sheep came huddling through the broken door, across the prostrate men, and scampered away into the open. Captain Claiborne, running toward the fold with his lantern and not looking for obstacles, stumbled over their bewildered advance guard and plunged headlong into the gray fleeces. Meanwhile into the pockets of his prostrate foe went Oscar's hands with no result. Then he remembered the man's gesture in pulling the hat close upon his ears,

and off came the hat and with it a blood-stained envelope. The last sheep in the pen trooped out and galloped
toward its comrades.

Oscar, making off with the letter, plunged into the
rear guard of the sheep, fell, stumbled to his feet, and
confronted Captain Claiborne as that gentleman, in
soiled evening dress, fumbled for his lantern and swore
in language unbecoming an officer and a gentleman.

"Damn the sheep!" roared Claiborne.

"It is sheep—yes?" and Oscar started to bolt.

"Halt!"

The authority of the tone rang familiarly in Oscar's
ears. He had, after considerable tribulation, learned to
stop short when an officer spoke to him, and the gentleman of the sheepfold stood straight in the starlight
and spoke like an officer.

"What in the devil are you doing here, and who fired
that shot?"

Oscar saluted and summoned his best English.

"It was an accident, sir."

"Why are you running and why did you fire? Understand you are a trespasser here, and I am going to
turn you over to the constable."

"There was a sheep-stealer—yes? He is yonder by the

pens—and we had some little fighting; but he is not dead—no?"

At that moment Claiborne's eyes caught sight of a burly figure rising and threshing about by the broken pen door.

"That is the sheep-stealer," said Oscar. "We shall catch him—yes?"

Zmai peered toward them uncertainly for a moment; then turned abruptly and ran toward the road. Oscar started to cut off his retreat, but Claiborne caught the sergeant by the shoulder and flung him back.

"One of you at a time! They can turn the hounds on the other rascal. What's that you have there? Give it to me—quick!"

"It's a piece of wool—"

But Claiborne snatched the paper from Oscar's hand, and commanded the man to march ahead of him to the house. So over the meadow and through the pergola they went, across the veranda and into the library. The power of army discipline was upon Oscar; if Claiborne had not been an officer he would have run for it in the garden. As it was, he was taxing his wits to find some way out of his predicament. He had not the slightest idea as to what the paper might be. He had risked his life to secure it, and now the crumpled, blood-stained paper had been taken away from him by a person whom it could not interest in any way whatever.

He blinked under Claiborne's sharp scrutiny as they faced each other in the library.

"You are the man who brought a horse back to our stable an hour ago."

"Yes, sir."

"You have been a soldier."

"In the cavalry, sir. I have my discharge at home."

"Where do you live?"

"I work as teamster in the coal mines—yes?—they are by Lamar, sir."

Claiborne studied Oscar's erect figure carefully.

"Let me see your hands," he commanded; and Oscar extended his palms.

"You are lying; you do not work in the coal mines. Your clothes are not those of a miner; and a discharged soldier doesn't go to digging coal. Stand where you are, and it will be the worse for you if you try to bolt."

Claiborne turned to the table with the envelope. It was not sealed, and he took out the plain sheet of note-paper on which was written:

CABLEGRAM

WINKELRIED, VIENNA.

Not later than Friday.

CHAUVENET.

Claiborne read and re-read these eight words; then he spoke bluntly to Oscar.

"Where did you get this?"

"From the hat of the sheep-stealer up yonder."

"Who is he and where did he get it?"

"I don't know, sir. He was of Servia, and they are an ugly race—yes?"

"What were you going to do with the paper?"

Oscar grinned.

"If I could read it—yes; I might know; but if Austria is in the paper, then it is mischief; and maybe it would be murder; who knows?"

Claiborne looked frowningly from the paper to Oscar's tranquil eyes.

"Dick!" called Shirley from the hall, and she appeared in the doorway, drawing on her gloves; but paused at seeing Oscar.

"Shirley, I caught this man in the sheepfold. Did you ever see him before?"

"I think not, Dick."

"It was he that brought your horse home."

"To be sure it is! I hadn't recognized him. Thank you very much;" and she smiled at Oscar.

Dick frowned fiercely and referred again to the paper.

"Where is Monsieur Chauvenet—have you any idea?"

"If he isn't at the hotel or in Washington, I'm sure I don't know. If we are going to the dance—"

"Plague the dance! I heard a shot in the sheep pasture a bit ago and ran out to find this fellow in a row with another man, who got away."

"I heard the shot and the dogs from my window. You seem to have been in a fuss, too, from the looks of your clothes;" and Shirley sat down and smoothed her gloves with provoking coolness.

Dick sent Oscar to the far end of the library with a gesture, and held up the message for Shirley to read.

"Don't touch it!" he exclaimed; and when she nodded her head in sign that she had read it, he said, speaking earnestly and rapidly:

"I suppose I have no right to hold this message; I must send the man to the hotel telegraph office with it. But where is Chauvenet? What is his business in the valley? And what is the link between Vienna and these hills?"

"Don't you know what *you* are doing here?" she asked, and he flushed.

"I know what, but not *why!*" he blurted irritably; "but that's enough!"

"You know that Baron von Marhof wants to find Mr. John Armitage; but you don't know why."

"I have my orders and I'm going to find him, if it takes ten years."

Shirley nodded and clasped her fingers together. Her elbows resting on the high arms of her chair caused her cloak to flow sweepingly away from her shoulders. At the end of the room, with his back to the portières, stood Oscar, immovable. Claiborne reëxamined the message, and extended it again to Shirley.

"There's no doubt of that being Chauvenet's writing, is there?"

"I think not, Dick. I have had notes from him now and then in that hand. He has taken pains to write this with unusual distinctness."

The color brightened in her cheeks suddenly as she looked toward Oscar. The curtains behind him swayed, but so did the curtain back of her. A May-time languor had crept into the heart of April, and all the windows were open. The blurred murmurs of insects stole into the house. Oscar, half-forgotten by his captor, heard a sound in the window behind him and a hand touched him through the curtain.

Claiborne crumpled the paper impatiently.

"Shirley, you are against me! I believe you have seen Armitage here, and I want you to tell me what you know of him. It is not like you to shield a scamp of an adventurer—an unknown, questionable character. He has followed you to this valley and will involve you in his affairs without the slightest compunction, if he can. It's most infamous, outrageous, and when I find him I'm going to thrash him within an inch of his life before I turn him over to Marhof!"

Shirley laughed for the first time in their interview, and rose and placed her hands on her brother's shoulders.

"Do it, Dick! He's undoubtedly a wicked, a terribly wicked and dangerous character."

"I tell you I'll find him," he said tensely, putting up his hands to hers, where they rested on his shoulders. She laughed and kissed him, and when her hands fell to her side the message was in her gloved fingers.

"I'll help you, Dick," she said, buttoning her glove.

"That's like you, Shirley."

"If you want to find Mr. Armitage—"

"Of course I want to find him—" His voice rose to a roar.

"Then turn around; Mr. Armitage is just behind you!"

"Yes; I needed my man for other business," said Armitage, folding his arms, "and as you were very much occupied I made free with the rear veranda and changed places with him."

Claiborne walked slowly toward him, the anger glowing in his face.

"You are worse than I thought—eavesdropper, housebreaker!"

"Yes; I am both those things, Captain Claiborne. But I am also in a great hurry. What do you want with me?"

"You are a rogue, an impostor—"

"We will grant that," said Armitage quietly. "Where is your warrant for my arrest?"

"That will be forthcoming fast enough! I want you to understand that I have a personal grievance against you."

"It must wait until day after to-morrow, Captain

Claiborne. I will come to you here or wherever you say on the day after to-morrow."

Armitage spoke with a deliberate sharp decision that was not the tone of a rogue or a fugitive. As he spoke he advanced until he faced Claiborne in the center of the room. Shirley still stood by the window, holding the soiled paper in her hand. She had witnessed the change of men at the end of the room; it had touched her humor; it had been a joke on her brother; but she felt that the night had brought a crisis: she could not continue to shield a man of whom she knew nothing save that he was the object of a curious enmity. Her idle prayer that her own land's commonplace sordidness might be obscured by the glamour of Old World romance came back to her; she had been in touch with an adventure that was certainly proving fruitful of diversion. The *coup de théâtre* by which Armitage had taken the place of his servant had amused her for a moment; but she was vexed and angry now that he had dared come again to the house.

"You are under arrest, Mr. Armitage; I must detain you here," said Claiborne.

"In America—in free Virginia—without legal process?" asked Armitage, laughing.

"You are a housebreaker, that is enough. Shirley, please go!"

"You were not detached from the army to find a housebreaker. But I will make your work easy for you —day after to-morrow I will present myself to you wherever you say. But now—that cable message which my man found in your sheep pasture is of importance. I must trouble you to read it to me."

"No!" shouted Claiborne.

Armitage drew a step nearer.

"You must take my word for it that matters of importance, of far-reaching consequence, hang upon that message. I must know what it is."

"You certainly have magnificent cheek! I am going to take that paper to Baron von Marhof at once."

"Do so!—but *I* must know first! Baron von Marhof and I are on the same side in this business, but he doesn't understand it, and it is clear you don't. Give me the message!"

He spoke commandingly, his voice thrilling with earnestness, and jerked out his last words with angry impatience. At the same moment he and Claiborne stepped toward each other, with their hands clenched at their sides.

"I don't like your tone, Mr. Armitage!"

"I don't like to use that tone, Captain Claiborne."

Shirley walked quickly to the table and put down the message. Then, going to the door, she paused as though by an afterthought, and repeated quite slowly the words:

"Winkelried—Vienna—not later than Friday—Chauvenet."

"Shirley!" roared Claiborne.

John Armitage bowed to the already vacant doorway; then bounded into the hall out upon the veranda and ran through the garden to the side gate, where Oscar waited.

Half an hour later Captain Claiborne, after an interview with Baron von Marhof, turned his horse toward the hills.

CHAPTER XXII

So, exultant of heart, with front toward the bridges of
    battle,
Sat they the whole night long, and the fires that they kin-
    dled were many.
E'en as the stars in her train, with the moon as she walketh
    in splendor,
Blaze forth bright in the heavens on nights when the welkin
    is breathless,
Nights when the mountain peaks, their jutting cliffs, and
    the valleys,
All are disclosed to the eye, and above them the fathomless
    ether
Opens to star after star, and glad is the heart of the shep-
    herd—
Such and so many the fires 'twixt the ships and the streams
    of the Xanthus
Kept ablaze by the Trojans in front of the darkening city.
Over the plains were burning a thousand fires, and beside
    them
Each sat fifty men in the firelight glare; and the horses,
Champing their fodder and barley white, and instant for
    action,
Stood by the chariot-side and awaited the glory of morning.
        The Iliad: Translation of Prentiss Cummings.

"In Vienna, Friday!"

"There should be great deeds, my dear Jules;" and

Monsieur Durand adjusted the wick of a smoking brass lamp that hung suspended from the ceiling of a room of the inn, store and post-office at Lamar.

"Meanwhile, this being but Wednesday, we have our work to do."

"Which is not so simple after all, as one studies the situation. Mr. Armitage is here, quite within reach. We suspect him of being a person of distinction. He evinced unusual interest in a certain document that was once in your own hands—"

"*Our* own hands, if you would be accurate!"

"You are captious; but granted so, we must get them back. The gentleman is dwelling in a bungalow on the mountain side, for greater convenience in watching events and wooing the lady of his heart's desire. We employed a clumsy clown to put him out of the world; but he dies hard, and now we have got to get rid of him. But if he hasn't the papers on his clothes then you have this pleasant scheme for kidnapping him, getting him down to your steamer at Baltimore and cruising with him until he is ready to come to terms. The American air has done much for your imagination, my dear Jules; or possibly the altitude of the hills has over-stimulated it."

"You are not the fool you look, my dear Durand. You have actually taken a pretty fair grasp of the situation."

"But the adorable young lady, the fair Mademoiselle Claiborne,—what becomes of her in these transactions?"

"That is none of your affair," replied Chauvenet, frowning. "I am quite content with my progress. I have not finished in that matter."

"Neither, it would seem, has Mr. John Armitage! But I am quite well satisfied to leave it to you. In a few days we shall know much more than we do now. I should be happier if you were in charge in Vienna. A false step there—ugh! I hesitate to think of the wretched mess there would be."

"Trust Winkelried to do his full duty. You must not forget that the acute Stroebel now sleeps the long sleep and that many masses have already been said for the repose of his intrepid soul."

"The splendor of our undertaking is enough to draw his ghost from the grave. Ugh! By this time Zmai should have filed our cablegram at the Springs and got your mail at the hotel. I hope you have not misplaced your confidence in the operator there. Coming back, our giant must pass Armitage's house."

"Trust him to pass it! His encounters with Armitage have not been to his credit."

The two men were dressed in rough clothes, as for an outing, and in spite of the habitual trifling tone of their talk, they wore a serious air. Durand's eyes danced with excitement and he twisted his mustache nervously. Chauvenet had gone to Washington to meet Durand, to get from him news of the progress of the conspiracy in Vienna, and, not least, to berate him for crossing the Atlantic. "I do not require watching, my dear Durand," he had said.

"A man in love, dearest Jules, sometimes forgets;" but they had gone into the Virginia hills amicably and were quartered with the postmaster. They waited now for Zmai, whom they had sent to the Springs with a message and to get Chauvenet's mail. Armitage, they had learned, used the Lamar telegraph office and they had decided to carry their business elsewhere.

While they waited in the bare upper room of the inn for Zmai, the big Servian tramped up the mountain side with an aching head and a heart heavy with dread. The horse he had left tied in a thicket when he plunged down through the Claiborne place had broken free and run away; so that he must now trudge back afoot to report to his masters. He had made a mess of his errands and nearly lost his life besides. The bullet from Oscar's revolver had cut a neat furrow in his scalp, which was growing sore and stiff as it ceased bleeding. He would undoubtedly be dealt with harshly by Chauvenet and Durand, but he knew that the sooner he reported his calamities the better; so he stumbled toward Lamar, pausing at times to clasp his small head in his great hands. When he passed the wild tangle that hid Armitage's bungalow he paused and cursed the two occupants in his own dialect with a fierce vile tongue. It was near midnight when he reached the tavern and climbed the rickety stairway to the room where the two men waited.

Chauvenet opened the door at his approach, and they cried aloud as the great figure appeared before them and the lamplight fell upon his dark blood-smeared face.

"The letters!" snapped Chauvenet.

"Is the message safe?" demanded Durand.

"Lost; lost; they are lost! I lost my way and he nearly killed me,—the little soldier,—as I crossed a strange field."

When they had jerked the truth from Zmai, Chauvenet flung open the door and bawled through the house for the innkeeper.

"Horses; saddle our two horses quick—and get another if you have to steal it," he screamed. Then he turned into the room to curse Zmai, while Durand with a towel and water sought to ease the ache in the big fellow's head and cleanse his face.

"So that beggarly little servant did it, did he? He stole that paper I had given you, did he? What do you imagine I brought you to this country for if you are to let two stupid fools play with you as though you were a clown?"

The Servian, on his knees before Durand, suffered the torrent of abuse meekly. He was a scoundrel, hired to do murder; and his vilification by an angered employer did not greatly trouble him, particularly since he understood little of Chauvenet's rapid German.

In half an hour Chauvenet was again in a fury, learning at Lamar that the operator had gone down the road twenty miles to a dance and would not be back until morning.

The imperturbable Durand shivered in the night air and prodded Chauvenet with ironies.

"We have no time to lose. That message must go tonight. You may be sure Monsieur Armitage will not send it for us. Come, we've got to go down to Storm Springs."

They rode away in the starlight, leaving the postmaster alarmed and wondering. Chauvenet and Durand were well mounted on horses that Chauvenet had sent into the hills in advance of his own coming. Zmai rode grim and silent on a clumsy plow-horse, which was the best the publican could find for him. The knife was not the only weapon he had known in Servia; he carried a potato sack across his saddle-bow. Chauvenet and Durand sent him ahead to set the pace with his inferior mount. They talked together in low tones as they followed.

"He is not so big a fool, this Armitage," remarked Durand. "He is quite deep, in fact. I wish it were he we are trying to establish on a throne, and not that pitiful scapegrace in Vienna."

"I gave him his chance down there in the valley and he laughed at me. It is quite possible that he is not a fool; and quite certain that he is not a coward."

"Then he would not be a safe king. Our young friend in Vienna is a good deal of a fool and altogether a coward. We shall have to provide him with a spine at his coronation."

"If we fail—" began Chauvenet.

"You suggest a fruitful but unpleasant topic. If we fail we shall be fortunate if we reach the hospitable shores of the Argentine for future residence. Paris and Vienna would not know us again. If Winkelried succeeds in Vienna and we lose here, where do we arrive?"

"We arrive quite where Mr. Armitage chooses to land us. He is a gentleman of resources; he has money; he laughs cheerfully at misadventures; he has had you watched by the shrewdest eyes in Europe,—and you are considered a hard man to keep track of, my dear Durand. And not least important,—he has to-night snatched away that little cablegram that was the signal to Winkelried to go ahead. He is a very annoying and vexatious person, this Armitage. Even Zmai, whose knife made him a terror in Servia, seems unable to cope with him."

"And the fair daughter of the valley—"

"Pish! We are not discussing the young lady."

"I can understand how unpleasant the subject must be to you, my dear Jules. What do you imagine *she* knows of Monsieur Armitage? If he is the man we think he is and a possible heir to a great throne it would be impossible for her to marry him."

"His tastes are democratic. In Montana he is quite popular."

Durand flung away his cigarette and laughed suddenly.

"Has it occurred to you that this whole affair is decidedly amusing? Here we are, in one of the free American states, about to turn a card that will dethrone a king, if we are lucky. And here is a man we are trying to get out of the way—a man we might make king if he were not a fool! In America! It touches my sense of humor, my dear Jules!"

An exclamation from Zmai arrested them. The Servian jerked up his horse and they were instantly at his side. They had reached a point near the hunting preserve in the main highway. It was about half-past one o'clock, an hour at which Virginia mountain roads are usually free of travelers, and they had been sending their horses along as briskly as the uneven roads and the pace of Zmai's laggard beast permitted.

The beat of a horse's hoofs could be heard quite distinctly in the road ahead of them. The road tended downward, and the strain of the ascent was marked in the approaching animal's walk; in a moment the three men heard the horse's quick snort of satisfaction as it reached leveler ground; then scenting the other animals, it threw up its head and neighed shrilly.

In the dusk of starlight Durand saw Zmai dismount and felt the Servian's big rough hand touch his in passing the bridle of his horse.

"Wait!" said the Servian.

The horse of the unknown paused, neighed again, and refused to go farther. A man's deep voice encouraged him in low tones. The horses of Chauvenet's party danced about restlessly, responsive to the nervousness of the strange beast before them.

"Who goes there?"

The stranger's horse was quiet for an instant and the rider had forced him so near that the beast's up-reined head and the erect shoulders of the horseman were quite clearly defined.

"Who goes there?" shouted the rider; while Chauvenet and Durand bent their eyes toward him, their hands tight on their bridles, and listened, waiting for Zmai. They heard a sudden rush of steps, the impact of his giant body as he flung himself upon the shrinking horse; and then a cry of alarm and rage. Chauvenet slipped down and ran forward with the quick, soft glide of a cat and caught the bridle of the stranger's horse. The

horseman struggled in Zmai's great arms, and his beast
plunged wildly. No words passed. The rider had kicked
his feet out of the stirrups and gripped the horse hard
with his legs. His arms were flung up to protect his
head, over which Zmai tried to force the sack.

"The knife?" bawled the Servian.

"No!" answered Chauvenet.

"The devil!" yelled the rider; and dug his spurs into
the rearing beast's flanks.

Chauvenet held on valiantly with both hands to the
horse's head. Once the frightened beast swung him clear
of the ground. A few yards distant Durand sat on his
own horse and held the bridles of the others. He soothed
the restless animals in low tones, the light of his cigarette shaking oddly in the dark with the movement of
his lips.

The horse ceased to plunge; Zmai held its rider erect
with his left arm while the right drew the sack down
over the head and shoulders of the prisoner.

"Tie him," said Chauvenet; and Zmai buckled a strap
about the man's arms and bound them tight.

The dust in the bag caused the man inside to cough,
but save for the one exclamation he had not spoken.
Chauvenet and Durand conferred in low tones while

Zmai drew out a tether strap and snapped it to the curb-bit of the captive's horse.

"The fellow takes it pretty coolly," remarked Durand, lighting a fresh cigarette. "What are you going to do with him?"

"We will take him to his own place—it is near—and coax the papers out of him; then we'll find a precipice and toss him over. It is a simple matter."

Zmai handed Chauvenet the revolver he had taken from the silent man on the horse.

"I am ready," he reported.

"Go ahead; we follow;" and they started toward the bungalow, Zmai riding beside the captive and holding fast to the led-horse. Where the road was smooth they sent the horses forward at a smart trot; but the captive accepted the gait; he found the stirrups again and sat his saddle straight. He coughed now and then, but the hemp sack was sufficiently porous to give him a little air. As they rode off his silent submission caused Durand to ask:

"Are you sure of the man, my dear Jules?"

"Undoubtedly. I didn't get a square look at him, but he's a gentleman by the quality of his clothes. He is the same build; it is not a plow-horse, but a thoroughbred he's riding. The gentlemen of the valley are in their beds long ago."

"Would that we were in ours! The spring nights are cold in these hills!"

"The work is nearly done. The little soldier is yet to reckon with; but we are three; and Zmai did quite well with the potato sack."

Chauvenet rode ahead and addressed a few words to Zmai.

"The little man must be found before we finish. There must be no mistake about it."

They exercised greater caution as they drew nearer the wood that concealed the bungalow, and Chauvenet dismounted, opened the gate and set a stone against it to insure a ready egress; then they walked their horses up the driveway.

Admonished by Chauvenet, Durand threw away his cigarette with a sigh.

"You are convinced this is the wise course, dearest Jules?"

"Be quiet and keep your eyes open. There's the house."

He halted the party, dismounted and crept forward to the bungalow. He circled the veranda, found the blinds open, and peered into the long lounging-room, where a few embers smoldered in the broad fireplace, and an oil lamp shed a faint light. One man they held captive; the other was not in sight; Chauvenet's courage rose at the prospect of easy victory. He tried the door, found it unfastened, and with his revolver ready in his hand, threw it open. Then he walked slowly toward the table, turned the wick of the lamp high, and surveyed the room carefully. The doors of the rooms that opened from the apartment stood ajar; he followed the wall cautiously, kicked them open, peered into the room where Armitage's things were scattered about, and found his iron bed empty. Then he walked quickly to the veranda and summoned the others.

"Bring him in!" he said, without taking his eyes from the room.

A moment later Zmai had lifted the silent rider to the veranda, and flung him across the threshold. Durand, now aroused, fastened the horses to the veranda rail.

Chauvenet caught up some candles from the mantel and lighted them.

"Open the trunks in those rooms and be quick; I will join you in a moment;" and as Durand turned into Armitage's room, Chauvenet peered again into the other chambers, called once or twice in a low tone; then turned to Zmai and the prisoner.

"Take off the bag," he commanded.

Chauvenet studied the lines of the erect, silent figure as Zmai loosened the strap, drew off the bag, and stepped back toward the table on which he had laid his revolver for easier access.

"Mr. John Armitage—"

Chauvenet, his revolver half raised, had begun an ironical speech, but the words died on his lips. The man who stood blinking from the sudden burst of light was not John Armitage, but Captain Claiborne.

The perspiration on Claiborne's face had made a paste of the dirt from the potato sack, which gave him a weird appearance. He grinned broadly, adding a fantastic horror to his visage which caused Zmai to leap back toward the door. Then Chauvenet cried aloud, a cry of anger, which brought Durand into the hall at a jump. Claiborne shrugged his shoulders, shook the blood into his numbed arms; then turned his besmeared face toward Durand and laughed. He laughed long and loud as the stupefaction deepened on the faces of the two men.

The objects which Durand held caused Claiborne to

stare, and then he laughed again. Durand had caught up from a hook in Armitage's room a black cloak, so long that it trailed at length from his arms, its red lining glowing brightly where it lay against the outer black. From the folds of the cloak a sword, plucked from a trunk, dropped upon the floor with a gleam of its bright scabbard. In his right hand he held a silver box of orders, and as his arm fell at the sight of Claiborne, the gay ribbons and gleaming pendants flashed to the floor.

"It is not Armitage; we have made a mistake!" muttered Chauvenet tamely, his eyes falling from Claiborne's face to the cloak, the sword, the tangled heap of ribbons on the floor.

Durand stepped forward with an oath.

"Who is the man?" he demanded.

"It is my friend Captain Claiborne. We owe the gentleman an apology—" Chauvenet began.

"You put it mildly," cried Claiborne in English, his back to the fireplace, his arms folded, and the smile gone from his face. "I don't know your companions, Monsieur Chauvenet, but you seem inclined to the gentle arts of kidnapping and murder. Really, Monsieur—"

"It is a mistake! It is unpardonable! I can only offer you reparation—anything you ask," stammered Chauvenet.

"You are looking for John Armitage, are you?" demanded Claiborne hotly, without heeding Chauvenet's words. "Mr. Armitage is not here; he was in Storm Springs to-night, at my house. He is a brave gentleman, and I warn you that you will injure him at your peril. You may kill me here or strangle me or stick a knife into me, if you will be better satisfied that way; or you may kill him and hide his body in these hills; but, by God, there will be no escape for you! The highest powers of my government know that I am here; Baron von Marhof knows that I am here. I have an engagement to breakfast with Baron von Marhof at his house at eight o'clock in the morning, and if I am not there every agency of the government will be put to work to find you, Mr. Jules Chauvenet, and these other scoundrels who travel with you."

"You are violent, my dear sir—" began Durand, whose wits were coming back to him much quicker than Chauvenet's.

"I am not as violent as I shall be if I get a troop of cavalry from Fort Myer down here and hunt you like rabbits through the hills. And I advise you to cable Winkelried at Vienna that the game is all off !"

Chauvenet suddenly jumped toward the table, the revolver still swinging at arm's length.

"You know too much !"

"I don't know any more than Armitage, and Baron von Marhof and my father, and the Honorable Secretary of State, to say nothing of the equally Honorable Secretary of War."

Claiborne stretched out his arms and rested them along the shelf of the mantel, and smiled with a smile which the dirt on his face weirdly accented. His hat was gone, his short hair rumpled; he dug the bricks of the hearth with the toe of his riding-boot as an emphasis of his contentment with the situation.

"You don't understand the gravity of our labors. The peace of a great Empire is at stake in this business. We are engaged on a patriotic mission of great importance."

It was Durand who spoke. Outside, Zmai held the horses in readiness.

"You are a fine pair of patriots, I swear," said Claiborne. "What in the devil do you want with John Armitage ?"

"He is a menace to a great throne—an impostor
—a—"

Chauvenet's eyes swept with a swift glance the cloak,
the sword, the scattered orders. Claiborne followed the
man's gaze, but he looked quickly toward Durand and
Chauvenet, not wishing them to see that the sight of
these things puzzled him.

"Pretty trinkets! But such games as yours, these
pretty baubles—are not for these free hills."

"Where is John Armitage?"

Chauvenet half raised his right arm as he spoke and
the steel of his revolver flashed.

Claiborne did not move; he smiled upon them, re-
crossed his legs, and settled his back more comfortably
against the mantel-shelf.

"I really forget where he said he would be at this
hour. He and his man may have gone to Washington,
or they may have started for Vienna, or they may be in
conference with Baron von Marhof at my father's, or
they may be waiting for you at the gate. The Lord only
knows!"

"Come; we waste time," said Durand in French. "It
is a trap. We must not be caught here!"

"Yes; you'd better go," said Claiborne, yawning and

settling himself in a new pose with his back still to the fireplace. "I don't believe Armitage will care if I use his bungalow occasionally during my sojourn in the hills; and if you will be so kind as to leave my horse well tied out there somewhere I believe I'll go to bed. I'm sorry, Mr. Chauvenet, that I can't just remember who introduced you to me and my family. I owe that person a debt of gratitude for bringing so pleasant a scoundrel to my notice."

He stepped to the table, his hands in his pockets, and bowed to them.

"Good night, and clear out," and he waved his arm in dismissal.

"Come!" said Durand peremptorily, and as Chauvenet hesitated, Durand seized him by the arm and pulled him toward the door.

As they mounted and turned to go they saw Claiborne standing at the table, lighting a cigarette from one of the candles. He walked to the veranda and listened until he was satisfied that they had gone; then went in and closed the door. He picked up the cloak and sword and restored the insignia to the silver box. The sword he examined with professional interest, running his hand over the embossed scabbard, then drawing the bright blade and trying its balance and weight.

As he held it thus, heavy steps sounded at the rear of the house, a door was flung open and Armitage sprang into the room with Oscar close at his heels.

CHAPTER XXIII

THE VERGE OF MORNING

O to mount again where erst I haunted;
Where the old red hills are bird-enchanted,
    And the low green meadows
        Bright with sward;
And when even dies, the million-tinted,
And the night has come, and planets glinted,
    Lo! the valley hollow,
        Lamp-bestarr'd.

—R. L. S.

"I hope you like my things, Captain Claiborne!"

Armitage stood a little in advance, his hand on Oscar's arm to check the rush of the little man.

Claiborne sheathed the sword, placed it on the table and folded his arms.

"Yes; they are very interesting."

"And those ribbons and that cloak,—I assure you they are of excellent quality. Oscar, put a blanket on this gentleman's horse. Then make some coffee and wait."

As Oscar closed the door, Armitage crossed to the

314

table, flung down his gauntlets and hat and turned to Claiborne.

"I didn't expect this of you; I really didn't expect it. Now that you have found me, what in the devil do you want?"

"I don't know—I'll be *damned* if I know!" and Claiborne grinned, so that the grotesque lines of his soiled countenance roused Armitage's slumbering wrath.

"You'd better find out damned quick! This is my busy night and if you can't explain yourself I'm going to tie you hand and foot and drop you down the well till I finish my work. Speak up! What are you doing on my grounds, in my house, at this hour of the night, prying into my affairs and rummaging in my trunks?"

"I didn't *come* here, Armitage; I was brought—with a potato sack over my head. There's the sack on the floor, and any of its dirt that isn't on my face must be permanently settled in my lungs."

"What are you doing up here in the mountains—why are you not at your station? The potato-sack story is pretty flimsy. Do better than that and hurry up!"

"Armitage"—as he spoke, Claiborne walked to the table and rested his finger-tips on it—"Armitage, you and I have made some mistakes during our short acquaintance. I will tell you frankly that I have blown hot and cold about you as I never did before with another man in my life. On the ship coming over and when I met you in Washington I thought well of you. Then your damned cigarette case shook my confidence in you there at the Army and Navy Club that night; and now—"

"Damn my cigarette case!" bellowed Armitage, clapping his hand to his pocket to make sure of it.

"That's what I say! But it was a disagreeable situation,—you must admit that."

"It was, indeed!"

"It requires some nerve for a man to tell a circumstantial story like that to a tableful of gentlemen, about one of the gentlemen!"

"No doubt of it whatever, Mr. Claiborne."

Armitage unbuttoned his coat, and jerked back the lapels impatiently.

"And I knew as much about Monsieur Chauvenet as I did about you, or as I do about you!"

"What you know of him, Mr. Claiborne, is of no consequence. And what you don't know about me would fill a large volume. How did you get here, and what do you propose doing, now that you are here? I am in a

hurry and have no time to waste. If I can't get anything satisfactory out of you within two minutes I'm
going to chuck you back into the sack."

"I came up here in the hills to look for you—you—
you—! Do you understand?" began Claiborne angrily.
"And as I was riding along the road about two miles
from here I ran into three men on horseback. When I
stopped to parley with them and find out what they were
doing, they crept up on me and grabbed my horse and
put that sack over my head. They had mistaken me
for you; and they brought me here, into your house,
and pulled the sack off and were decidedly disagreeable
at finding they had made a mistake. One of them had
gone in to ransack your effects and when they pulled off
the bag and disclosed the wrong hare, he dropped his
loot on the floor; and then I told them to go to the devil,
and I hope they've done it! When you came in I was
picking up your traps, and I submit that the sword is
handsome enough to challenge anybody's eye. And
there's all there is of the story, and I don't care a damn
whether you believe it or not."

Their eyes were fixed upon each other in a gaze of
anger and resentment. Suddenly, Armitage's tense fig-

ure relaxed; the fierce light in his eyes gave way to a gleam of humor and he laughed long and loud.

"Your face—your face, Claiborne; it's funny. It's too funny for any use. When your teeth show it's something ghastly. For God's sake go in there and wash your face!"

He made a light in his own room and plied Claiborne with towels, while he continued to break forth occasionally in fresh bursts of laughter. When they went into the hall both men were grave.

"Claiborne—"

Armitage put out his hand and Claiborne took it in a vigorous clasp.

"You don't know who I am or what I am; and I haven't got time to tell you now. It's a long story; and I have much to do, but I swear to you, Claiborne, that my hands are clean; that the game I am playing is no affair of my own, but a big thing that I have pledged myself to carry through. I want you to ride down there in the valley and keep Marhof quiet for a few hours; tell him I know more of what's going on in Vienna than he does, and that if he will only sit in a rocking-chair and tell you fairy stories till morning, we can all be

happy. Is it a bargain—or—must I still hang your
head down the well till I get through?"

"Marhof may go to the devil! He's a lot more mysterious than even you, Armitage. These fellows that
brought me up here to kill me in the belief that I was
you can not be friends of Marhof's cause."

"They are not; I assure you they are not! They are
blackguards of the blackest dye."

"I believe you, Armitage."

"Thank you. Now your horse is at the door—run
along like a good fellow."

Armitage dived into his room, caught up a cartridge
belt and reappeared buckling it on.

"Oscar!" he yelled, "bring in that coffee—with cups
for two."

He kicked off his boots and drew on light shoes and
leggings.

"Light marching orders for the rough places. Con-
found that buckle."

He rose and stamped his feet to settle the shoes.

"Your horse is at the door; that rascal Oscar will take
off the blanket for you. There's a bottle of fair whisky
in the cupboard, if you'd like a nip before starting.
Bless me! I forgot the coffee! There on the table, Os-

car, and never mind the chairs," he added as Oscar came
in with a tin pot and the cups on a piece of plank.

"I'm taking the rifle, Oscar; and be sure those revolvers are loaded with the real goods."

There was a great color in Armitage's face as he strode
about preparing to leave. His eyes danced with excitement, and between the sentences that he jerked out half
to himself he whistled a few bars from a comic opera
that was making a record run on Broadway. His steps
rang out vigorously from the bare pine floor.

"Watch the windows, Oscar; you may forgive a general anything but a surprise—isn't that so, Claiborne?—
and those fellows must be pretty mad by this time. Excuse the coffee service, Claiborne. We always pour the
sugar from the paper bag—original package, you understand. And see if you can't find Captain Claiborne a
hat, Oscar—"

With a tin-cup of steaming coffee in his hand he sat
on the table dangling his legs, his hat on the back of his
head, the cartridge belt strapped about his waist over a
brown corduroy hunting-coat. He was in a high mood,
and chaffed Oscar as to the probability of their breakfasting another morning. "If we die, Oscar, it shall be
in a good cause!"

" Excuse the coffee service, Claiborne" *Page 320*

He threw aside his cup with a clatter, jumped down and caught the sword from the table, examined it critically, then sheathed it with a click.

Claiborne had watched Armitage with a growing impatience; he resented the idea of being thus ignored; then he put his hand roughly on Armitage's shoulder.

Armitage, intent with his own affairs, had not looked at Claiborne for several minutes, but he glanced at him now as though just recalling a duty.

"Lord, man! I didn't mean to throw you into the road! There's a clean bed in there that you're welcome to—go in and get some sleep."

"I'm not going into the valley," roared Claiborne, "and I'm not going to bed; I'm going with you, damn you!"

"But bless your soul, man, you can't go with me; you are as ignorant as a babe of my affairs, and I'm terribly busy and have no time to talk to you. Oscar, that coffee scalded me. Claiborne, if only I had time, you know, but under existing circumstances—"

"I repeat that I'm going with you. I don't know why I'm in this row, and I don't know what it's all about, but I believe what you say about it; and I want you to understand that I can't be put in a bag like a prize potato without taking a whack at the man who put me there."

"But if you should get hurt, Claiborne, it would spoil my plans. I never could face your family again," said Armitage earnestly. "Take your horse and go."

"I'm going back to the valley when you do."

"Humph! Drink your coffee! Oscar, bring out the rest of the artillery and give Captain Claiborne his choice."

He picked up his sword again, flung the blade from the scabbard with a swish, and cut the air with it, humming a few bars of a German drinking-song. Then he broke out with:

> "I do not think a braver gentleman,
> More active-valiant or more valiant-young,
> More daring or more bold, is now alive
> To grace this latter age with noble deeds.
> For my part, I may speak it to my shame,
> I have a truant been to chivalry;—

"Lord, Claiborne, you don't know what's ahead of us! It's the greatest thing that ever happened. I never expected anything like this—not on my cheerfulest days. Dearest Jules is out looking for a telegraph office to pull off the Austrian end of the rumpus. Well, little good it will do him! And we'll catch him and Durand and that

Servian devil and lock them up here till Marhof decides
what to do with him. We're off!"

"All ready, sir;" said Oscar briskly.

"It's half-past two. They didn't get off their message
at Lamar, because the office is closed and the operator
gone, and they will keep out of the valley and away from
the big inn, because they are rather worried by this time
and not anxious to get too near Marhof. They've probably decided to go to the next station below Lamar to
do their telegraphing. Meanwhile they haven't got me!"

"They had me and didn't want me," said Claiborne,
mounting his own horse.

"They'll have a good many things they don't want in
the next twenty-four hours. If I hadn't enjoyed this
business so much myself we might have had some secret
service men posted all along the coast to keep a lookout
for them. But it's been a great old lark. And now to
catch them!"

Outside the preserve they paused for an instant.

"They're not going to venture far from their base,
which is that inn and post-office, where they have been
rummaging my mail. I haven't studied the hills for
nothing, and I know short cuts about here that are not
on maps. They haven't followed the railroad north, because the valley broadens too much and there are too

many people. There's a trail up here that goes over the
ridge and down through a wind gap to a settlement
about five miles south of Lamar. If I'm guessing right,
we can cut around and get ahead of them and drive them
back here to my land."

"To the Port of Missing Men! It was made for the
business," said Claiborne.

"Oscar, patrol the road here, and keep an eye on the
bungalow, and if you hear us forcing them down, charge
from this side. I'll fire twice when I get near the Port
to warn you; and if you strike them first, give the same
signal. Do be careful, Sergeant, how you shoot. We
want prisoners, you understand, not corpses."

Armitage found a faint trail, and with Claiborne
struck off into the forest near the main gate of his own
grounds. In less than an hour they rode out upon a low-
wooded ridge and drew up their panting, sweating horses
—two shadowy videttes against the lustral dome of
stars. A keen wind whistled across the ridge and the
horses pawed the unstable ground restlessly. The men
jumped down to tighten their saddle-girths, and they
turned up their coat collars before mounting again.

"Come! We're on the verge of morning," said Armitage, "and there's no time to lose."

CHAPTER XXIV

THE ATTACK IN THE ROAD

Cowards and laggards fall back; but alert to the saddle,
Straight, grim and abreast, vault our weather-worn gallop-
    ing legion,
With a stirrup-cup each to the one gracious woman that
    loves him.
                —*Louise Imogen Guiney.*

"There's an abandoned lumber camp down here, if
I'm not mistaken, and if we've made the right turns we
ought to be south of Lamar and near the railroad."

Armitage passed his rein to Claiborne and plunged
down the steep road to reconnoiter.

"It's a strange business," Claiborne muttered half-
aloud.

The cool air of the ridge sobered him, but he reviewed the events of the night without regret. Every
young officer in the service would envy him this adventure. At military posts scattered across the continent
men whom he knew well were either abroad on duty, or
slept the sleep of peace. He lifted his eyes to the paling

325

stars. Before long bugle and morning gun would announce the new day at points all along the seaboard.
His West Point comrades were scattered far, and the
fancy seized him that the bugle brought them together
every day of their lives as it sounded the morning calls
that would soon begin echoing down the coast from
Kennebec Arsenal and Fort Preble in Maine, through
Myer and Monroe, to McPherson, in Georgia, and back
through Niagara and Wayne to Sheridan, and on to
Ringgold and Robinson and Crook, zigzagging back and
forth over mountain and plain to the Pacific, and thence
ringing on to Alaska, and echoing again from Hawaii
to lonely outposts in Asian seas.

He was so intent with the thought that he hummed
reveille, and was about to rebuke himself for unsoldierly
behavior on duty when Armitage whistled for him to advance.

"It's all right; they haven't passed yet. I met a railroad track-walker down there and he said he had seen
no one between here and Lamar. Now they're handi-
capped by the big country horse they had to take for
that Servian devil, and we can push them as hard as we
like. We must get them beyond Lamar before we crowd
them; and don't forget that we want to drive them into

my land for the round-up. I'm afraid we're going to have a wet morning."

They rode abreast beside the railroad through the narrow gap. A long freight-train rumbled and rattled by, and a little later they passed a coal shaft, where a begrimed night shift loaded cars under flaring torches.

"Their message to Winkelried is still on this side of the Atlantic," said Armitage; "but Winkelried is in a strong room by this time, if the existing powers at Vienna are what they ought to be. I've done my best to get him there. The message would only help the case against him if they sent it."

Claiborne groaned mockingly.

"I suppose I'll know what it's all about when I read it in the morning papers. I like the game well enough, but it might be more amusing to know what the devil I'm fighting for."

"You enlisted without reading the articles of war, and you've got to take the consequences. You've done what you set out to do—you've found me; and you're traveling with me over the Virginia mountains to report my capture to Baron von Marhof. On the way you are going to assist in another affair that will be equally to your credit; and then if all goes well with us I'm going

to give myself the pleasure of allowing Monsieur Chauvenet to tell you exactly who I am. The incident appeals
to my sense of humor—I assure you I have one! Of
course, if I were not a person of very great distinction
Chauvenet and his friend Durand would not have
crossed the ocean and brought with them a professional
assassin, skilled in the use of smothering and knifing, to
do away with me. You are in luck to be alive. We are
dangerously near the same size and build—and in the
dark—on horseback—"

"That was funny. I knew that if I ran for it they'd
plug me for sure, and that if I waited until they saw
their mistake they would be afraid to kill me. Ugh! I
still taste the red soil of the Old Dominion."

"Come, Captain! Let us give the horses a chance to
prove their blood. These roads will be paste in a few
hours."

The dawn was breaking sullenly, and out of a gray,
low-hanging mist a light rain fell in the soft, monotonous fashion of mountain rain. Much of the time it
was necessary to maintain single file; and Armitage
rode ahead. The fog grew thicker as they advanced; but
they did not lessen their pace, which had now dropped
to a steady trot.

Suddenly, as they swept on beyond Lamar, they heard the beat of hoofs and halted.

"Bully for us! We've cut in ahead of them! Can you count them, Claiborne?"

"There are three horses all right enough, and they're forcing the beasts. What's the word?"

"Drive them back! Ready—here we go!" roared Armitage in a voice intended to be heard.

They yelled at the top of their voices as they charged, plunging into the advancing trio after a forty-yard gallop.

" 'Not later than Friday'—back you go!" shouted Armitage, and laughed aloud at the enemy's rout. One of the horses—it seemed from its rider's yells to be Chauvenet's—turned and bolted, and the others followed back the way they had come.

Soon they dropped their pace to a trot, but the trio continued to fly before them.

"They're rattled," said Claiborne, "and the fog isn't helping them any."

"We're getting close to my place," said Armitage; and as he spoke two shots fired in rapid succession cracked faintly through the fog and they jerked up their horses.

"It's Oscar! He's a good way ahead, if I judge the shots right."

"If he turns them back we ought to hear their horses in a moment," observed Claiborne. "The fog muffles sounds. The road's pretty level in here."

"We must get them out of it and into my territory for safety. We're within a mile of the gate and we ought to be able to crowd them into that long open strip where the fences are down. Damn the fog!"

The agreed signal of two shots reached them again, but clearer, like drum-taps, and was immediately answered by scattering shots. A moment later, as the two riders moved forward at a walk, a sharp volley rang out quite clearly and they heard shouts and the crack of revolvers again.

"By George! They're coming—here we go!"

They put their horses to the gallop and rode swiftly through the fog. The beat of hoofs was now perfectly audible ahead of them, and they heard, quite distinctly, a single revolver snap twice.

"Oscar has them on the run—bully for Oscar! They're getting close—thank the Lord for this level stretch—now howl and let 'er go!"

They went forward with a yell that broke weirdly and

chokingly on the gray cloak of fog, their horses' hoofs
pounding dully on the earthen road. The rain had almost ceased, but enough had fallen to soften the ground.

"They're terribly brave or horribly scared, from their
speed," shouted Claiborne. "Now for it!"

They rose in their stirrups and charged, yelling lustily, riding neck and neck toward the unseen foe, and
with their horses at their highest pace they broke upon
the mounted trio that now rode upon them grayly out
of the mist.

There was a mad snorting and shrinking of horses.
One of the animals turned and tried to bolt, and his
rider, struggling to control him, added to the confusion.
The fog shut them in with each other; and Armitage
and Claiborne, having flung back their own horses at the
onset, had an instant's glimpse of Chauvenet trying to
swing his horse into the road; of Zmai half-turning, as
his horse reared, to listen for the foe behind; and of
Durand's impassive white face as he steadied his horse
with his left hand and leveled a revolver at Armitage
with his right.

With a cry Claiborne put spurs to his horse and drove
him forward upon Durand. His hand knocked the leveled revolver flying into the fog. Then Zmai fired twice,

and Chauvenet's frightened horse, panic-stricken at the shots, reared, swung round and dashed back the way he had come, and Durand and Zmai followed.

The three disappeared into the mist, and Armitage and Claiborne shook themselves together and quieted their horses.

"That was too close for fun—are you all there?" asked Armitage.

"Still in it; but Chauvenet's friend won't miss every time. There's murder in his eye. The big fellow seemed to be trying to shoot his own horse."

"Oh, he's a knife and sack man and clumsy with the gun."

They moved slowly forward now and Armitage sent his horse across the rough ditch at the roadside to get his bearings. The fog seemed at the point of breaking, and the mass about them shifted and drifted in the growing light.

"This is my land, sure enough. Lord, man, I wish you'd get out of this and go home. You see they're an ugly lot and don't use toy pistols."

"Remember the potato sack! That's my watchword," laughed Claiborne.

They rode with their eyes straight ahead, peering

through the breaking, floating mist. It was now so clear
and light that they could see the wood at either hand,
though fifty yards ahead in every direction the fog still
lay like a barricade.

"I should value a change of raiment," observed Armitage. "There was an advantage in armor—your duds
might get rusty on a damp excursion, but your shirt
wouldn't stick to your hide."

"Who cares? Those devils are pretty quiet, and the
little sergeant is about due to bump into them again."

They had come to a gradual turn in the road at a
point where a steep, wooded incline swept up on the left.
On the right lay the old hunting preserve and Armitage's bungalow. As they drew into the curve they heard
a revolver crack twice, as before, followed by answering
shots and cries and the thump of hoofs.

"Ohee! Oscar has struck them again. Steady now!
Watch your horse!" And Armitage raised his arm high
above his head and fired twice as a warning to Oscar.

The distance between the contending parties was
shorter now than at the first meeting, and Armitage and
Claiborne bent forward in their saddles, talking softly
to their horses, that had danced wildly at Armitage's
shots.

"Lord! if we can crowd them in here now and back
to the Port!"

"There!"

Exclamations died on their lips at the instant. Ahead
of them lay the fog, rising and breaking in soft folds,
and behind it men yelled and several shots snapped
spitefully on the heavy air. Then a curious picture disclosed itself just at the edge of the vapor, as though it
were a curtain through which actors in a drama emerged
upon a stage. Zmai and Chauvenet flashed into view
suddenly, and close behind them, Oscar, yelling like
mad. He drove his horse between the two men, threw
himself flat as Zmai fired at him, and turned and waved
his hat and laughed at them; then, just before his horse
reached Claiborne and Armitage, he checked its speed
abruptly, flung it about and then charged back, still
yelling, upon the amazed foe.

"He's crazy—he's gone clean out of his head!" muttered Claiborne, restraining his horse with difficulty.
"What do you make of it?"

"He's having fun with them. He's just rattling them
to warm himself up—the little beggar. I didn't know
it was in him."

Back went Oscar toward the two horsemen he had

passed less than a minute before, still yelling, and this time he discharged his revolver with seeming unconcern for the value of ammunition, and as he again dashed between them, and back through the gray curtain, Armitage gave the word, and he and Claiborne swept on at a gallop.

Durand was out of sight, and Chauvenet turned and looked behind him uneasily; then he spoke sharply to Zmai. Oscar's wild ride back and forth had demoralized the horses, which were snorting and plunging wildly. As Armitage and Claiborne advanced Chauvenet spoke again to Zmai and drew his own revolver.

"Oh, for a saber now!" growled Claiborne.

But it was not a moment for speculation or regret. Both sides were perfectly silent as Claiborne, leading slightly, with Armitage pressing close at his left, galloped toward the two men who faced them at the gray wall of mist. They bore to the left with a view of crowding the two horsemen off the road and into the preserve, and as they neared them they heard cries through the mist and rapid hoof-beats, and Durand's horse leaped the ditch at the roadside just before it reached Chauvenet and Zmai and ran away through the rough underbrush into the wood, Oscar close behind and silent now, grimly intent on his business.

The revolvers of Zmai and Chauvenet cracked together, and they, too, turned their horses into the wood, and away they all went, leaving the road clear.

"My horse got it that time!" shouted Claiborne.

"So did I," replied Armitage; "but never you mind, old man, we've got them cornered now."

Claiborne glanced at Armitage and saw his right hand, still holding his revolver, go to his shoulder.

"Much damage?"

"It struck a hard place, but I am still fit."

The blood streamed from the neck of Claiborne's horse, which threw up its head and snorted in pain, but kept bravely on at the trot in which Armitage had set the pace.

"Poor devil! We'll have a reckoning pretty soon," cried Armitage cheerily. "No kingdom is worth a good horse!"

They advanced at a trot toward the Port.

"You'll be afoot any minute now, but we're in good shape and on our own soil, with those carrion between us and a gap they won't care to drop into! I'm off for the gate—you wait here, and if Oscar fires the signal, give the answer."

Armitage galloped off to the right and Claiborne jumped from his horse just as the wounded animal trembled for a moment, sank to its knees and rolled over dead.

CHAPTER XXV

THE PORT OF MISSING MEN

Fast they come, fast they come;
  See how they gather!
Wide waves the eagle plume,
  Blended with heather.
Cast your plaids, draw your blades,
  Forward each man set!
Pibroch of Donuil Dhu
  Knell for the onset!
                              —*Sir Walter Scott.*

Claiborne climbed upon a rock to get his bearings, and as he gazed off through the wood a bullet sang close to his head and he saw a man slipping away through the underbrush a hundred yards ahead of him. He threw up his rifle and fired after the retreating figure, jerked the lever spitefully and waited. In a few minutes Oscar rode alertly out of the wood at his left.

"It was better for us a dead horse than a dead man—yes?" was the little sergeant's comment. "We shall come back for the saddle and bridle."

"Humph! Where do you think those men are?"

"Behind some rocks near the edge of the gap. It is a poor position."

"I'm not sure of that. They'll escape across the old bridge."

"*Nein.* A sparrow would shake it down. Three men at once—they would not need our bullets!"

Far away to the right two reports in quick succession gave news of Armitage.

"It's the signal that he's got between them and the gate. Swing around to the left and I will go straight to the big clearing, and meet you."

"You will have my horse—yes?" Oscar began to dismount.

"No; I do well enough this way. Forward!—the word is to keep them between us and the gap until we can sit on them."

The mist was fast disappearing and swirling away under a sharp wind, and the sunlight broke warmly upon the drenched world. Claiborne started through the wet undergrowth at a dog trot. Armitage, he judged, was about half a mile away, and to make their line complete Oscar should traverse an equal distance. The soldier blood in Claiborne warmed at the prospect of a definite contest. He grinned as it occurred to him

that he had won the distinction of having a horse shot
under him in an open road fight, almost within sight
of the dome of the Capitol.

The brush grew thinner and the trees fewer, and he
dropped down and crawled presently to the shelter of a
boulder, from which he could look out upon the open
and fairly level field known as the Port of Missing
Men. There as a boy he had dreamed of battles as he
pondered the legend of the Lost Legion. At the far edge
of the field was a fringe of stunted cedars, like an
abatis, partly concealing the old barricade where, in
the golden days of their youth, he had played with
Shirley at storming the fort; and Shirley, in these
fierce assaults, had usually tumbled over upon the im-
aginary enemy ahead of him !

As he looked about he saw Armitage, his horse at a
walk, ride slowly out of the wood at his right. Claiborne
jumped up and waved his hat and a rifle-ball flicked
his coat collar as lightly as though an unseen hand had
tried to brush a bit of dust from it. As he turned toward
the marksman behind the cedars three shots, fired in a
volley, hummed about him. Then it was very still, with
the Sabbath stillness of early morning in the hills, and
he heard faintly the mechanical click and snap of the

rifles of Chauvenet's party as they expelled their ex-
ploded cartridges and refilled their magazines.

"They're really not so bad—bad luck to them!" he
muttered. "I'll be ripe for the little brown men after
I get through with this;" and Claiborne laughed a
little and watched Armitage's slow advance out into
the open.

The trio behind the barricade had not yet seen the
man they had crossed the sea to kill, as the line of his
approach closely paralleled the long irregular wall with
its fringe of cedars; but they knew from Claiborne's
signal that he was there. The men had picketed their
horses back of the little fort, and Claiborne commended
their good generalship and wondered what sort of be-
ings they were to risk so much upon so wild an adventure.

Armitage rode out farther into the opening, and
Claiborne, with his eyes on the barricade, saw a man
lean forward through the cedars in an effort to take
aim at the horseman. Claiborne drew up his own rifle
and blazed away. Bits of stone spurted into the air below the target's elbow, and the man dropped back out
of sight without firing.

"I've never been the same since that fever," growled

Claiborne, and snapped out the shell spitefully, and watched for another chance.

Being directly in front of the barricade, he was in a position to cover Armitage's advance, and Oscar, meanwhile, had taken his cue from Armitage and ridden slowly into the field from the left. The men behind the cedars fired now from within the enclosure at both men without exposing themselves; but their shots flew wild, and the two horsemen rode up to Claiborne, who had emptied his rifle into the cedars and was reloading.

"They are all together again, are they?" asked Armitage, pausing a few yards from Claiborne's rock, his eyes upon the barricade.

"The gentleman with the curly hair—I drove him in. He is a damned poor shot—yes?"

Oscar tightened his belt and waited for orders, while Armitage and Claiborne conferred in quick pointed sentences.

"Shall we risk a rush or starve them out? I'd like to try hunger on them," said Armitage.

"They'll all sneak off over the bridge to-night if we pen them up. If they all go at once they'll break it down, and we'll lose our quarry. But you want to capture them—alive?"

"I certainly do!" Armitage replied, and turned to laugh at Oscar, who had fired at the barricade from the back of his horse, which was resenting the indignity by trying to throw his rider.

The enemy now concentrated a sharp fire upon Armitage, whose horse snorted and pawed the ground as the balls cut the air and earth.

"For God's sake, get off that horse, Armitage!" bawled Claiborne, rising upon the rock. "There's no use in wasting yourself that way."

"My arm aches and I've got to do something. Let's try storming them just for fun. It's a cavalry stunt, Claiborne, and you can play being the artillery that's supporting our advance. Fall away there, Oscar, about forty yards, and we'll race for it to the wall and over. That barricade isn't as stiff as it looks from this side— I know all about it. There are great chunks out of it that can't be seen from this side."

"Thank me for that, Armitage. I tumbled down a good many yards of it when I played up here as a kid. Get off that horse, I tell you! You've got a hole in you now! Get down!"

"You make me tired, Claiborne. This beautiful row will all be over in a few minutes. I never intended to waste much time on those fellows when I got them where I wanted them."

His left arm hung quite limp at his side and his face was very white. He had dropped his rifle in the road at the moment the ball struck his shoulder, but he still carried his revolver. He nodded to Oscar, and they both galloped forward over the open ground, making straight for the cedar covert.

Claiborne was instantly up and away between the two riders. Their bold advance evidently surprised the trio beyond the barricade, who shouted hurried commands to one another as they distributed themselves along the wall and awaited the onslaught. Then they grew still and lay low out of sight as the silent riders approached. The hoofs of the onrushing horses rang now and then on the harsh outcropping rock, and here and there struck fire. Armitage sat erect and steady in his saddle, his horse speeding on in great bounds toward the barricade. His lips moved in a curious stiff fashion, as though he were ill, muttering:

"For Austria! For Austria! He bade me do something for the Empire!"

Beyond the cedars the trio held their fire, watching

with fascinated eyes the two riders, every instant drawing closer, and the runner who followed them.

"They can't jump this—they'll veer off before they
get here," shouted Chauvenet to his comrades. "Wait
till they check their horses for the turn."

"We are fools. They have got us trapped;" and Durand's hands shook as he restlessly fingered a revolver.
The big Servian crouched on his knees near by, his
finger on the trigger of his rifle. All three were hatless
and unkempt. The wound in Zmai's scalp had broken
out afresh, and he had twisted a colored handkerchief
about it to stay the bleeding. A hundred yards away
the waterfall splashed down the defile and its faint
murmur reached them. A wild dove rose ahead of
Armitage and flew straight before him over the barricade. The silence grew tense as the horses galloped
nearer; the men behind the cedar-lined wall heard only
the hollow thump of hoofs and Claiborne's voice calling
to Armitage and Oscar, to warn them of his whereabouts.

But the eyes of the three conspirators were fixed on
Armitage; it was his life they sought; the others did not
greatly matter. And so John Armitage rode across the
little plain where the Lost Legion had camped for a
year at the end of a great war; and as he rode on the

defenders of the boulder barricade saw his white face
and noted the useless arm hanging and swaying, and
felt, in spite of themselves, the strength of his tall erect
figure.

Chauvenet, watching the silent rider, said aloud,
speaking in German, so that Zmai understood:

"It is in the blood; he is like a king."

But they could not hear the words that John Armitage kept saying over and over again as he crossed the
field:

"He bade me do something for Austria—for Austria!"

"He is brave, but he is a great fool. When he turns
his horse we will fire on him," said Zmai.

Their eyes were upon Armitage; and in their intentness they failed to note the increasing pace of Oscar's
horse, which was spurting slowly ahead. When they
saw that he would first make the sweep which they assumed to be the contemplated strategy of the charging
party, they leveled their arms at him, believing that he
must soon check his horse. But on he rode, bending forward a little, his rifle held across the saddle in front of
him.

"Take him first," cried Chauvenet. "Then be ready for Armitage!"

Oscar was now turning his horse, but toward them and across Armitage's path, with the deliberate purpose of taking the first fire. Before him rose the cedars that concealed the line of wall; and he saw the blue barrels of the waiting rifles. With a great spurt of speed he cut in ahead of Armitage swiftly and neatly; then on, without a break or a pause—not heeding Armitage's cries—on and still on, till twenty, then ten feet lay between him and the wall, at a place where the cedar barrier was thinnest. Then, as his horse crouched and rose, three rifles cracked as one. With a great crash the horse struck the wall and tumbled, rearing and plunging, through the tough cedar boughs. An instant later, near the same spot, Armitage, with better luck clearing the wall, was borne on through the confused line. When he flung himself down and ran back Claiborne had not yet appeared.

Oscar had crashed through at a point held by Durand, who was struck down by the horse's forefeet. He lay howling with pain, with the hind quarters of the prostrate beast across his legs. Armitage, running back toward the wall, kicked the revolver from his hand and left him. Zmai had started to run as Oscar gained the wall and Chauvenet's curses did not halt the Servian when he found Oscar at his heels.

Chauvenet stood impassively by the wall, his revolver raised and covering Armitage, who walked slowly and doggedly toward him. The pallor in Armitage's face gave him an unearthly look; he appeared to be trying to force himself to a pace of which his wavering limbs were incapable. At the moment that Claiborne sprang upon the wall behind Chauvenet Armitage swerved and stumbled, then swayed from side to side like a drunken man. His left arm swung limp at his side, and his revolver remained undrawn in his belt. His gray felt hat was twitched to one side of his head, adding a grotesque touch to the impression of drunkenness, and he was talking aloud:

"Shoot me, Mr. Chauvenet. Go on and shoot me! I am John Armitage, and I live in Montana, where real people are. Go on and shoot! Winkelried's in jail and the jig's up and the Empire and the silly King are safe. Go on and shoot, I tell you!"

He had stumbled on until he was within a dozen steps of Chauvenet, who lifted his revolver until it covered Armitage's head.

"Drop that gun—drop it damned quick!" and Dick Claiborne swung the butt of his rifle high and brought it down with a crash on Chauvenet's head; then Armitage paused and glanced about and laughed.

It was Claiborne who freed Durand from the dead horse, which had received the shots fired at Oscar the moment he rose at the wall. The fight was quite knocked out of the conspirator, and he swore under his breath, cursing the unconscious Chauvenet and the missing Zmai and the ill fortune of the fight.

"It's all over but the shouting—what's next?" demanded Claiborne.

"Tie him up—and tie the other one up," said Armitage, staring about queerly. "Where the devil is Oscar?"

"He's after the big fellow. You're badly fussed, old man. We've got to get out of this and fix you up."

"I'm all right. I've got a hole in my shoulder that feels as big and hot as a blast furnace. But we've got them nailed, and it's all right, old man!"

Durand continued to curse things visible and invisible as he rubbed his leg, while Claiborne watched him impatiently.

"If you start to run I'll certainly kill you, Monsieur."

"We have met, my dear sir, under unfortunate circumstances. You should not take it too much to heart about the potato sack. It was the fault of my dear colleagues. Ah, Armitage, you look rather ill, but I trust you will harbor no harsh feelings."

Armitage did not look at him; his eyes were upon the prostrate figure of Chauvenet, who seemed to be regaining his wits. He moaned and opened his eyes.

"Search him, Claiborne, to make sure. Then get him on his legs and pinion his arms, and tie the gentlemen together. The bridle on that dead horse is quite the thing."

"But, Messieurs," began Durand, who was striving to recover his composure—"this is unnecessary. My friend and I are quite willing to give you every assurance of our peaceable intentions."

"I don't question it," laughed Claiborne.

"But, my dear sir, in America, even in delightful America, the law will protect the citizens of another country."

"It will, indeed," and Claiborne grinned, put his revolver into Armitage's hand, and proceeded to cut the reins from the dead horse. "In America such amiable scoundrels as you are given the freedom of cities, and little children scatter flowers in their path. You ought to write for the funny papers, Monsieur."

"I trust your wounds are not serious, my dear Armitage—"

Armitage, sitting on a boulder, turned his eyes wearily upon Durand, whose wrists Claiborne was knotting together with a strap. The officer spun the man around viciously.

"You beast, if you address Mr. Armitage again I'll choke you!"

Chauvenet, sitting up and staring dully about, was greeted ironically by Durand:

"Prisoners, my dearest Jules; prisoners, do you understand? Will you please arrange with dear Armitage to let us go home and be good?"

Claiborne emptied the contents of Durand's pockets upon the ground and tossed a flask to Armitage.

"We will discuss matters at the bungalow. They always go to the nearest farm-house to sign the treaty of peace. Let us do everything according to the best traditions."

A moment later Oscar ran in from the direction of the gap, to find the work done and the party ready to leave.

"Where is the Servian?" demanded Armitage.

The soldier saluted, glanced from Chauvenet to Durand, and from Claiborne to Armitage.

"He will not come back," said the sergeant quietly.

"That is bad," remarked Armitage. "Take my horse and ride down to Storm Springs and tell Baron von Marhof and Judge Claiborne that Captain Claiborne has found John Armitage, and that he presents his compliments and wishes them to come to Mr. Armitage's house at once. Tell them that Captain Claiborne sent you and that he wants them to come back with you immediately."

"But Armitage—not Marhof—for God's sake, not Marhof." Chauvenet staggered to his feet and his voice choked as he muttered his appeal. "Not Marhof!"

"We can fix this among ourselves—just wait a little, till we can talk over our affairs. You have quite the wrong impression of us, I assure you, Messieurs," protested Durand.

"That is your misfortune! Thanks for the brandy, Monsieur Durand. I feel quite restored," said Armitage, rising; and the color swept into his face and he spoke with quick decision.

"Oh, Claiborne, will you kindly give me the time?"

Claiborne laughed. It was a laugh of real relief at the change in Armitage's tone.

"It's a quarter of seven. This little scrap didn't take as much time as you thought it would."

Oscar had mounted Armitage's horse and Claiborne stopped him as he rode past on his way to the road.

"After you deliver Mr. Armitage's message, get a doctor and tell him to be in a hurry about getting here."

"No!" began Armitage. "Good Lord, no! We are not going to advertise this mess. You will spoil it all. I don't propose to be arrested and put in jail, and a doctor would blab it all. I tell you, no!"

"Oscar, go to the hotel at the Springs and ask for Doctor Bledsoe. He's an army surgeon on leave. Tell him I want him to bring his tools and come to me at the bungalow. Now go!"

The conspirators' horses were brought up and Claiborne put Armitage upon the best of them.

"Don't treat me as though I were a sick priest! I tell you, I feel bully! If the prisoners will kindly walk ahead of us, we'll graciously ride behind. Or we might put them both on one horse! Forward!"

Chauvenet and Durand, as they marched ahead of their captors, divided the time between execrating each other and trying to make terms with Armitage. The thought of being haled before Baron von Marhof gave them great concern.

"Wait a few hours, Armitage—let us sit down and talk it all over. We're not as black as your imagination paints us!"

"Save your breath! You've had your fun so far, and now I'm going to have mine. You fellows are all right to sit in dark rooms and plot murder and treason; but you're not made for work in the open. Forward!"

They were a worn company that drew up at the empty bungalow, where the lamp and candles flickered eerily. On the table still lay the sword, the cloak, the silver box, the insignia of noble orders.

CHAPTER XXVI

"WHO ARE YOU, JOHN ARMITAGE?"

"Morbleu, Monsieur, you give me too much majesty," said the Prince.—*The History of Henry Esmond.*

"These gentlemen doubtless wish to confer—let them sequester themselves!" and Armitage waved his hand to the line of empty sleeping-rooms. "I believe Monsieur Durand already knows the way about—he may wish to explore my trunks again," and Armitage bowed to the two men, who, with their wrists tied behind them and a strap linking them together, looked the least bit absurd.

"Now, Claiborne, that foolish Oscar has a first-aid kit of some sort that he used on me a couple of weeks ago. Dig it out of his simple cell back there and we'll clear up this mess in my shoulder. Twice on the same side,— but I believe they actually cracked a bone this time."

He lay down on a long bench and Claiborne cut off his coat.

"I'd like to hold a little private execution for this," growled the officer. "A little lower and it would have caught you in the heart."

"Don't be spiteful! I'm as sound as wheat. We have them down and the victory is ours. The great fun is to come when the good Baron von Marhof gets here. If I were dying I believe I could hold on for that."

"You're not going to die, thank God! Just a minute more until I pack this shoulder with cotton. I can't do anything for that smashed bone, but Bledsoe is the best surgeon in the army, and he'll fix you up in a jiffy."

"That will do now. I must have on a coat when our honored guests arrive, even if we omit one sleeve—yes, I guess we'll have to, though it does seem a bit affected. Dig out the brandy bottle from the cupboard there in the corner, and then kindly brush my hair and straighten up the chairs a bit. You might even toss a stick on the fire. That potato sack you may care to keep as a souvenir."

"Be quiet, now! Remember, you are my prisoner, Mr. Armitage."

"I am, I am! But I will wager ten courses at Sherry's the Baron will be glad to let me off."

He laughed softly and began repeating:

With their wrists tied behind them, they looked the least bit absurd *Page 356*

" 'Why, hear you, my masters: was it for me to kill the heir apparent? Should I turn upon the true prince? Why, thou knowest I am as valiant as Hercules; but beware instinct; the lion will not touch the true prince. Instinct is a great matter; I was a coward on instinct. I shall think the better of myself and thee during my life; I for a valiant lion, and thou for a true prince.' "

Claiborne forced him to lie down on the bench, and threw a blanket over him, and in a moment saw that he slept. In an inner room the voices of the prisoners occasionally rose shrilly as they debated their situation and prospects. Claiborne chewed a cigar and watched and waited. Armitage wakened suddenly, sat up and called to Claiborne with a laugh:

"I had a perfectly bully dream, old man. I dreamed that I saw the ensign of Austria-Hungary flying from the flag-staff of this shanty; and by Jove, I'll take the hint! We owe it to the distinguished Ambassador who now approaches to fly his colors over the front door. We ought to have a trumpeter to herald his arrival— but the white and red ensign with the golden crown— it's in the leather-covered trunk in my room—the one with the most steamer labels on it—go bring it, Claiborne, and we'll throw it to the free airs of Virginia. And be quick—they ought to be here by this time!"

He stood in the door and watched Claiborne haul up the flag, and he made a mockery of saluting it as it snapped out in the fresh morning air.

"The Port of Missing Men! It was designed to be extra-territorial, and there's no treason in hauling up an alien flag," and his high spirits returned, and he stalked back to the fireplace, chaffing Claiborne and warning him against ever again fighting under an unknown banner.

"Here they are," called Claiborne, and flung open the door as Shirley, her father and Baron von Marhof rode up under the billowing ensign. Dick stepped out to meet them and answer their questions.

"Mr. Armitage is here. He has been hurt and we have sent for a doctor; but"—and he looked at Shirley.

"If you will do me the honor to enter—all of you!" and Armitage came out quickly and smiled upon them.

"We had started off to look for Dick when we met your man," said Shirley, standing on the steps, rein in hand.

"What has happened, and how was Armitage injured?" demanded Judge Claiborne.

"There was a battle," replied Dick, grinning, "and Mr. Armitage got in the way of a bullet."

Her ride through the keen morning air had flooded Shirley's cheeks with color. She wore a dark blue skirt and a mackintosh with the collar turned up about her neck, and a red scarf at her throat matched the band of her soft felt hat. She drew off her gauntlets and felt in her pocket for a handkerchief with which to brush some splashes of mud that had dried on her cheek, and the action was so feminine, and marked so abrupt a transition from the strange business of the night and morning, that Armitage and Dick laughed and Judge Claiborne turned upon them frowningly.

Shirley had been awake much of the night. On returning from the ball at the inn she found Dick still absent, and when at six o'clock he had not returned she called her father and they had set off together for the hills, toward which, the stablemen reported, Dick had ridden. They had met Oscar just outside the Springs, and had returned to the hotel for Baron von Marhof. Having performed her office as guide and satisfied herself that Dick was safe, she felt her conscience eased, and could see no reason why she should not ride home and leave the men to their council. Armitage saw her turn to her horse, whose nose was exploring her mackintosh pockets, and he stepped quickly toward her.

"You see, Miss Claiborne, your brother is quite safe, but I very much hope you will not run away. There are some things to be explained which it is only fair you should hear."

"Wait, Shirley, and we will all go down together," said Judge Claiborne reluctantly.

Baron von Marhof, very handsome and distinguished, but mud-splashed, had tied his horse to a post in the driveway, and stood on the veranda steps, his hat in his hand, staring, a look of bewilderment on his face. Armitage, bareheaded, still in his riding leggings, his trousers splashed with mud, his left arm sleeveless and supported by a handkerchief swung from his neck, shook hands with Judge Claiborne.

"Baron von Marhof, allow me to present Mr. Armitage," said Dick, and Armitage walked to the steps and bowed. The Ambassador did not offer his hand.

"Won't you please come in?" said Armitage, smiling upon them, and when they were seated he took his stand

by the fireplace, hesitated a moment, as though weigh-
ing his words, and began:

"Baron von Marhof, the events that have led to this
meeting have been somewhat more than unusual—they
are unique. And complications have arisen which require prompt and wise action. For this reason I am glad
that we shall have the benefit of Judge Claiborne's ad-
vice."

"Judge Claiborne is the counsel of our embassy," said
the Ambassador. His gaze was fixed intently on Armitage's face, and he hitched himself forward in his chair
impatiently, grasping his crop nervously across his
knees.

"You were anxious to find me, Baron, and I may have
seemed hard to catch, but I believe we have been work-
ing at cross-purposes to serve the same interests."

The Baron nodded.

"Yes, I dare say," he remarked dryly.

"And some other gentlemen, of not quite your own
standing, have at the same time been seeking me. It will
give me great pleasure to present one of them—one, I
believe, will be enough. Mr. Claiborne, will you kindly
allow Monsieur Jules Chauvenet to stand in the door for
a moment? I want to ask him a question."

Shirley, sitting farthest from Armitage, folded her hands upon the long table and looked toward the door into which her brother vanished. Then Jules Chauvenet stood before them all, and as his eyes met hers for a second the color rose to his face, and he broke out angrily:

"This is infamous! This is an outrage! Baron von Marhof, as an Austrian subject, I appeal to you for protection from this man!"

"Monsieur, you shall have all the protection Baron von Marhof cares to give you; but first I wish to ask you a question—just one. You followed me to America with the fixed purpose of killing me. You sent a Servian assassin after me—a fellow with a reputation for doing dirty work—and he tried to stick a knife into me on the deck of the *King Edward*. I shall not recite my subsequent experiences with him or with you and Monsieur Durand. You announced at Captain Claiborne's table at the Army and Navy Club in Washington that I was an impostor, and all the time, Monsieur, you have really believed me to be some one—some one in particular."

Armitage's eyes glittered and his voice faltered with intensity as he uttered these last words. Then he thrust his hand into his coat pocket, stepped back, and concluded:

"Who am I, Monsieur?"

Chauvenet shifted uneasily from one foot to another under the gaze of the five people who waited for his answer; then he screamed shrilly:

"You are the devil—an impostor, a liar, a thief!"

Baron von Marhof leaped to his feet and roared at Chauvenet in English:

"Who is this man? Whom do you believe him to be?"

"Answer and be quick about it!" snapped Claiborne.

"I tell you"—began Chauvenet fiercely.

"*Who am I?*" asked Armitage again.

"I don't know who you are—"

"You do not! You certainly do not!" laughed Armitage; "but whom have you believed me to be, Monsieur?"

"I thought—"

"Yes; you thought—"

"I thought—there seemed reasons to believe—"

"Yes; and you believe it; go on!"

Chauvenet's eyes blinked for a moment as he considered the difficulties of his situation. The presence of Baron von Marhof sobered him. America might not, after all, be so safe a place from which to conduct an Old World conspiracy, and this incident must, if possible, be turned to his own account. He addressed the Baron in German:

"This man is a designing plotter; he is bent upon mischief and treason; he has contrived an attempt against the noble ruler of our nation—he is a menace to the throne—"

"Who is he?" demanded Marhof impatiently; and his eyes and the eyes of all fell upon Armitage.

"I tell you we found him lurking about in Europe, waiting his chance, and we drove him away—drove him here to watch him. See these things—that sword— those orders! They belonged to the Archduke Karl. Look at them and see that it is true! I tell you we have rendered Austria a high service. One death—one death —at Vienna—and this son of a madman would be king! He is Frederick Augustus, the son of the Archduke Karl!"

The room was very still as the last words rang out. The old Ambassador's gaze clung to Armitage; he stepped nearer, the perspiration breaking out upon his brow, and his lips trembled as he faltered:

"He would be king; he would be king!"

Then Armitage spoke sharply to Claiborne.

"That will do. The gentleman may retire now."

As Claiborne thrust Chauvenet out of the room, Armitage turned to the little company, smiling.

"I am not Frederick Augustus, the son of the Archduke Karl," he said quietly; "nor did I ever pretend that I was, except to lead those men on in their conspiracy. The cigarette case that caused so much trouble at Mr. Claiborne's supper-party belongs to me. Here it is."

The old Ambassador snatched it from him eagerly.

"This device—the falcon poised upon a silver helmet! You have much to explain, Monsieur."

"It is the coat-of-arms of the house of Schomburg. The case belonged to Frederick Augustus, Karl's son; and this sword was his; and these orders and that cloak lying yonder—all were his. They were gifts from his father. And believe me, my friends, I came by them honestly."

The Baron bent over the table and spilled the orders from their silver box and scanned them eagerly. The colored ribbons, the glittering jewels, held the eyes of all. Many of them were the insignia of rare orders no longer conferred. There were the crown and pendant cross of the Invincible Knights of Zaringer; the white falcon upon a silver helmet, swung from a ribbon of cloth of gold—the familiar device of the house of Schomburg, the gold Maltese cross of the Chevaliers of the Blessed Sacrament; the crossed swords above an iron crown of the Ancient Legion of Saint Michael and All Angels; and the full-rigged ship pendant from triple anchors—the decoration of the rare Spanish order of the Star of the Seven Seas. Silence held the company as the Ambassador's fine old hands touched one after another. It seemed to Shirley that these baubles again bound the New World, the familiar hills of home, the Virginia shores, to the wallowing caravels of Columbus.

The Ambassador closed the silver box the better to examine the white falcon upon its lid. Then he swung about and confronted Armitage.

"Where is he, Monsieur?" he asked, his voice sunk to a whisper, his eyes sweeping the doors and windows.

"The Archduke Karl is dead; his son Frederick Augustus, whom these conspirators have imagined me to be—he, too, is dead."

"You are quite sure—you are quite sure, Mr. Armitage?"

"I am quite sure."

"That is not enough! We have a right to ask more than your word!"

"No, it is not enough," replied Armitage quietly. "Let me make my story brief. I need not recite the peculiarities of the Archduke—his dislike of conventional society, his contempt for sham and pretense. After living a hermit life at one of the smallest and most obscure of the royal estates for several years, he vanished utterly. That was fifteen years ago."

"Yes; he was mad—quite mad," blurted the Baron.

"That was the common impression. He took his oldest son and went into exile. Conjectures as to his whereabouts have filled the newspapers sporadically ever since. He has been reported as appearing in the South Sea Islands, in India, in Australia, in various parts of this country. In truth he came directly to America and established himself as a farmer in western Canada. His son was killed in an accident; the Archduke died within the year."

Judge Claiborne bent forward in his chair as Armitage paused.

"What proof have you of this story, Mr. Armitage?"

"I am prepared for such a question, gentlemen. His identity I may establish by various documents which he gave me for the purpose. For greater security I locked them in a safety box of the Bronx Loan and Trust

Company in New York. To guard against accidents I
named you jointly with myself as entitled to the contents of that box. Here is the key."

As he placed the slim bit of steel on the table and
stepped back to his old position on the hearth, they saw
how white he was, and that his hand shook, and Dick
begged him to sit down.

"Yes; will you not be seated, Monsieur?" said the
Baron kindly.

"No; I shall have finished in a moment. The Archduke gave those documents to me, and with them a paper
that will explain much in the life of that unhappy gentleman. It contains a disclosure that might in certain
emergencies be of very great value. I beg of you, believe that he was not a fool, and not a madman. He
sought exile for reasons—for the reason that his son
Francis, who has been plotting the murder of the new
Emperor-king, *is not his son!*"

"What!" roared the Baron.

"It is as I have said. The faithlessness of his wife,
and not madness, drove him into exile. He intrusted
that paper to me and swore me to carry it to Vienna if
Francis ever got too near the throne. It is certified by
half a dozen officials authorized to administer oaths in

Canada, though they, of course, never knew the contents of the paper to which they swore him. He even carried it to New York and swore to it there before the consul-general of Austria-Hungary in that city. There was a certain grim humor in him; he said he wished to have the affidavit bear the seal of his own country, and the consul-general assumed that it was a document of mere commercial significance."

The Baron looked at the key; he touched the silver box; his hand rested for a moment on the sword.

"It is a marvelous story—it is wonderful! Can it be true—can it be true?" murmured the Ambassador.

"The documents will be the best evidence. We can settle the matter in twenty-four hours," said Judge Claiborne.

"You will pardon me for seeming incredulous, sir," said the Baron, "but it is all so extraordinary. And these men, these prisoners—"

"They have pursued me under the impression that I am Frederick Augustus. Oddly enough, I, too, am Frederick Augustus," and Armitage smiled. "I was within a few months of his age, and I had a little brush with Chauvenet and Durand in Geneva in which they captured my cigarette case—it had belonged to Frederick, and the Archduke gave it to me—and my troubles began. The Emperor-king was old and ill; the disorders in Hungary were to cloak the assassination of his successor; then the Archduke Francis, Karl's reputed son, was to be installed upon the throne."

"Yes; there has been a conspiracy; I—"

"And there have been conspirators! Two of them are safely behind that door; and, somewhat through my efforts, their chief, Winkelried, should now be under arrest in Vienna. I have had reasons, besides my pledge to Archduke Karl, for taking an active part in these affairs. A year ago I gave Karl's repudiation of his second son to Count Ferdinand von Stroebel, the prime minister. The statement was stolen from him for the Winkelried conspirators by these men we now have locked up in this house."

The Ambassador's eyes blazed with excitement as these statements fell one by one from Armitage's lips; but Armitage went on:

"I trust that my plan for handling these men will meet with your approval. They have chartered the *George W. Custis,* a fruit-carrying steamer lying at Morgan's wharf in Baltimore, in which they expected to make off after they had finished with me. At one time they had some idea of kidnapping me; and it isn't my fault they failed at that game. But I leave it to you, gentlemen, to deal with them. I will suggest, however, that the presence just now in the West Indies, of the cruiser *Sophia Margaret,* flying the flag of Austria-Hungary, may be suggestive."

He smiled at the quick glance that passed between the Ambassador and Judge Claiborne.

Then Baron von Marhof blurted out the question that was uppermost in the minds of all.

"Who are *you,* John Armitage?"

And Armitage answered, quite simply and in the quiet tone that he had used throughout:

"I am Frederick Augustus von Stroebel, the son of your sister and of the Count Ferdinand von Stroebel. The Archduke's son and I were school-fellows and playmates; you remember as well as I my father's place near the royal lands. The Archduke talked much of democracy and the New World, and used to joke about the divine right of kings. Let me make my story short— I found out their plan of flight and slipped away with them. It was believed that I had been carried away by gipsies."

"Yes, that is true; it is all true! And you never saw your father—you never went to him?"

"I was only thirteen when I ran away with Karl. When I appeared before my father in Paris last year he would have sent me away in anger, if it had not been that I knew matters of importance to Austria—Austria, always Austria!"

"Yes; that was quite like him," said the Ambassador. "He served his country with a passionate devotion. He hated America—he distrusted the whole democratic idea. It was that which pointed his anger against you— that you should have chosen to live here."

"Then when I saw him at Geneva—that last interview—he told me that Karl's statement had been stolen, and he had his spies abroad looking for the thieves. He was very bitter against me. It was only a few hours before he was killed, as a part of the Winkelried conspiracy. He had given his life for Austria. He told me never to see him again—never to claim my own name until I had done something for Austria. And I went to Vienna and knelt in the crowd at his funeral, and no one knew me, and it hurt me, oh, it hurt me to know that he had grieved for me; that he had wanted a son to carry on his own work, while I had grown away from the whole idea of such labor as his. And now—"

He faltered, his hoarse voice broke with stress of feeling, and his pallor deepened.

"It was not my fault—it was really not my fault! I did the best I could, and, by God, I've got them in the room there where they can't do any harm!—and Dick Claiborne, you are the finest fellow in the world, and the squarest and bravest, and I want to take your hand before I go to sleep; for I'm sick—yes, I'm sick—and sleepy—and you'd better haul down that flag over the door—it's treason, I tell you!—and if you see Shirley, tell her I'm John Armitage—tell her I'm John Armitage, John Arm—"

The room and its figures rushed before his eyes, and as he tried to stand erect his knees crumpled under him, and before they could reach him he sank to the floor with a moan. As they crowded about he stirred slightly, sighed deeply, and lay perfectly still.

CHAPTER XXVII

DECENT BURIAL

To-morrow? 'Tis not ours to know
That we again shall see the flowers.
To-morrow is the gods'—but, oh!
To-day is ours.

—*C. E. Merrill, Jr.*

Claiborne called Oscar through the soft dusk of the April evening. The phalanx of stars marched augustly across the heavens. Claiborne lifted his face gratefully to the cool night breeze, for he was worn with the stress and anxiety of the day, and there remained much to do. The bungalow had been speedily transformed into a hospital. One nurse, borrowed from a convalescent patient at the Springs, was to be reinforced by another summoned by wire from Washington. The Ambassador's demand to be allowed to remove Armitage to his own house at the Springs had been promptly rejected by the surgeon. A fever had hold of John Armitage, who was ill enough without the wound in his shoulder, and

374

the surgeon moved his traps to the bungalow and took charge of the case. Oscar had brought Claiborne's bag, and all was now in readiness for the night.

Oscar's erect figure at salute and his respectful voice brought Claiborne down from the stars.

"We can get rid of the prisoners to-night—yes?"

"At midnight two secret service men will be here from Washington to travel with them to Baltimore to their boat. The Baron and my father arranged it over the telephone from the Springs. The prisoners understand that they are in serious trouble, and have agreed to go quietly. The government agents are discreet men. You brought up the buckboard?"

"But the men should be hanged—for they shot our captain, and he may die."

The little man spoke with sad cadence. A pathos in his erect, sturdy figure, his lowered tone as he referred to Armitage, touched Claiborne.

"He will get well, Oscar. Everything will seem brighter to-morrow. You had better sleep until it is time to drive to the train."

Oscar stepped nearer and his voice sank to a whisper.

"I have not forgotten the tall man who died; it is not·

well for him to go unburied. You are not a Catholic—
no?"

"You need not tell me how—or anything about it—
but you are sure he is quite dead?"

"He is dead; he was a bad man, and died very terribly," said Oscar, and he took off his hat and drew
his sleeve across his forehead. "I will tell you just how it
was. When my horse took the wall and got their bullets
and tumbled down dead, the big man they called Zmai
saw how it was, that we were all coming over after
them, and ran. He kept running through the brambles
and over the stones, and I thought he would soon turn
and we might have a fight, but he did not stop; and I
could not let him get away. It was our captain who
said, 'We must take them prisoners,' was it not so?"

"Yes; that was Mr. Armitage's wish."

"Then I saw that we were going toward the bridge,
the one they do not use, there at the deep ravine. I had
crossed it once and knew that it was weak and shaky,
and I slacked up and watched him. He kept on, and just
before he came to it, when I was very close to him, for
he was a slow runner—yes? being so big and clumsy, he
turned and shot at me with his revolver, but he was in
a hurry and missed; but he ran on. His feet struck the

planks of the bridge with a great jar and creaking, but he kept running and stumbled and fell once with a mad clatter of the planks. He was a coward with a heart of water, and would not stop when I called, and come back for a little fight. The wires of the bridge hummed and the bridge swung and creaked. When he was almost midway of the bridge the big wires that held it began to shriek out of the old posts that held them—though I had not touched them—and it seemed many years that passed while the whole of it dangled in the air like a bird-nest in a storm; and the creek down below laughed at that big coward. I still heard his hoofs thumping the planks, until the bridge dropped from under him and left him for a long second with his arms and legs flying in the air. Yes; it was very horrible to see. And then his great body went down, down—God! It was a very dreadful way for a wicked man to die."

And Oscar brushed his hat with his sleeve and looked away at the purple and gray ridges and their burden of stars.

"Yes, it must have been terrible," said Claiborne.

"But now he can not be left to lie down there on the rocks, though he was so wicked and died like a beast. I am a bad Catholic, but when I was a boy I used to serve mass, and it is not well for a man to lie in a wild place where the buzzards will find him."

"But you can not bring a priest. Great harm would be done if news of this affair were to get abroad. You understand that what has passed here must never be known by the outside world. My father and Baron von Marhof have counseled that, and you may be sure there are reasons why these things must be kept quiet, or they would seek the law's aid at once."

"Yes; I have been a soldier; but after this little war I shall bury the dead. In an hour I shall be back to drive the buckboard to Lamar station."

Claiborne looked at his watch.

"I will go with you," he said.

They started through the wood toward the Port of Missing Men; and together they found rough niches in the side of the gap, down which they made their way toilsomely to the boulder-lined stream that laughed and tumbled foamily at the bottom of the defile. They found the wreckage of the slender bridge, broken to fragments where the planking had struck the rocks. It was very quiet in the mountain cleft, and the stars seemed withdrawn to newer and deeper arches of heaven as they sought in the debris for the Servian. They kindled a

fire of twigs to give light for their search, and soon found
the great body lying quite at the edge of the torrent,
with arms flung out as though to ward off a blow. The
face twisted with terror and the small evil eyes, glassed
in death, were not good to see.

"He was a wicked man, and died in sin. I will dig a
grave for him by these bushes."

When the work was quite done, Oscar took off his hat
and knelt down by the side of the strange grave and
bowed his head in silence for a moment. Then he began
to repeat words and phrases of prayers he had known
as a peasant boy in a forest over seas, and his voice rose
to a kind of chant. Such petitions of the Litany of the
Saints as he could recall he uttered, his voice rising
mournfully among the rocks.

*"From all evil; from all sin; from Thy wrath; from
sudden and unprovided death, O Lord, deliver us!"*

Then he was silent, though in the wavering flame of
the fire Claiborne saw that his lips still muttered prayers
for the Servian's soul. When again his words grew audible he was saying:

*"—That Thou wouldst not deliver it into the hand of
the enemy, nor forget it unto the end, but wouldst command it to be received by the Holy Angels, and con-*

ducted to paradise, its true country; that, as in Thee it hath hoped and believed, it may not suffer the pains of hell, but may take possession of eternal joys."

He made the sign of the cross, rose, brushed the dirt from his knees and put on his hat.

"He was a coward and died an ugly death, but I am glad I did not kill him."

"Yes, we were spared murder," said Claiborne; and when they had trodden out the fire and scattered the embers into the stream, they climbed the steep side of the gap and turned toward the bungalow. Oscar trudged silently at Claiborne's side, and neither spoke. Both were worn to the point of exhaustion by the events of the long day; the stubborn patience and fidelity of the little man touched a chord in Claiborne. Almost unconsciously he threw his arm across Oscar's shoulders and walked thus beside him as they traversed the battle-field of the morning.

"You knew Mr. Armitage when he was a boy?" asked Claiborne.

"Yes; in the Austrian forest, on his father's place— the Count Ferdinand von Stroebel. The young captain's mother died when he was a child; his father was the great statesman, and did much for the Schomburgs and Austria; but it did not aid his disposition—no?"

The secret service men had come by way of the Springs, and were waiting at the bungalow to report to Claiborne. They handed him a sealed packet of instructions from the Secretary of War. The deportation of Chauvenet and Durand was to be effected at once under Claiborne's direction, and he sent Oscar to the stables for the buckboard and sat down on the veranda to discuss the trip to Baltimore with the two secret agents. They were to gather up the personal effects of the conspirators at the tavern on the drive to Lamar. The rooms occupied by Chauvenet at Washington had already been ransacked and correspondence and memoranda of a startling character seized. Chauvenet was known to be a professional blackmailer and plotter of political mischief, and the embassy of Austria-Hungary had identified Durand as an ex-convict who had only lately been implicated in the launching of a dangerous issue of forged bonds in Paris. Claiborne had been carefully coached by his father, and he answered the questions of the officers readily:

"If these men give you any trouble, put them under arrest in the nearest jail. We can bring them back here

for attempted murder, if nothing worse; and these
mountain juries will see that they're put away for a long
time. You will accompany them on board the *George W.
Custis,* and stay with them until you reach Cape Charles.
A lighthouse tender will follow the steamer down Chesa-
peake Bay and take you off. If these gentlemen do not
give the proper orders to the captain of the steamer, you
will put them all under arrest and signal the tender."

Chauvenet and Durand had been brought out and
placed in the buckboard, and these orders were intended
for their ears.

"We will waive our right to a writ of *habeas corpus,"*
remarked Durand cheerfully, as Claiborne flashed a lantern over them. "Dearest Jules, we shall not forget Monsieur Claiborne's courteous treatment of us."

"Shut up!" snapped Chauvenet.

"You will both of you do well to hold your tongues,"
remarked Claiborne dryly. "One of these officers under-
stands French, and I assure you they can not be
bought or frightened. If you try to bolt, they will certainly shoot you. If you make a row about going on
board your boat at Baltimore, remember they are government agents, with ample authority for any emer-

gency, and that Baron von Marhof has the American State Department at his back."

"You are wonderful, Captain Claiborne," drawled Durand.

"There is no trap in this? You give us the freedom of the sea?" demanded Chauvenet.

"I gave you the option of a Virginia prison for conspiracy to murder, or a run for your life in your own boat beyond the Capes. You have chosen the second alternative; if you care to change your decision—"

Oscar gathered up the reins and waited for the word. Claiborne held his watch to the lantern.

"We must not miss our train, my dear Jules!" said Durand.

"Bah, Claiborne! this is ungenerous of you. You know well enough this is an unlawful proceeding—kidnapping us this way—without opportunity for counsel."

"And without benefit of clergy," laughed Claiborne. "Is it a dash for the sea, or the nearest county jail? If you want to tackle the American courts, we have nothing to venture. The Winkelried crowd are safe behind the bars in Vienna, and publicity can do us no harm."

"Drive on!" ejaculated Chauvenet.

As the buckboard started, Baron von Marhof and

Judge Claiborne rode up, and watched the departure from their saddles.

"That's the end of one chapter," remarked Judge Claiborne.

"They're glad enough to go," said Dick. "What's the latest word from Vienna?"

"The conspirators were taken quietly; about one hundred arrests have been made in all, and the Hungarian uprising has played out utterly—thanks to Mr. John Armitage," and the Baron sighed and turned toward the bungalow.

When the two diplomats rode home half an hour later, it was with the assurance that Armitage's condition was satisfactory.

"He is a hardy plant," said the surgeon, "and will pull through."

CHAPTER XXVIII

JOHN ARMITAGE

If so be, you can discover a mode of life more desirable than the being a king, for those who shall be kings; then the true Ideal of the State will become a possibility; but not otherwise.—Marius the Epicurean.

June roses overflowed the veranda rail of Baron von Marhof's cottage at Storm Springs. The Ambassador and his friend and counsel, Judge Hilton Claiborne, sat in a cool corner with a wicker table between them. The representative of Austria-Hungary shook his glass with an impatience that tinkled the ice cheerily.

"He's as obstinate as a mule!"

Judge Claiborne laughed at the Baron's vehemence.

"He comes by it honestly. I can imagine his father doing the same thing under similar circumstances."

"What! This rot about democracy! This light tossing away of an honest title, a respectable fortune! My dear sir, there is such a thing as carrying democracy too far!"

385

"I suppose there is; but he's of age; he's a grown man. I don't see what you're going to do about it."

"Neither do I! But think what he's putting aside. The boy's clever—he has courage and brains, as we know; he could have position—the home government is under immense obligations to him. A word from me to Vienna and his services to the crown would be acknowledged in the most generous fashion. And with his father's memory and reputation behind him—"

"But the idea of reward doesn't appeal to him. We canvassed that last night."

"There's one thing I haven't dared to ask him: to take his own name—to become Frederick Augustus von Stroebel, even if he doesn't want his father's money or the title. Quite likely he will refuse that, too."

"It is possible. Most things seem possible with Armitage."

"It's simply providential that he hasn't become a citizen of your republic. That would have been the last straw!"

They rose as Armitage called to them from a French window near by.

"Good afternoon, gentlemen! When two diplomats

get their heads together on a summer afternoon, the universe is in danger."

He came toward them hatless, but trailing a stick that had been the prop of his later convalescence. His blue serge coat, a negligée shirt and duck trousers had been drawn a few days before from the trunks brought by Oscar from the bungalow. He was clean-shaven for the first time since his illness, and the two men looked at him with a new interest. His deepened temples and lean cheeks and hands told their story; but his step was regaining its old assurance, and his eyes were clear and bright. He thrust the little stick under his arm and stood erect, gazing at the near gardens and then at the hills. The wind tumbled his brown newly-trimmed hair, and caught the loose ends of his scarf and whipped them free.

"Sit down. We were just talking of you. You are getting so much stronger every day that we can't be sure of you long," said the Baron.

"You have spoiled me,—I am not at all anxious to venture back into the world. These Virginia gardens are a dream world, where nothing is really quite true."

"Something must be done about your father's estate soon. It is yours, waiting and ready."

The Baron bent toward the young man anxiously.

Armitage shook his head slowly, and clasped the stick with both hands and held it across his knees.

"No,—no! Please let us not talk of that any more. I could not feel comfortable about it. I have kept my pledge to do something for his country—something that we may hope pleases him if he knows."

The three were silent for a moment. A breeze, sweet with pine-scent of the hills, swept the valley, taking tribute of the gardens as it passed. The Baron was afraid to venture his last request.

"But the name—the honored name of the greatest statesman Austria has known—a name that will endure with the greatest names of Europe—surely you can at least accept that."

The Ambassador's tone was as gravely importunate as though he were begging the cession of a city from a harsh conqueror. Armitage rose and walked the length of the veranda. He had not seen Shirley since that morning when the earth had slipped from under his feet at the bungalow. The Claibornes had been back and forth often between Washington and Storm Springs. The Judge had just been appointed a member of the Brazilian boundary commission which was to meet shortly in Ber-

lin, and Mrs. Claiborne and Shirley were to go with him.
In the Claiborne garden, beyond and below, he saw a
flash of white here and there among the dark green
hedges. He paused, leaned against a pillar, and waited
until Shirley crossed one of the walks and passed slowly
on, intent upon the rose trees; and he saw—or thought
he saw—the sun searching out the gold in her brown
hair. She was hatless. Her white gown emphasized
the straight line of her figure. She paused to ponder
some new arrangement of a line of hydrangeas, and he
caught a glimpse of her against a pillar of crimson
ramblers. Then he went back to the Baron.

"How much of our row in the hills got into the newspapers?" he asked, sitting down.

"Nothing,—absolutely nothing. The presence of the
Sophia Margaret off the capes caused inquiries to be
made at the embassy, and several correspondents came
down here to interview me. Then the revenue officers
made some raids in the hills opportunely and created a
local diversion. You were hurt while cleaning your gun,
—please do not forget that!—and you are a friend of my
family,—a very eccentric character, who has chosen to
live in the wilderness."

The Judge and Armitage laughed at these explana-

tions, though there was a little constraint upon them all.
The Baron's question was still unanswered.

"You ceased to be of particular interest some time
ago. While you were sick the fraudulent Von Kissel was
arrested in Australia, and I believe some of the newspapers apologized to you handsomely."

"That was very generous of them;" and Armitage
shifted his position slightly. A white skirt had flashed
again in the Claiborne garden and he was trying to follow it. At the same time there were questions he
wished to ask and have answered. The Baroness von
Marhof had already gone to Newport; the Baron lingered merely out of good feeling toward Armitage—for
it was as Armitage that he was still known to the people
of Storm Springs, to the doctor and nurses who tended
him.

"The news from Vienna seems tranquil enough," remarked Armitage. He had not yet answered the Baron's
question, and the old gentleman grew restless at the delay. "I read in the *Neue Freie Presse* a while ago that
Charles Louis is showing an unexpected capacity for affairs. It is reported, too, that an heir is in prospect. The
Winkelried conspiracy is only a bad dream and we may
safely turn to other affairs."

"Yes; but the margin by which we escaped is too narrow to contemplate."

"We have a saying that a miss is as good as a mile," remarked Judge Claiborne. "We have never told Mr. Armitage that we found the papers in the safety box at New York to be as he described them."

"They are dangerous. We have hesitated as to whether there was more risk in destroying them than in preserving them," said the Baron.

Armitage shrugged his shoulders and laughed.

"They are out of my hands. I positively decline to accept their further custody."

A messenger appeared with a telegram which the Baron opened and read.

"It's from the commander of the *Sophia Margaret,* who is just leaving Rio Janeiro for Trieste, and reports his prisoners safe and in good health."

"It was a happy thought to have him continue his cruise to the Brazilian coast before returning homeward. By the time he delivers those two scoundrels to his government their fellow conspirators will have forgotten they ever lived. But"—and Judge Claiborne shrugged his shoulders and smiled disingenuously—"as a lawyer I deplore such methods. Think what a stir would be

made in this country if it were known that two men had
been kidnapped in the sovereign state of Virginia and
taken out to sea under convoy of ships carrying our flag
for transfer to an Austrian battle-ship! That's what we
get for being a free republic that can not countenance
the extradition of a foreign citizen for a political offense."

Armitage was not listening. Questions of international law and comity had no interest for him whatever.
The valley breeze, the glory of the blue Virginia sky,
the far-stretching lines of hills that caught and led the
eye like sea billows; the dark green of shrubbery, the
slope of upland meadows, and that elusive, vanishing
gleam of white,—before such things as these the splendor of empire and the might of armies were unworthy of
man's desire.

The Baron's next words broke harshly upon his mood.

"The gratitude of kings is not a thing to be despised.
You could go to Vienna and begin where most men leave
off! Strong hands are needed in Austria,—you could
make yourself the younger—the great Stroebel—"

The mention of his name brought back the Baron's
still unanswered question. He referred to it now, as he
stood before them smiling.

"I have answered all your questions but one; I shall answer that a little later,—if you will excuse me for just a few minutes I will go and get the answer,—that is, gentlemen, I hope I shall be able to bring it back with me."

He turned and ran down the steps and strode away through the long shadows of the garden. They heard the gate click after him as he passed into the Claiborne grounds and then they glanced at each other with such a glance as may pass between two members of a peace commission sitting on the same side of the table, who will not admit to each other that the latest proposition of the enemy has been in the nature of a surprise. They did not, however, suffer themselves to watch Armitage, but diplomatically refilled their glasses.

Through the green walls went Armitage. He had not been out of the Baron's grounds before since he was carried thence from the bungalow; and it was pleasant to be free once more, and able to stir without a nurse at his heels; and he swung along with his head and shoulders erect, walking with the confident stride of a man who has no doubt whatever of his immediate aim.

At the pergola he paused to reconnoiter, finding on the bench certain *vestigia* that interested him deeply,—

a pink parasol, a contrivance of straw, lace and pink roses that seemed to be a hat, and a June magazine. He jumped upon the bench where once he had sat, an exile, a refugee, a person discussed in disagreeable terms by the newspapers, and studied the landscape. Then he went on up the gradual slope of the meadow, until he came to the pasture wall. It was under the trees beneath which Oscar had waited for Zmai that he found her.

"They told me you wouldn't dare venture out for a week," she said, advancing toward him and giving him her hand.

"That was what they told me," he said, laughing; "but I escaped from my keepers."

"You will undoubtedly take cold,—without your hat!"

"Yes; I shall undoubtedly have pneumonia from exposure to the Virginia sunshine. I take my chances."

"You may sit on the wall for three minutes; then you must go back. I can not be responsible for the life of a wounded hero."

"Please!" He held up his hand. "That's what I came to talk to you about."

"About being a hero? You have taken an unfair advantage. I was going to send for the latest designs in laurel wreaths to-morrow."

She sat down beside him on the wall. The sheep were a grayish blur against the green. A little negro boy was shepherding them, and they scampered before him toward the farther end of the pasture. The faint and vanishing tinkle of a bell, and the boy's whistle, gave emphasis to the country-quiet of the late afternoon. They spoke rapidly and impersonally of his adventures in the hills and of his illness. When they looked at each other it was with swift laughing glances. Her cheeks and hands were already brown,—an honest brown won from May and June in the open field,—not that blistered, peeling scarlet that marks the insincere devotee of racket, driver and oar, who jumps into the game in August, but the real brown conferred by the dear mother of us all upon the faithful who go forth to meet her in April. Her hands interested him particularly. They were long, slender and supple; and she had a pretty way of folding them upon her knees that charmed him.

"I didn't know, Miss Claiborne, that I was going to lose my mind that morning at the bungalow or I should have asked your brother to conduct you to the conservatory while I fainted. From what they told me I must have been a little light-headed for a day or two. If I had been in my right mind I shouldn't have let Captain

Dick mix up in my business and run the risk of getting killed in a nasty little row. Dear old Dick! I made a mess of that whole business; I ought to have telegraphed for the Storm Springs constable in the beginning, and told him that if he wasn't careful the noble house of Schomburg would totter and fall."

"Yes; and just imagine the effect on our constable of telling him that the fate of an empire lay in his hands. It's hard enough to get a man arrested who beats his horse. But you must go back to your keepers. You haven't your hat—"

"Neither have you; you shan't outdo me in recklessness. I inspected your hat as I came through the pergola. I liked it immensely; I came near seizing it as spoil of war,—the loot of the pergola!"

"There would be cause for another war; I have rarely liked any hat so much. But the Baron will be after you in a moment. I can't be responsible for you."

"The Baron annoys me. He has given me a lot of worry. And that's what I have come to ask you about."

"Then I should say that you oughtn't to quarrel with a dear old man like Baron von Marhof. Besides, he's your uncle."

"No! No! I don't want him to be my uncle! I don't need any uncle!"

He glanced about with an anxiety that made her laugh.

"I understand perfectly! My father told me that the events of April in these hills were not to be mentioned. But don't worry; the sheep won't tell—and I won't."

He was silent for a moment as he thought out the words of what he wished to say to her. The sun was dipping down into the hills; the mellow air was still; the voice of a negro singing as he crossed a distant field stole sweetly upon them.

"Shirley!"

He touched her hand.

"Shirley!" and his fingers closed upon hers.

"I love you, Shirley! From those days when I saw you in Paris,—before the great Gettysburg battle picture, I loved you. You had felt the cry of the Old World, the story that is in its battle-fields, its beauty and romance, just as I had felt the call of this new and more wonderful world. I understood—I knew what was in your heart; I knew what those things meant to you;—but I had put them aside; I had chosen another life for myself. And the poor life that you saved, that is yours if

you will take it. I have told your father and Baron von
Marhof that I would not take the fortune my father left
me; I would not go back there to be thanked or to get a
ribbon to wear in my coat. But my name, the name I
bore as a boy and disgraced in my father's eyes,—his
name that he made famous throughout the world, the
name I cast aside with my youth, the name I flung away
in anger,—they wish me to take that."

She withdrew her hand and rose and looked away toward the western hills.

"The greatest romance in the world is here, Shirley.
I have dreamed it all over,—in the Canadian woods, on
the Montana ranch as I watched the herd at night. My
father spent his life keeping a king upon his throne; but
I believe there are higher things and finer things than
steadying a shaking throne or being a king. And the
name that has meant nothing to me except dominion and
power,—it can serve no purpose for me to take it now.
I learned much from the poor Archduke; he taught me
to hate the sham and shame of the life he had fled from.
My father was the last great defender of the divine right
of kings; but I believe in the divine right of men. And
the dome of the Capitol in Washington does not mean to
me force or hatred or power, but faith and hope and